THE
OTHER

THE
OTHER

JEFF MARKOWITZ

Author Photo Credit: Jeff Markowitz

First edition

ISBN: 978-1-68512-804-3

Cover art by Level Best Designs

This book was professionally typeset on Reedsy.
Find out more at reedsy.com

To the Memory of Tom O'Day, a friend to writers everywhere

Praise for The Other

"Jeff Markowitz's powerful and poignant novel addresses hate, that scourge of human experience, and how it poisons what should be the joy we all deserve in simply being alive. It's in his exquisitely drawn characters' quest for joy that Markowitz finds beauty despite the darkness overtaking two interconnected eras: one past, and one present. It is a quest we all need, and which Markowitz has gifted us."—Ann Aptaker, award-winning author of the Cantor Gold series

"Both contemporary and historical, *The Other*, will grab you from the first page. Written with the tension of a murder mystery, which it is as well, this riveting tale of heroism in the face of bigotry takes a fresh look at an age old problem. Set in the serenity of pastoral New Jersey, its characters reflect the symmetry of hate and reconciliation shaking our world then and now. A not-to-be-missed book."—A. J. Sidransky, author of *The Incident at San Miguel*

"*The Other* is the kind of book that we need right now. *Markowitz* investigates what national identity means, seamlessly weaving two storylines at the same lock tender's house, ninety years apart. The narrative judiciously navigates the seeds of Nazism, the Iranian Revolution, and the rise of twenty-first-century militias with a level of historical accuracy often lacking in modern literature. The wisdom contained within these pages simply can't be ignored."—Robert Creekmore, author of the Manly Wade Wellman Award finalist, *Prophet's Debt*

"Are a people chosen or marked? Are we fated for suffering or destined to love? When do the differences that make us unique become a signal for escalating hatred? Jeff Markowitz explores these factors and looks at the core of humanity in his novel The Other which, with its dual timelines, looks at the progress—or lack of it over ninety years of human activity in a rural New Jersey town.

"It weaves a complex tale of hate with a deep love between family members that even reaches beyond the veil that separates life from death. With the spirit of his dead wife Zoya, (or is it just her memory) to advise him Charlie Levenson sets out to unravel the thread that connects two Gordian knots threaded together through time. A buried box and a seemingly senseless murder. He faces a hydra of bigotry and antisemitism with internal courage and the love of his family.

"*The Other* is an important work deeply personal, and completely accessible. I cannot recommend it strongly enough as a book about crime, about humanity and a book about the power of love."—Teel James Glenn

Chapter One

2023

Charlie lost himself in the sound of his paddle as it sliced through the water, each stroke another syllable in his morning meditation. He was not by nature an early riser, but there was something about being out on the water at sunrise that pulled him from his bed. No one fished this stretch of the canal, maybe a few kids, but none of them would be out on the water at this hour. Charlie was alone on the canal. As the sun began to burn a hole through the early morning mist, turtles climbed onto mud-streaked logs, basking in the first heat of the day. Charlie envied the turtles their simple life, half asleep on a fallen tree branch, munching on pondweed and woodfern. He took a hint from the turtles, closing his eyes, letting the canoe drift. Low-hanging tree branches slapped against his face. He looked up just in time to see the eight-foot drop at the lock. The paddle slipped from his hands.

Charlie told himself not to panic. He had canoed this spot too many times to make an amateur mistake. He grabbed for the paddle, up to his elbows now in water, the canoe careening wildly, nearly capsizing. Jamming the paddle into wooden pilings, he managed to swing the canoe sideways toward the canal bank. His paddle splintered from the force. He grabbed at the foliage that grew along the edge. The canoe banged hard against the pilings, but he found the strength to pull himself to the edge of the lock. He held on until he regained his composure. Another foot and Charlie would have taken a nasty eight-foot spill.

He wiped the sweat from his face and dragged the canoe up out of the water. There was a nasty ding on the side of the canoe where it had hit the piling. The piling itself carried damage from a century of boats bumping up against it as they navigated the dangerous lock. Charlie looked across the towpath at the lowlands that bordered the canal. A tall man with dark hair and a darker scowl appeared just beyond the towpath, perhaps fifty feet away. Even at that distance, Charlie had the unmistakable impression of the stranger's eyes peering out at him from beneath a low-slung ballcap. Had he been watching the whole time? Charlie pretended not to notice.

The area hadn't changed dramatically since Charlie's last visit. In fact, he told himself, it probably hadn't changed much in a hundred years. Small farms and old homes dotted the landscape. The canoe rested in what had once been a small vegetable garden attached to a modest two-story clapboard house with a damaged gable roof and the remains of a simple brick chimney. Charlie peeked down the towpath. The stranger was gone.

The home was abandoned, shuttered, with a for sale sign tacked to the front door. Charlie jiggled the door, and the lock gave way. He let himself in.

Despite the layers of dirt and grime, Charlie could tell that the first floor of the building was structurally sound. There was enough space, he calculated, for a small kitchen and parlor. The bathroom was serviceable, at best. An old wooden staircase led to the upstairs bedrooms. The steps creaked but held. Sunlight poured in through a hole in the roof.

It would take a lot of work to transform the old building into a habitable home, but Charlie wasn't afraid of work. To be honest, he needed something to keep him busy, to take his mind off...

He ripped the for sale sign from the door and shoved it in his pocket.

Chapter Two

1933

Manny Dubinski was sitting at the kitchen table, his head buried in his schoolwork, when his father climbed down from the second-floor bedroom.

"Emanuel," he asked, "are you doing your studies?"

"Yes, father. What else would I be doing?"

Manny's twin sister, Rachel, grinned. "What indeed?" She paused, considering whether or not to say anything more. "So how is Joe Palook—"

"That's none of your concern, my dearest sister." Manny slammed the book shut, before his father could catch a glimpse of the comic hidden inside.

"Don't tease your brother. One day, he's going to be a famous scientist." Abe Dubinski looked fondly at his son. He had high hopes for his son's future. Manny would be more than just a lock tender. "You still plan to become a scientist, isn't that right?"

Manny didn't know what to say. Of course, he wanted to be a scientist, just like his hero Albert Einstein. But what was the point? His father couldn't afford to send him to college. And even if he could, Manny had heard all about the backlash that was building against Einstein and the other Jewish scientists.

"It's my plan, but perhaps it is not realistic. I could do worse than to become the next lock tender here on the canal. Like you." He smiled at his father. "When the time comes."

"No, my son. You are destined for greater things." Mr. Dubinski allowed himself a moment, daydreaming about his son's future, working side-by-side with Dr. Einstein. Mr. Dubinski's reverie was interrupted by the sound of one blast from a conch horn.

Rachel and Manny jumped up, grabbed a bucket, and ran down to the canal. Their father followed close behind. He stopped just long enough to sound three loud blasts on his whistle. There was an eight-foot drop in the water level at the lock. Three blasts meant it was not safe for the barge to proceed. Boys and girls were already running along the canal, laughing and shouting at the tow boys who were tending to the mules on the towpath. Canallers waiting on the barge passed the time by tossing small chunks of anthracite into the buckets.

When Abe had taken the job as lock tender, families who lived along the canal would heat their homes all winter with the anthracite that was tossed from the barges. These days, most anthracite traveled by rail. The buckets were little more than a children's game. Barges were fast becoming obsolete. Abe was not a stupid man. He understood that there was nothing he could do to stop the forward thrust of progress. He shook his head in disgust. Abe couldn't stop the future, but that didn't mean he had to like it.

Moving carefully, Abe Dubinski stepped out onto the narrow wooden planking that abutted the lock. On his signal, the tow boys gave the mules a tug. Once the barge was safely inside the lock, Dubinski closed the miter gate. Then he pushed on a lever that engaged the vertical rods, opening wickets, allowing water to escape. Slowly, the water level in the lock began to drop, and with it, the barge. When the water level inside the lock matched the level "down canal," Dubinski opened the gate, allowing the barge to continue on its way. The barge captain appreciated his efforts. "Thanks, Rabbi."

Abe Dubinski chuckled. He was the only Jew these canallers knew. The nickname was a sign of their affection and respect. Well, most of the time. Abe was not so naïve as to forget that there was a time not so very long ago when one of the canallers had asked him about his horns.

Chapter Three

2023

The realtor told Charlie that he already had an interested buyer but was still waiting for a firm offer. Charlie was a cash buyer. He floated a more than reasonable number. The seller wanted a quick closing, and Charlie was only too happy to comply. He had one final hoop to jump through before signing the contract. He needed to talk to his wife. He should have had the conversation sooner. Now, he could only imagine what Zoya might have said.

"The house is small…. Okay, the house is tiny. But it's time for us to downsize." He did his best to make downsizing sound like a good thing.

Charlie looked up at the silver maple tree that dominated the landscape. The tree was the reason they had selected this spot. Helicopter seeds blanketed the ground below the branches. Without thinking, Charlie picked up a seed and stuck it to the end of his nose. Zoya had taught him that.

Zoya didn't agree. "We've created a lifetime of memories in our home."

He lowered his eyes and examined the headstone. Zoya Aziz Levenson. Beloved wife – mother – friend. February 7, 1967 – October 5, 2022. Is there any reward for goodness except goodness?

"Yes. We did. And I promise you, those memories, every one of them, will come with me to the tiny house." Charlie lost himself momentarily in the memories. "But memories don't require much in the way of square footage."

Zoya had to admit, in her current condition, material things were less important to her than they once had been. "What about Ben and Olivia? What about Jamila?"

"There's enough space for two small bedrooms. One for me. And one for the kids when they come to visit."

Eventually, Zoya got to her real objection. "Will I be able to find the place? You know I've got a lousy sense of direction."

Charlie didn't believe in ghosts, but Zoya did. He had no doubt that she intended to visit him from time to time. "Surely, where you are now, you have access to GPS."

"That's not funny, Charlie."

Charlie snorted. The helicopter seed blew off his nose, spinning as it fell to the earth.

* * *

As promised, the deal closed quickly. Charlie wasted no time getting started on the renovations. His first project was the roof. Charlie erected a bit of scaffolding along the side of the house and rigged a hoist to raise and lower his supplies. His plan was simple enough. He'd rip up the damaged shingles, create a clean edge, and then fashion a temporary repair using peel-and-stick starter shingles. It would be neither pretty nor permanent, but it would eliminate the hole in the roof. It was, Charlie decided, a reasonable start to a long list of home repairs. At least, it would have been reasonable if the peel-and-stick product had performed as advertised. But try as he might, it stuck when it was supposed to peel, and it peeled when it was supposed to stick. Charlie muttered a few well-chosen epithets, set aside his tools, and climbed down off the roof.

His face was streaked with dirt and sweat. His clothes were stained black from the old asbestos roofing. Zoya would have admonished him to clean up before going into town. It would have led to an argument. Charlie had always enjoyed arguing with his wife. They never argued about important stuff, but they could argue for hours about what the important stuff was. If Zoya said that her new shirt was green, Charlie would insist it was blue.

Eventually, they would settle on teal. But was it teal blue or teal green? He rinsed his face and dragged a brush through his hair. He drew the line on changing into clean clothes. After all, he was only heading back to the building supply store. He jumped into his car and drove back to the store.

Charlie explained his problem. The manager was happy to upsell him. Charlie left with a product that promised to do the trick. He got back to the house just in time to see his son Ben jump off the roof, the repair complete, the hole gone.

"Hey, Pops, you weren't here, but the repair looked pretty simple. Next time, read the directions."

Charlie was always surprised by his son's skills as a craftsman. He had not inherited that from his father. "Thanks. I figured I must have screwed up."

"You were placing the shingles improperly. Once I figured that out, it was a pretty simple repair. The peel and stick should hold up nicely now." Ben popped the trunk of his car, reached into a cooler, and grabbed two beers. He tossed one to his father and chugged the other. "What's next on the list?"

"Where's Jami?" Charlie looked around for any sign of his darling granddaughter. "You didn't come alone, did you?"

"I left Olivia and Jamila at the hotel. Olivia is up against a deadline, and Jamila needed a nap." Charlie started to complain, but Ben waved his father off. "C'mon Pops, this place isn't ready for houseguests. Hell, it isn't even ready for you. Anyway, they'll join us for dinner."

"Okay then. That should give us enough time to take a closer look at the foundation."

Before Charlie had time to start digging, he was interrupted by a man walking along the towpath.

"Hey, buddy!" It was the stranger, the same one who had been watching him that first morning when he nearly pitched his canoe into the lock. The stranger veered off the towpath and approached Charlie and Ben. "Are you the new owner?"

Charlie wiped the beer foam from his lips. "That would be me. Name's Charlie."

The stranger grunted hello. "What are your plans here?"

"My plans?" Charlie was puzzled. "I plan to fix the place up."

"And then."

"I plan to live here." Charlie stared into the stranger's eyes. "Have you been watching me?"

The stranger thought about that for a while. "Look, it's none of my business, but you might want to re-think your plan."

"Why is that?" Charlie smacked the side of his head. "Where are my manners? Ben, get a beer for our guest."

"I don't drink pisswater." But the stranger accepted the can of beer. "Bad things have been known to happen here. You never can tell when bad things might happen again." The stranger took a swig of beer. "How much do you know about the lock tender?"

Charlie laughed nervously, but he made eye contact with the stranger, and the laugh got stuck in his throat. "The lock tender?"

The stranger smiled. "Back in the day, this was the lock tender's house. When the canal was the center of the village's economic life, it was the lock tender who kept everything moving safely on the canal. You know, the water drops eight feet at the lock."

"I know. I nearly took that eight-foot drop last time I was on the water."

"It's best to be careful hereabouts." The stranger chuckled. "The house has sat empty for a very long time." The scowl returned to the stranger's face. "Anyway, thanks for the pisswater."

Charlie and Ben watched as the tall man walked off, heading back the way he came.

"Pisswater!" Ben offered up a halfhearted laugh. "That was odd."

Charlie wasn't about to let the strange encounter ruin his day. "Probably a nice enough fellow, having a bad day." He finished his beer and crumpled the can. "Happens to all of us from time to time."

"Maybe, but I'd be careful." Ben stared down the towpath. "Mr. Pisswater."

Chapter Four

A be kissed his wife on the cheek. He had one more chore before his day's work was complete. "I won't be long."

Every lock on the canal had a tender, like Abe Dubinski, who was responsible for the safe operation of the lock. The same was true for the swing bridges. The bridges spanned the canal, allowing for pedestrian traffic, as well as horse-drawn wagons and, more recently, automobiles, to travel across the canal. The barges were too tall to pass under the bridge. So, the canal company employed bridge tenders who were responsible for swinging the bridge open and closed. Otto Becker tended a swing bridge less than a mile from Abe's lock. He was as close to being a friend as Abe had in the village.

The king post swing bridge had only recently replaced the original A-frame bridge. The new design was intended to handle the increased weight of automobile traffic, but in Otto's experience, it required more maintenance. Once every few months, he needed to climb the king post in order to adjust the tension in the cables. The adjustment itself was simple, but it was not without risk, especially for a man like Otto. He was afraid of heights. At the apex of the king post, Otto would be some thirty feet above the canal, standing on a ladder, leaning against the king post for support, keeping his hands free to complete the adjustment. He never looked down. But he knew that an ill-timed gust of wind could send him on a thirty-foot drop. If the swing bridge malfunctioned, the canal company would have little sympathy for an acrophobic bridge tender. Otto wanted to be certain, in the event that he did fall, that someone would be there to complete the repair. And, if necessary, to help him up off the deck. Abe had promised Otto that he would come "up canal" and keep watch while Otto made the necessary adjustments. In return, Otto's wife, Gertrude, would send him home with a pot of her famous sauerbraten.

Otto had already pulled a ladder up against the king post and was pacing and muttering under his breath. He clutched his toolbox in one hand and climbed to the top of the post. The repair itself was a simple adjustment, but while checking the tension, Otto needed to swivel on the ladder, in an eerie imitation of the bridge itself. Momentarily, he lost his footing. As he reached out to regain his balance, the toolbox slipped from his hand, landing with a thud at the base of the bridge. A second thud followed rapidly, and Otto lay on his back, next to the toolbox.

Abe helped him to a sitting position. "Are you alright?"

"I think so." Otto patted his arms and legs and rubbed his back. "Don't say anything to Gertrude."

Abe looked over toward the bridge tender's house. Gertrude was already coming out the front door. Otto struggled to his feet.

"Are you okay mein Barchen?" Gertrude brushed the dirt off her husband's jacket.

He kissed her sweetly on the forehead. "Yes, mein Liebling."

"Come inside. I'll make you a cup of coffee."

As Otto and Gertrude walked toward the house, Abe hung back, waiting for an invitation.

Gertrude looked over her shoulder. "You too, Mr. Dubinski."

* * *

Abe and Otto sat at the table sipping their coffee, black with two sugars, while Gertrude hovered over her husband.

"I'm fine, mein Liebling. Leave the men to talk."

Otto waited for his wife to step out into their little garden. "I believe the Company has made plans to shut the canal."

Abe put down his coffee. "Why?"

"They're losing business to the railroads."

Abe was skeptical. "There's enough business to support the railroads and the canal."

"You might think so. But everything these days is controlled by the Jew bankers." Otto blushed, adding quickly, "I'm sorry, my friend, but that's what I've been told."

Abe didn't know what to say. "Miriam will be expecting me."

"Gertrude left something for you, there, by the door."

A small pot of food was sitting on a table by the front door. Above the table, there was a picture tacked to the wall. Abe felt a sudden chill.

"Who is that?"

"That, my friend, is the future of Germany."

Abe left without taking the sauerbraten.

Chapter Five

2023

Ben's eyes stung from the mixture of dirt and sweat. "Damn, Pops, this is a bitch to clear."

They were digging a narrow trench around the perimeter of the house, the better to examine the foundation. Ben's wife, Olivia, and his toddler, Jamila, were in the garden. Olivia was digging holes and planting perennials. Jamila was rolling in the potting soil. Olivia looked at her daughter and frowned. "You're going to need a bath before dinner." She turned to Ben. "I'm taking Jami back to the hotel to get cleaned up. We'll meet you at the tavern. Don't be late."

Ben didn't think his little girl was too dirty to go to the tavern, but he smiled and nodded his head.

Olivia grinned. "You might want to clean up a bit yourself before dinner."

"Yes, dear."

Charlie chuckled. "I'll make sure he's presentable. Anyway, we've got work to do." Charlie grunted, just thinking about the effort. "The last thing I need is water damage."

It hadn't happened since he'd closed on the property, but Charlie knew that four, maybe five times a year, the lowlands adjacent to the canal were likely to flood. It was critical that he be ready.

So they dug, pulling dirt and rock and small chunks of concrete away from the foundation.

Ben was struggling with a bit of hardpack. Jamming his spade down hard into the earth, he heard a clunk. The clunk reverberated in his arms.

Charlie called over to his son. "Did you hit something?"

Ben cleared away the dirt. A wooden box was nestled up against the foundation.

"I found buried treasure." Ben grinned. "It must be from the days that pirate ships reigned on the canal."

It was an ancient wooden box with rusted metal hinges. Carefully, Charlie pried open the lid. He didn't know what he would find inside.

Ben looked at the box and then at his father. "What is it?"

Charlie examined the contents. The discovery tugged at Charlie, something he felt, but didn't quite comprehend, something he couldn't or perhaps wouldn't put into words. "We can deal with this later." He set the box aside and picked up his shovel. "I'd like to finish the job before dinner."

* * *

When Charlie and Ben got to the tavern, Olivia and Jamila were waiting out front. The establishment was a recent addition to the community, designed to resemble an old-time neighborhood tavern. Inside, the walls were covered with photographs that documented a century of life along the canal. The hostess led them to a booth along the far wall.

Charlie was a fast eater. While he waited for the rest of the family to finish their meals, he examined the photos. There were pictures of barges, of buildings, of locks and bridges, and lots of photos of the canallers themselves. He spotted a photograph of a couple standing in front of their house. They must be the lock tenders, he decided, studying the photo.

He got up to take a closer look. As he slid out of the booth, his arm brushed against a plate and sent it flying. He tried unsuccessfully to catch the plate before it hit the floor. In the attempt to save the plate, he knocked over a carafe. Hot coffee was pooling on the table and dripping onto the floor below. Pieces of broken dinnerware were strewn across the tavern. In the next booth, a gentleman was picking beef stew from his pants. Charlie mumbled his apologies and left the mess for the restaurant staff to clean. He made his way closer to the photo of the lock tenders. In the photo, Charlie spotted candlesticks in the front window. They looked familiar. By the time he returned to the booth, staff had cleaned the mess he had left behind.

Charlie signaled the waitress and pantomimed pouring a cup of coffee. The waitress frowned, but complied, and, moments later, was at their table with a fresh carafe. She refilled Charlie's coffee and topped up Ben's cup as well. This time, she took the carafe with her when she retreated. Jamila sat in a highchair and played with her tippy cup. Olivia reached over to intercept the cup before it set sail across the tavern. She adopted her sternest expression. "That's enough of that."

Jamila squirmed in her seat and giggled.

"Are you sure you want to stay at the house tonight?" Ben didn't agree with his father's plans. "We can get a room for you at the motel."

Charlie put down his coffee. "No. The house is ready."

Ben laughed. "Ready? The roof repair is temporary, at best. The bedroom is a work in process."

"I've made up my mind. I bought a mattress and put it in the parlor."

With that, Charlie pulled out his wallet, counting out enough twenties to cover the bill and an overly generous tip. "I'll probably eat here a lot," he said, to explain the size of the tip. And then he re-opened his wallet, adding one more twenty to the folio. "I want the waitress to remember me."

Olivia looked at her father-in-law. "Trust me, Pops, they're gonna remember you."

"I imagine you're right." Charlie's face reddened. "If I get in any trouble here, at least, I have a good lawyer. Right?"

Olivia grinned. "As long as you pay my retainer."

* * *

Charlie didn't spook easily, but it was his first night, alone, in the lock tender's house. The sky was overcast, with just an occasional star peeking through the clouds. The rain started just after ten. The first clap of thunder followed close behind. The peel-and-stick tiles were not intended for such a storm. It was nearly midnight when the temporary roof repair succumbed to the high winds and driving rain. Charlie climbed the stairs to the second floor, surveying the damage. Rain was pouring in through the gaping hole.

"Damn it." Charlie pulled on his boots and rain slicker. "I'm way too old for this shit." He knew it was crazy, but he had no other option. He retrieved his extension ladder from the shed, propped it up against the side of the house, and lashed it down. He rummaged through the shed for an old tarp. The rain swirling around him, Charlie dragged the tarp over to the ladder. Lightning struck a tree on the far side of the canal. A massive branch crashed down into the water. Charlie struggled with the tarp. Ever careful about the footing, he climbed out onto the roof and managed to secure the tarp. He hurried down the ladder. Water was puddling under his feet. Charlie retreated to the relative safety of the house.

Inside, he climbed the stairs to the second floor. The tarp was keeping the rain from pouring into the house. It was, he figured, even money that the tarp would survive the storm, but it was the best he could do.

He made his way back down to the first-floor parlor and poured himself a glass of cheap whiskey. He had better choices, smooth sipping whiskies, but he wanted to feel the burn in his throat.

"Damn!"

He poured himself another.

That's when he felt her presence in the house. "Is that you, Zoya?"

"You didn't think I'd let you stay here alone, your first night, in this terrible storm."

"So, what do you think of our new home?"

"I think it's a dump."

Charlie poured himself a third glass of whiskey.

"Don't you think you've had enough?"

"If I thought I'd had enough, I wouldn't have poured this one." Charlie raised his glass. "To our new home." He tossed down the glass of whiskey. It went down hard, and nearly came back up.

"I told you so."

Charlie smiled. He missed arguing with Zoya. Even if it was only in his imagination, the argument made him feel alive, made him feel like Zoya was still alive. "Yes, you did."

"Anyway," Zoya said, getting to the point of her visit, "what's in the box?"

"What box?"

"Don't play games with me, Charlie Levenson. The box you found when you were digging around in the dirt."

"That box."

"Yes. That box." Zoya was growing impatient. "What did you find in the box?"

Charlie knew he could only push Zoya so far. "Candlesticks."

"Anything else."

"No. Maybe a bit of dried-up candle wax."

"Show me."

Charlie retrieved the box.

"Be careful with that!"

Months after her death, Zoya was still telling him what to do. He opened the box slowly and showed the contents to his wife.

Zoya examined the pair of candlesticks. "Shabbos candles," she exclaimed.

"I thought so." Charlie paused. "But what are they doing here, buried under the foundation?"

Zoya had an answer for everything. "Maybe the lock tender was Jewish."

"I don't think there were many Jews living in this area back in the day. Or, for that matter, now."

"I grant you, it would have been unusual, but not impossible."

"You're probably right. You always were." Charlie corrected himself. "You always are."

"Do you remember the prayer?"

"What is this, a test?"

"Do you?"

Charlie rubbed his beard, recalling the Friday nights of his childhood, his mother lighting the candles and saying the prayer. He considered himself a secular Jew, but that didn't mean he didn't remember. "Baruch Atah Adonai,

16

Eloheinu Melech haolam. Asher kid'shanu b'mitzvotav v'zivanu l'hadlik ner shel Shabbat."

"Blessed art Thou, O Lord our God, Ruler of the Universe who sanctifies us with His commandments and commands us to kindle the Shabbos light."

"Why did you give up on the temple?"

Why did you stay? But Charlie wouldn't give voice to his question. He shoved the words down in his throat. He wished he could shove the words out of his head completely.

Chapter Six

1933

"I heard a rumor that the Company has made plans to close the canal."

Miriam looked up from her knitting. "Don't be silly. They close the canal every winter."

"That's not what I mean. What I heard is they don't intend to re-open the canal next spring."

"They can't do that!" Miriam was adamant. "What about the barges?"

"How many barges did we see this season?" Abe shook his head. "No, Miriam. The barges are done."

"But there's still plenty of private boats."

"The pleasure boats don't pay enough to keep the canal open." Abe scratched his beard while he decided how much to tell his wife. After a lengthy and awkward silence, he made up his mind. "I think this season will be the last." He saw the fear in his Miri's eyes. "Of course, I could be wrong."

"But your job! Omigod! What about the house?"

"Not so loud, my sweet." Abe patted his wife's arm. "The children are in the next room."

Miriam forced herself to whisper. "What about the house?"

What about the house? Abe had thought of little else since Otto told him about the rumor. Neither of them had heard anything directly from the Company. To Abe, that was further evidence that the rumor was true.

* * *

No barges came for the rest of the season, no mule teams, no steam engines, no anthracite. By fall, it was obvious that the rumors were true. The company intended to close the canal for good. Late in the fall, not long before the first freeze, two pleasure boats made their way south for the winter. With the arrival of the private boats, there was talk in the village that the wealthy pleasure boaters might sue to keep the canal open, but the optimism was short-lived. The yachts were the property of the principal owner of the canal company. He had promised his family and friends one final pleasure cruise. To his employees, he had promised nothing. As the boats approached the lock, the owner himself blew the conch horn. Abe responded with three toots on his whistle. The very last boat that made its way safely through the lock before the winter freeze was the property of Abe's boss.

* * *

Manny and Rachel were ice skating on the frozen canal when Abe Dubinski got the official word. The canal would not re-open.

Abe wasn't especially worried about the job. Every winter, when the canal closed, he took odd jobs to keep some money coming in. He had a knack for small engine repair. He thought perhaps he could make a living working on automobiles. Certainly, there were enough cars in the area to keep a good mechanic busy. He was confident he could turn that into year-round income. At least he feigned confidence when he explained his plans to Miriam. There was no reason, he decided, for them both to worry about money.

It was enough to worry about their home. Abe read the letter three times, searching for a clue about the house. The letter offered no additional information. Would the company kick the Dubinskis out of the lock tender's house? He checked with Otto. The bridge tender had the same questions. The company didn't have a reputation for taking care of its employees. But the air was clean and crisp. The ice was several inches thick. There would be plenty of time to worry come spring.

The canal was a different place in the winter, crowded not with barges, but with boys and girls on skates, gliding on the ice. Firepits were dug along the canal, offering the skaters a place to warm up. Manny and Rachel called to their Papa to join them on the canal. He retrieved his ancient ice skates. He loved the feel of the soft leather. He got Miriam's figure skates as well.

"What about you, my dear? Will you skate today?"

"Not today."

"Are you sure? You love to skate!"

"Go." Miriam looked up from her knitting. "Maybe later." She didn't want to tell her husband that the dizzy spells had returned. "Go skate with the children."

Abe stood in the doorway, waiting, knowing that his patience would eventually be rewarded. Miriam would not deny her husband. She put down her knitting and feigned a smile. "Perhaps just for a few minutes."

Abe took her hand, and together, they walked down to the canal. Miriam sat on a bench by the firepit and laced up her skates. Abe was eager to get out on the ice. Miriam smiled at her husband, a real smile this time. "I'll join you in a moment."

A group of young children were playing freeze tag on the ice under the watchful gaze of their mothers. The older boys set up a small net below the swing bridge and practiced taking shots on goal. Manny joined the would-be hockey stars. He imagined himself to be the great Sammy Rothschild. Sammy played left wing for the Montreal Maroons, the 1926 Stanley Cup Champions. He was the first Jewish player in the National Hockey League. In season, Manny aspired to be a professional hockey player. During the off-season, he would be a theoretical physicist. He liked to picture himself talking particle theory with Rothschild, comparing slapshots with Einstein. Pretty girls would fight for the opportunity to go out on a date with the famous Jewish hockey player-physicist. Manny was still at an age when that seemed to be a perfectly reasonable dream. His teachers had often told the class that anyone could grow up to be President, but Manny knew better. A Jew would never be President. But a Jew could be a hockey player. A Jew could be a physicist. Perhaps a Jew could be both.

Rachel joined the teenage girls practicing their pirouettes, trying their best to distract the boys. Abe took his wife by the hand and together, they weaved their way around the children, taking pleasure in their synchronous movements. It was a simple routine, mastered over many winters skating on the canal.

With the slightest nudge from Abe, Miriam began her pirouette. The world was spinning around her, but her head remained clear. She said a private thank you to the One who kept her dizziness at bay. She let the physical world slip away.

A line of boys was skating quickly, holding hands, forming a human whip. When the last boy in line let go, his momentum sent him flying across the canal. Too late, Miriam spotted the human projectile. The boy did his best to avoid hitting her, but even the glancing blow sent Miriam crashing to the ice. A red puddle formed on the ice beneath her head.

Abe stared at the puddle of red. For just a moment, his world stood still. Abe had been selfish. He knew his wife was bothered by dizzy spells. She had been to the doctor one time but had kept silent about the diagnosis. Abe never pressured her for more information. He assumed that she was experiencing some sort of woman's sickness, and, to be honest, he really didn't want to know what that meant. He only knew that he had been selfish, under the circumstances, dragging her out onto the ice. In that moment, he promised to be a better husband. Then he heard the ice crack.

Chapter Seven

2023

Charlie had been canoeing on the canal on and off since he was a young man. He was aware of the canal's historical significance but had never given it much thought. Out on the water, approaching a bridge, he'd sing out, "Low bridge, everybody down, low bridge 'cause we're going thru a town," even though it was a different bridge, a different town, a different canal. Now, as the new owner of the lock tender's house, Charlie found himself obsessing about the house and its inhabitants. He thought of himself as the keeper of the lock tender's house, responsible for maintaining its historical significance. He read everything he could find about life along the canal back in its heyday. He imagined the barges, loaded down with cargo—dry goods, foodstuff, and mostly, anthracite. He pictured the pleasure boaters—wealthy families on vacation making their way to the bay. He studied the design and maintenance of the lock and went down a rabbit hole searching for personal stories of the lock tenders. He was especially curious about the last of the lock tenders. What was his life like, all those years managing safe passage for the barges and the pleasure boats? What happened to the lock tender when the canal ceased to do business? How did he survive the closing of the canal? What was it like to preside over the end of an era?

When Charlie bought the house, his intention had been to make it habitable and then to live out what was left of his life as a hermit in his clapboard home on the edge of the canal.

He was not unfriendly, but after Zoya's death, Charlie found it uncomfortable to be around new people. He would nod at passersby, but he had lost interest in meeting people, making friends, becoming part of a community. He certainly had no intention of joining any of the local organizations. But if he wanted to know more about life on the canal, he would do well to listen to the personal accounts of the people whose families had lived on this canal for generations. He had seen posters promoting the Conservatorship for a Clean Canal. Perhaps they could help. The Conservatorship had an office less than a mile away. His curiosity overcame his desire to be left alone with his memories.

Charlie dropped his canoe into the canal. When he was a young boy, he had been taught to kneel in the bottom of the canoe. Now, it hurt just to bend. He wasn't an old man, not really, but his knees cracked as he climbed into the canoe. He plopped a cushion onto the rattan seat, sat down on the adjustable seat back, stretched his left leg out straight ahead, and paddled lazily up the canal, heading for the brand-new home of the Conservatorship. When he spotted the building just beyond a low bridge, Charlie docked his canoe on the boat ramp, stowed his paddle, and examined the building. It was not a new building, just new to the CCC. In fact, it looked much like the lock tender's house—a simple two-story structure, stone instead of clapboard, but the same general design. Charlie realized, back in the day, this must have been the bridge tender's house. Out front, a sign announced the future home of the Conservatorship for a Clean Canal. Future home. Charlie rebuked himself for the mistake.

With no expectations, he reached for the doorknob. The door swung open. He stepped inside. Like the lock tender's house, it had suffered from years of neglect. The parlor room floor was piled deep with debris. Ashtrays filled with cigarette butts and empty beer cans adorned the windowsills. Mildew stains dotted the walls. The home had, until recently, been home to squatters.

A note tacked to the wall announced the Conservatorship's plan to renovate the building, but there was no building permit on display, and no drawings. The renovation of the bridge tender's house was expected to take the rest of the year. In the interim, the CCC maintained a small office at the public library. The public library conjured up a vision of more interactions with more strangers. He would need to brush up on his social skills.

Charlie heard voices coming from outside the house. Had they seen his canoe on the bank of the canal? He didn't think he was violating any laws, but he was uncomfortable being caught inside the house without a good explanation. He looked around for a place to hide. The first floor was mostly open, empty space. He studied the center stairway. It was missing more than a few of its steps, but if he could make his way up the steps, he had a good chance to remain undetected. Charlie trusted that the steps would hold. Just shy of the second-floor landing, a step cracked under his weight. He fell forward, landing in the dirt in the second-floor hallway. Had the men outside heard him tumble? He rubbed a bruise on his shin. It was rapidly turning a nasty shade of purple. Charlie made a mental note to ice it down when he got home.

Charlie listened as the front door swung open. He crawled to the back of the hallway. Through a crack in the floor, he could see one man's scuffed boots and the other man's plaid jacket.

"I heard something. Didn't you hear it?"

"You're being paranoid. It was probably a muskrat, rooting through the garbage."

Upstairs, Charlie broke out in a cold sweat. He couldn't see either of the men clearly, but he recognized one of the voices. It was Mr. Pisswater, the stranger from the towpath, the one who had questioned his plan to buy the lock tender's house. He didn't want a confrontation here with the stranger, or to be honest, with a muskrat either.

"Muskrats don't drink beer. And they don't smoke cigarettes."

"Look at that stuff. The beer cans...the ashtrays...does any of it look recent?"

"Well, no. But, as long as we're here, we should probably check upstairs."

Charlie looked around. There was no place for him to hide, certainly no place he could get to without making noise.

"You can if you want to. But I'll wait here." Mr. Pisswater laughed. "That way, when you injure yourself falling through the stairs, I'll be able to call 911."

"Maybe you're right." The man paused. "It's probably a muskrat."

Charlie waited until he heard the front door open and close. He could hear the men talking outside.

"What about the other house?"

Charlie couldn't hear the answer. He peeked out through a window. The men were walking away.

The other house. The words gave Charlie a chill. What was it Mr. Pisswater had said when Charlie told him that he planned to live in the lock tender's house. *Bad things have been known to happen there. You never can tell when bad things might happen again.* He forced himself to wait a few moments longer, just to be safe, alone in the old house, alone with an imaginary muskrat, a bruised shin, and a new cause for concern.

Chapter Eight

Miriam screamed. The canal was not deep, but it could be deadly. When the ice cracked, she managed to hold onto an edge, keeping her arms and, more importantly, her head, above the freezing canal water. She tried to crawl out onto the ice, but her fur-trimmed coat and long woolen skirt worn over heavy woolen leggings weighed her down. When she attempted to shed the heavy coat, she lost her grip on the ice and slipped further into the freezing water. Her head disappeared briefly. She managed to pull herself back up onto the edge of the ice. She was soaking wet, and dirty, her coat half-off, the fur-trim tangled in her hair. Abe rushed toward her, but a young man held him back.

"Stay back. The ice is not safe!" He spoke with the tone of a man who was used to giving orders. They heard another crack and watched in horror as Miriam once again slipped into the freezing water.

"Let me go," Abe wailed. "Hold on, Miriam, I'm coming."

The young man pushed Abe down onto the ice. "We will form a human chain." The young man joined Abe, prone on the dangerous ice. Manny joined them, as did the rest of the men and older boys. Lying flat on the ice, each one's arms securing the next man's legs, they were able to reach out to Miriam. Abe gently pulled on his wife's arms, and ever so slowly, they managed to drag her up out of the water. Abe resisted the urge to jump up and carry his wife to safety, allowing the human chain to do its work and

26

slide them back away from the open water.

Women stood ready on the bank, wrapping Miriam in a cocoon of woolen blankets. They sat her down on a bench next to the firepit and rubbed her arms and back. Abe shivered but refused a blanket for himself.

"Your wife is in shock," the young man said in a clipped German accent, "I must examine her before you go back to your house."

Abe knew everyone who lived along the canal, but he didn't know this young man. He had been helpful on the ice; in truth, Abe realized, the young man's quick thinking probably saved her life. Still, he was not about to let a stranger examine his injured wife.

"Listen to me," the young man continued. "I have had some training. It is necessary that I check her head." The young man turned to Miriam. "I'm just going to check the wound."

Miriam stared blankly at the handsome young man. "Okay," she mumbled, her eyes glassy, her voice subdued, her mind somewhere else entirely.

Expertly, the young man touched her head, tilting it ever so slightly, feeling the area around the wound. He turned to Abe. "The blood makes it look worse than it is." Then he turned back to Miriam. "You gave us all quite a fright." He smiled. "I'm going to carry you back to your house. Is that okay?"

Abe started to say something, but Rachel shushed her father. She draped a blanket across his shoulders. "It's going to be okay, papa."

Miriam wasn't sure where her house was. In truth, she wasn't sure where she was. But the young man seemed to know what he was doing, and, anyway, he had a nice smile, and, for the moment, that was enough. "Okay."

With Abe's assistance, the good-looking stranger carried Miriam back to the house. In the safety of their parlor, Miriam rallied. She pulled a cloth from some secret fold in her skirt and pressed it against the back of her head. The cloth was dripping wet and filthy with canal debris. The stranger removed the cloth and examined the wound, satisfied that the bleeding had stopped.

For the first time since he heard the ice crack, Abe allowed himself to exhale. "Thank you, young man." The stranger's clothing was soaking wet and dirty, but the fair-haired man himself appeared clean and dry. "I've never seen you here before."

The young man stood up ramrod straight, shoulders back, head held high. "My name is Helmut Fischer. I'm visiting with the bridge tender."

"You're friends with Otto! That is good."

The young man seemed puzzled. "Why is that good?"

"You are German, are you not?"

"Yes, I am. Does that matter?"

"I'm sure it does for Otto. He misses his homeland." Abe smiled. "It is good to have friends who remind you of home."

"Yes. It is." Helmut examined Abe closely. "And you, my new friend, where are you from?"

"My grandfather came from Russia. But we are Americans now." Abe put his hand on his heart. "We have made a new home here in the land of opportunity."

"And have you found your opportunity?"

Abe's head bounced up and down in affirmation. "I am the lock tender." Abe puffed out his chest. "It is enough for me, but for my children, there will be more." Abe looked fondly at his twins. "Abe is going to be a scientist."

"That is good. In Germany, we have many scientists. In the future, I believe we will need still more." Helmut looked from Abe to Manny and finally to Rachel. In her flared skirt and black leggings, still wearing her pert hat and warm gloves, Rachel reminded Helmut of Sonja Henie. Helmut admired Sonja Henie. "And your daughter? What will she be? Perhaps a champion figure skater?"

"My daughter will be a wife and mother. That is the most important job of all." Abe realized he needed to talk to Miriam about finding their daughter a husband. Rachel was growing up quickly. If Miriam did not find a proper husband for their daughter, Rachel would find one of her own.

Outside, the sun was going down. Miriam struggled to her feet. "I need to light the candles!"

Abe put his hand on Miriam's shoulder and gently nudged her back down onto the threadbare sofa. "You need to rest. Rachel can get the Shabbos candles." He turned to Helmut. "I am sorry, my new friend, it is nearly sundown."

"You are…Jewish?" Helmut frowned and took one step toward the door.

"Yes. And it is the Sabbath. We have been distracted by Miriam's unfortunate mishap on the ice, but our God commands us to light the Shabbos candles."

"You are…I mean to say…you are not a money lender?"

"I am the lock tender."

Helmut checked Miriam's wound one final time before leaving.

Abe couldn't shake the feeling that Helmut was looking for evidence of something other than his wife's ice-skating injury. Was a Jewish head so different? Was he looking for horns?

When Helmut left, Rachel placed the candles in the Shabbos candlesticks. "Baruch Atah Adonai, Eloheinu Melech haolam Asher kid'shanu b'mitzvotav v'zivanu l'hadlik ner shel Shabbat."

Chapter Nine

2023

Charlie paced back and forth in the parlor in his small home. It was only six steps from wall to wall. He was wearing out the floorboards as he paced, contemplating his near run-in with Mr. Pisswater at the future home of the Conservatorship. He couldn't decide what it was about the encounter that had so unnerved him. Charlie told himself that it was nothing more than a coincidence, the two of them showing up at the bridge tender's house at the same time. Charlie was hesitant around most strangers, but his encounters with this stranger had been especially uncomfortable. Something about the man gave Charlie the jitters. He had been rude to Charlie that first morning on the towpath, but that was no reason to blow things out of proportion. It was a coincidence, Charlie told himself, nothing more.

No matter how many times Charlie told himself that it was all in his imagination, he couldn't shake the feeling of impending doom. Was Mr. Pisswater the potential buyer that the realtor had talked about? That could explain the unpleasant conversation. But Charlie had assumed that the potential buyer was not real, a realtor's harmless lie, intended only to spur Charlie to make an offer. In any event, if the stranger really did want the house, he was too late. Charlie would not allow Mr. Pisswater to scare him from his new home.

If Zoya were there, she would have told him to breathe. Charlie's breathing would slow. His blood pressure would drop. His anxiety would pass. But Zoya was not there. During their marriage, Charlie depended on Zoya for many things. When she died, he was confronted with the challenge of learning how to depend on himself.

Charlie stepped outside. It was a beautiful day, sweatshirt weather and not a trace of humidity. He nudged his canoe into the water. It took but a few strokes for Charlie to steer clear of the lock. He loved the feeling of honest exercise, his back muscles unkinking with each stroke. He loved the sound the paddle made as it sliced through the water, loved the chorus of peepers that serenaded him as he made his way up canal. *"Low bridge everybody down. Low bridge 'cause we're going thru a town."* Charlie immediately felt better. He didn't have to worry about the stranger, *"'cause you'll always know your neighbor, you'll always know your pal."* The song may have been written about the Erie Canal, but the sentiment applied to any canal.

Charlie found refuge in his canoe. He set his mind adrift. Images of his late wife floated on the water. There were so many images. So many Zoyas. The book club Zoya, with her enormous TBR pile. The jazz club Zoya, beeping when she should have bopped. The obedient Zoya, offering prayers to Mohammed. The temple Zoya, a fish out of water, who'd somehow made the synagogue her own.

He smelled the smoke before he saw the fire. And then, all at once, the calm on the canal was shattered by the shriek of the fire trucks. Two shiny red pumpers raced across the bridge. There was no time to waste. The bridge tender's house, the future home of the Conservatorship, was on fire.

Charlie's thoughts returned to the two men he had seen inside the building, Mr. Pisswater, and the other man, the one he now thought of as Mr. Plaid Jacket.

Charlie docked his canoe on the far side of the canal and watched as fire engulfed the roof of the bridge tender's house. The renovation was still in the planning stage; the building itself was vacant. Any losses incurred as a result of the fire would be financial rather than human. The heat from the flames came, in waves, across the water, distorting Charlie's view of the events.

Firefighters worked in teams, some focused on putting out the fire, others deployed to prevent the fire from spreading to the underbrush and to nearby buildings. Another team made their way inside the house. Moments later, a firefighter rushed out the front door, a body slung over his shoulder. Someone had been inside the building, someone wearing a distinctive plaid jacket.

Charlie pushed his canoe away from the bank and paddled home.

Chapter Ten

1933

It had been two weeks since Miriam's injury. Although she claimed to be feeling better, Abe could see that she was moving slowly. He worried that her dizzy spells were getting worse. Also, her head wound had begun to ooze. He sent Rachel to the apothecary to purchase the latest salve.

Helmut had stopped by one time, to check on Miriam's progress. Manny watched him closely. It seemed to Manny that Helmut was spending more time looking at Rachel than he was looking at Miriam. Helmut was good-looking in that way that the new German Chancellor liked to talk about. Rachel didn't know much about the German Chancellor, but she would have agreed that Helmut was a good-looking man.

Being a twin, Manny often knew his sister's thoughts before she had time to fully think them. Recently, her thoughts had been about Helmut. It was not the first time that Rachel had thought about boys, but this time was different. This was no simple juvenile crush. Manny blushed. Sometimes, it was better not to know what his sister was thinking. The two of them were growing up the only Jewish teenagers in the village. Manny had had his own fantasies about a pretty goyishe villager. He had, on more than one occasion, admired her from afar. And once, from close up. Boys were allowed their dalliances. It was to be expected. But girls could ruin their lives in the blink of an eye. Manny promised himself that he would keep a close eye on his impressionable sister. When she set off on foot, en route to the local apothecary, Manny kept watch, from a distance.

He was startled by a honk coming from behind him. Manny turned in time to see a Duesenberg Model J Convertible approaching from the rear. He was surprised by the luxury car and even more so by the driver. Helmut barely slowed down as he passed Manny, smiling and nodding hello. When the Model J got further up the road, Manny could see the car stop. Rachel climbed into the seat beside Helmut.

It didn't take long for the Duesenberg to leave Manny in the dust. Just when it seemed that his surveillance was most needed, it was least effective.

* * *

"Do you know that your brother is following you?"

"My brother thinks he needs to protect me."

"In a quiet village such as this, what does he need to protect you from?"

Rachel laughed. It was a deep laugh, a guttural laugh. Helmut had never heard a Jewess laugh. Did all Jewesses have such a laugh, he wondered. Against his better judgment, he wanted to know more about her.

"What is it like?"

Rachel looked away, confused by Helmut's question.

He asked again. "What is it like?" This time, he recognized Rachel's confused expression. "Being a Jew? What is it like?"

"It is not so very different, I think." Rachel tried to recall a passage she had studied in school. "I am a Jew. Hath not a Jew eyes? Hath not a Jew hands, organs, dimensions, senses, affections, passions."

Helmut thought he might enjoy exploring Rachel's passions. "What does your brother need to protect you from?"

Rachel smiled. "From you!"

Neither of them spoke again until Helmut parked the car in front of the apothecary. "What do you think? Do you need to be protected from me?"

"I think that one day I will meet a nice Jewish man. We will be married and live a fine Jewish life. I will light the candles and say the prayers. I will make many Jewish babies." Rachel smiled at Helmut. "But today, I am not looking for a husband."

She gave him a sudden peck on the cheek and ran into the apothecary. "Wait for me."

Helmut's cheek felt hot where Rachel had kissed it. Sweat beaded up on his forehead and on his upper lip. He looked around, relieved that no one was staring at them. He considered driving off while Rachel was in the apothecary, but something about the Jewess made him stay.

She was not like the Jews that Helmut knew in New York. Old men, bankers, and jewelers mostly, with their long black coats and their enormous hats, with their strange hair and hooked noses. And their eyes. Eyes that looked through you like you didn't matter when, in truth, it was they who didn't matter. Rachel was most certainly not like them.

After a few minutes, she exited the apothecary, carrying a small tin of Dr. Martin's Magical Salve, an ointment guaranteed, according to the label, to cure all manner of wounds, burns, muscle pains, skin diseases, and heartache.

Helmut couldn't help but smile when he saw her. "You shouldn't have kissed me," he said.

"Is that what I did?" Rachel pretended innocence. "Did you like it?"

For a moment, Helmut thought that she was going to do it again. "People will gossip."

"What people? There's no one here."

"Still, you just shouldn't. It's not proper." Helmut frowned. "It's not feminine."

"Are you saying I kiss like a boy?"

"No...yes...I mean, no, a girl is supposed to wait for the boy."

Rachel laughed. "Don't make me wait too long, or I'll find another boy to kiss."

When they were a mile from the lock tender's house, Rachel told Helmut to stop the car. "I'll get out here."

"You're not mad at me, are you?"

"No, silly." She wanted to give him another peck on the cheek, but she had promised to wait for him to take the lead. "My father wouldn't like it if you pulled up in front of the house and he saw me in the passenger seat."

"Then he surely won't like this." Helmut leaned across the seat and gave Rachel a kiss. He pushed against her. He ached to impose himself on her, to explore all of her affections and passions, but she was not ready for that, not yet. Next time, he promised himself, ready or not.

"That was…" Rachel reminded herself to breathe. "…nice." She jumped from the car and set off briskly for home.

Helmut called after her. "Would you do me the honor of accompanying me to the movie theater?"

"Now?" Rachel gasped. "I couldn't."

Helmut chuckled. "But perhaps another time, you could?"

Rachel's face turned red. "Perhaps." She turned and ran home.

Chapter Eleven

C harlie was cooking dinner when he heard a knock on his front door. He didn't know many people in the village and, in any event, wouldn't have invited anyone to come by the house. He had a slew of onions caramelizing in Zoya's cast iron pot. He gave them a stir and decided they would be okay if the interruption was brief. Without putting down the wooden spoon, he opened the front door. An extraordinarily large man was standing on his front porch. Perhaps it was the mop of red hair and freckles, or the twinkle in his eyes, but the man managed to appear harmless enough to Charlie, despite his gargantuan size. The giant flashed a badge.

"May I come in?"

"Yes, yes, of course. Officer?"

"Detective Warren."

"This way." Without waiting, Charlie headed for the kitchen. He turned back, adding "I've got onions on the stove." Charlie wondered why he mentioned the onions. If the detective was an observant cop, he would have already made note of the aroma coming from the kitchen.

"I love the smell of onions on the stove. What are you making?"

"Ground beef with caramelized onions and smoked tomatoes." Charlie fussed with the ground beef, before adding it to the pot. "But I don't think you came here to swap recipes."

The officer pulled out his notepad. It looked like a miniature in his paw of a hand. "You were at the fire today."

"I was canoeing. I smelled smoke. I heard the shriek of the fire trucks. I stopped when I saw the flames."

"Did you see anything else?"

"Well, let me think… I watched the firemen battling the blaze. Those guys are pretty damn impressive."

"Yes, they are," Detective Warren agreed. "But I'm hoping that you saw something else."

"I'm not sure what you mean."

"Something the other witnesses might have missed. After all, you had a different line of sight, sitting in your canoe. I guess what I'm asking is, did you see anything suspicious?"

"Well, I guess the whole thing must be suspicious. Fires like that don't just happen, do they?" Charlie stirred the pot. "I saw a fireman carry the dead guy out of the building." Charlie paused, as if deep in thought. "Am I right? He was dead."

"Did you recognize the man?"

Charlie wondered if it meant anything, that the detective had ignored his question about the man's life, or lack thereof.

"Like I said, I was in my canoe, sitting on the other side of the canal."

"That's right. When you were out today on the canal, did you see anyone or anything that you would describe as unusual?"

Charlie was developing a bad feeling about the detective's line of questioning. "Am I a suspect in the fire?"

"No, of course not. But you are a witness. You might have seen something and not realized at the time that it was important."

"I saw the fire. I guess you could call that unusual." Charlie paused. "I wish I could be more helpful."

"Perhaps you can." The officer reached into a folder. "I'd like to show you a few photos."

"I need to add the smoked tomatoes to the pot first. Otherwise, the dish will be ruined."

"I wouldn't want to ruin your dinner. You might file a complaint." The detective grinned. "You'd be surprised by the things people file complaints about."

"It'll just take a moment. While the dish simmers, I can look."

Detective Warren agreed to wait. "As long as you tell me how you smoked the tomatoes." When Charlie was ready, the detective pulled out a photo of the man in the plaid jacket.

Charlie winced. "What an awful way to die, being burned to death."

"Can you identify the man?" Detective Warren paused, considering how much he wanted to say. "He's disappeared in the wind."

"Disappeared?" Charlie scratched his head. "I thought you said he was dead."

"I never said the man was dead."

"But I saw the fireman carry him out of the building."

"Yes. That's true. The EMTs gave him oxygen and some basic first aid and transported him to the hospital."

"I don't understand."

"Things were pretty busy in the emergency room. Best as I can tell, he simply got up and left." The detective looked closely at Charlie. "Do you recognize him?"

"No."

"Take your time, Charlie. Are you sure you don't know the man?"

Charlie studied the photo more closely. He didn't know the man. That much he could say without lying to the police.

"I'm sorry, detective. No."

"Sometimes, after a good night's sleep, witnesses will remember more about the scene. It may seem like an insignificant detail, but you never know what might turn out to be the critical clue. If you think of something, call me." Detective Warren handed Charlie his card.

Chapter Twelve

1934

"You can't go to the movies with Helmut!" They were sitting at the
kitchen table doing their schoolwork when Manny confronted his
sister. "What are you thinking?"

"Right now, I'm thinking about finishing this assignment." Rachel closed
her copy of *A la Recherche du Temps Perdu*, grateful to take a short break from
her struggles with French grammar and vocabulary. "Why do I need to learn
French anyway? It's not likely that I will ever visit Paris."

"A modern woman needs..." Manny was about to launch into a lecture
about the benefits of a well-rounded education when he realized that Rachel
was simply trying to distract him. "A modern woman needs to avoid certain
men."

"I know that. Helmut's not Jewish. Mama and Papa won't approve. But
what am I supposed to do, wait until a nice Jewish boy magically appears?"
She glared at her brother. "You're the only Jewish boy in the village. I'm not
going to the movies with you!"

"Of course, Mama and Papa won't approve. The fact that he's not Jewish
is a problem, but it's not an insurmountable problem."

"Then what is the problem? Why do you care whether I go out with
Helmut?"

Manny stood up and marched around the room before responding. He
mimicked a certain step he had seen in recent newsreels. "Because Helmut

is a Nazi!"

"You're being foolish." Rachel laughed at her brother's explanation. "Helmut is German. Not every German is a Nazi."

"Maybe not every German. Nevertheless, you've heard how he speaks of the Jews." Manny shook his head in disgust. "Helmut is a Nazi."

Rachel didn't want to believe her brother. "But he was so nice to Mama when she fell in the canal."

"Yes. I've given that a lot of thought." He paused, replaying the incident from beginning to end. He still got chills remembering the moment when he heard the ice crack. "When Mama fell through the ice, Helmut didn't know she was Jewish."

"Do you really think he would have let her go under, if he had known?"

"I don't think he would have shed a tear over the loss of one Jew."

Just at that moment, their mother entered the kitchen. Rachel shushed her brother before he could say any more.

"Are you children almost done with your schoolwork?"

"Yes, Mama. Almost."

Miriam checked the pot roast that had been simmering on the stove since the morning. She turned to Rachel. "I want to make a kugel. And I'll need you to help. We're having guests tonight."

"Guests for dinner! Who Mama?" It was an uncommon treat to entertain guests.

"Otto Becker and his wife."

Rachel put away her schoolbooks and put on an apron. She didn't ask whether the Becker's house guest might also be coming for dinner. Just in case, she wanted everything to be perfect.

Manny could read his twin sister's mind. "Don't forget what we discussed!"

Miriam looked from Manny to Rachel and back to Manny. She said nothing, choosing instead to focus on the kugel.

They didn't have time to make a proper broth, but Rachel chopped an onion and a few carrots and added them to a pot of water along with the leafy tops. She left the water to simmer. Miriam added a bit of paprika and before long, she deemed the water to be ready. She removed the vegetables, added a cup of buckwheat groats, and raised the heat. While the groats were cooking, Rachel beat the eggs with oil, salt, and pepper. When the groats were ready, Miriam mixed them with the eggs and placed the dish in the oven.

Miriam sat down at the kitchen table and patted the seat next to her. Rachel joined her at the table.

"Yes, Mama?"

Miriam cleared her throat. "Your father asked me to talk to you."

Rachel said nothing, waiting for her mother to gather her thoughts.

"How old are you?'

Rachel was surprised by the question. Surely, her mother knew how old her only daughter was.

"I'm seventeen, mama."

Miriam sat there, trying to remember what seventeen felt like. "When I was your age, I was already married to your father."

"Oh, Mama."

"I was pregnant with you and your brother."

"Oh, this is my sex talk!" Rachel blushed. "I know about the birds and the bees."

It was Miriam's turn to blush. "You know that the canal will not re-open this spring?"

Rachel nodded. "I have heard you and Papa talking about it."

"We do not know whether the canal company will allow us to remain in this house."

"But this is our home!" Rachel protested. "They have no right to kick us out of our home."

"I feel the same way." Miriam couldn't make eye contact with her daughter. "But your father tells me that is the way that business is conducted."

"I do not know anything about business, but I do know the difference between right and wrong. It would be wrong to put us out of our home."

Neither of them spoke for some time. Finally, Miriam spoke up. "Let us pray that the canal company knows right from wrong."

Rachel stood up and walked over to the oven. "The kugel is starting to smell good."

Miriam nodded. "How would you feel if we moved away from the village?"

Rachel didn't answer.

Miriam pushed ahead. "You are not a little girl anymore. Your father and I worry that you will never meet a nice Jewish boy if we stay here."

Still, Rachel said nothing.

"There is a temple not so very far from here. Perhaps an hour away. Where there's a temple, there are families. And where there are families, there are young Jewish men, looking for a bride."

"That sounds nice, Mama. But I am not ready to be a bride. Perhaps in a few years."

"I will tell your father that we talked." Miriam took her daughter's hand. "As your mother, I am pleased to know that I have a few more years before I have to worry about boys. But as a woman, I know how quickly that can change." She couldn't make eye contact with Rachel. "Please don't make a liar out of me."

Chapter Thirteen

2023

C harlie's first encounter with the stranger had been the morning when his canoe nearly capsized in the lock. The next time was the day he and Ben were repairing the house, getting it ready for Charlie to move in. That was the morning the stranger earned his nickname. Then there was the day he saw Mr. Pisswater at the future home of the Conservatorship for a Clean Canal. Charlie was hiding upstairs when the stranger walked into the house along with a second man. He could only see a bit of each man through the crack in the floor, but he recognized Mr. Pisswater's voice. Now that second man, the man that Charlie knew only from his distinctive plaid jacket, now Mr. Plaid Jacket had disappeared after being carried out of the burning building. The police had already questioned Charlie once, ostensibly as a witness. He had told them nothing of his encounter with the unidentified victim.

Charlie knew little about police procedures, other than what he saw on network TV. He was pretty sure that TV dramas made up a lot of stuff, but not everything. There were always a few things on the dramas that seemed to Charlie to be realistic. For example, on TV, the police never questioned a person of interest one time and one time only. Detective Warren had already questioned him once. Charlie assumed that the detective would return for a second spin of the wheel. When he did, Charlie was determined to know more than he currently knew. Because currently, he knew next to nothing.

That put him at a disadvantage.

So what did he know? Charlie mentally prepared a list of known facts. It was an exceedingly short list. Only that the building where Mr. Plaid Jacket had been found was the future home of the Conservatorship for a Clean Canal. Perhaps Mr. Plaid Jacket or Mr. Pisswater had a connection to the CCC. If so, he might find something useful. A thread that he could pull on. With a bit of luck, he might find a name. As a child, he loved scavenger hunts. Discovering Mr. Plaid Jacket's identity was nothing more than a high-stakes scavenger hunt.

He logged onto his computer and searched for the website of the CCC. He skimmed the About page and then clicked on a link to the organization's Board of Trustees. The link opened to a new page with a list of the trustees who managed the Conservatorship's activities. Unfortunately, the page was under construction. There were no bios and no images, just a list of names. One by one, Charlie googled the names of the men on the list. He followed wherever the Google search took him, slowly collecting identifying information about each of the men. Unfortunately, none of the men bore a resemblance to Mr. Plaid Jacket or, for that matter, to Mr. Pisswater. Charlie was no closer to identifying the missing man, but he did his best to convince himself that the search had not been a complete waste of time. As he bounced from one site to the next, hunting for the man's identity, he had learned quite a few random facts about life on the canal. Not useful facts, he had to admit, but interesting, nonetheless.

* * *

Charlie was still sitting in front of his computer, staring at his screensaver, when his late wife paid him a visit. "You really should get outside more."

"You really should mind your own business." Charlie immediately regretted the remark.

"You are my business!"

Charlie hung his head. "I'm sorry. I guess I'm just frustrated."

Zoya knew her husband wouldn't give up until he found what he was looking for. "Did you find anything?"

"Well, for one thing, I learned that boats paid two cents a mile to travel on the canal."

"Okay..."

"I may have gone down a rabbit hole." Charlie laughed. "If the boat was carrying tobacco, it was charged at a rate of a half penny per pound per mile. Liquor was six-tenths of a penny."

"Fascinating." Zoya smirked. "What else?"

"Nothing that will help me learn the identity of the missing man."

Zoya wondered sometimes about her husband's priorities. "Don't you think the missing man should have been your lede?"

"I was getting to it."

"I'm waiting..."

Charlie told her about the fire at the bridge tender's house. He told her about the visit from the police.

Zoya took it all in. "You told the detective that you didn't know the man."

"I don't."

"Let's not split hairs. There's something you chose not to tell the detective, something you're not telling me."

"I only saw the man one time, actually I only saw a bit of the man's back, through a crack in the floor."

"And yet, that was enough for you to recognize him in the police photo. So what is the insignificant detail that you're withholding?"

"I recognized the man's plaid jacket." Charlie ducked his head, avoiding Zoya's gaze. "There's nothing I could have told the police that would have been helpful."

"But it makes you look like you're involved... like you have something to hide."

"I know. That's why I'm trying to figure out who Mr. Plaid Jacket is." Charlie shook his head.

"Let me think."

Charlie sat quietly, waiting for Zoya to come up with a good idea. He didn't like to admit it, but most of his good ideas came from Zoya.

"Did you search the women on the list of trustees?"

"Aren't you listening? I'm looking for a man."

Zoya wished she could smack her husband upside the head. "Pay attention, Charlie. Most women have a man in their life. A husband. A boyfriend. Maybe a co-worker. A brother. Someone."

Chapter Fourteen

1934

There was a knock on the door.

"That will be the Beckers," said Miriam.

Rachel hurried to answer the door. It was, as expected, the Beckers. Just the Beckers. Rachel stood in the doorway, waiting, as if by waiting, she could cause Helmut to materialize.

"You're in the way."

"I'm sorry, Mama."

"Don't apologize to me. Apologize to the Beckers."

Rachel's face turned bright red. "Of course. How silly of me." She moved out of the doorway. "Please come in."

Manny knew who Rachel was looking for. He resisted the urge to scold his sister in front of the Beckers. He shook Mr. Becker's hand and helped Mrs. Becker with a tray she was carrying.

"I made dessert," Gertrude Becker said, smiling. "I hope you like Linzer cookies."

"I've never had them before." Manny could smell the raspberry filling. "Do we have to wait until dessert?"

Gertrude gave one to Manny to try, but Miriam stepped in. "That's very nice of you, Gertrude." She took the cookie from Manny. "It will spoil his appetite."

Miriam and Gertrude headed for the kitchen. Alone in the kitchen,

Miriam ate the Linzer cookie. "This is wonderful."

"Thank you." Gertrude blushed. "And thank you for inviting us for dinner."

"The men need to talk." Miriam smiled. "It is easier to talk with a full stomach."

Gertrude smiled. It was an infrequent, but not unpleasant expression. "I think perhaps the women need to talk as well."

"I think you may be right. Are you worried about your house?"

"I am. And you?"

Miriam nodded her head in agreement. "I am afraid we may have to find another place to live. Abe is talking about moving away."

Gertrude gasped. "I hope that won't be necessary. You are our only close friends."

Miriam hid her surprise as best she could manage. "How very nice of you to say so. But what about your house guest Helmut? Surely, he is your friend?"

"He is our guest, and if things work out, he will be Otto's new employer, but no, he is not our friend."

"A job is more important than a friend." Miriam was pleased to hear that Otto had a potential job lined up. "Do you think Helmut might have a job for my Abe?"

"I don't think that will be possible. Anyway, I think we should leave that to the men."

With that, Miriam invited everyone to sit at the kitchen table. Without waiting to be told a second time, the men hustled to their seats. Rachel helped serve the beef and kugel.

When dinner was finished, Miriam brought out Gertrude's cookies and a fresh pot of coffee. "Let's have dessert in the parlor."

After their first sip of coffee and their first bite of the raspberry cookies, the conversation turned serious.

"Have you decided what you are going to do in the spring?" asked Abe.

At first, Otto said nothing. "I thought I would always be the bridge tender."

"But surely you were not always a bridge tender. What did you do before you took the job with the canal company?"

"Bridge tender was my first job here in America. In Germany, I was a lumberman."

"When spring comes, it will be strange having no boats on the water."

Otto nodded his head in agreement. "Helmut has offered me a job."

The clatter of flatware hitting the floor punctuated Otto's announcement. Hurriedly, Rachel picked up the spoons. "I'm sorry."

Rachel was not the only one startled by the mention of Helmut.

"That's wonderful, Otto." Abe could not imagine what sort of job Helmut could offer.

"I thought so, too. Now I'm not so sure."

"If it's not prying, might I ask what sort of business Helmut has?"

"Helmut and his associates plan to open a camp for German youth. Helmut says that German boys in America have lost pride in the fatherland. Helmut wants to do something about that."

"Here? In the village?" Abe didn't say so, but it seemed like an unlikely business opportunity.

"Perhaps. At least that's why he was here. Looking for a suitable property."

Manny could see Rachel flinch at Otto's use of the past tense. He asked the question that she couldn't. "Helmut is no longer visiting with you?"

"He has moved on to inspect other properties." Otto looked at Rachel, adding, "But I expect he will return in the spring."

Before he could say anything more, their conversation was interrupted by the crash of rocks hitting the outside of their home. The men rushed outside in time to see two young thugs running down the towpath, laughing. The women stood in the doorway, nervously watching. One of the thugs turned toward them and yelled, "Kike!" The second man yanked on his partner's arm, and they ran off together into the night.

Chapter Fifteen

2023

"Look, Grandpa! Mamani's favorite flower!"

Charlie was walking with Jamila when she stopped to examine a single yellow flower growing on the edge of the towpath. "You're right." Charlie wiped a tear from the corner of his eye. "It was your grandmother's favorite."

Jami had been so young when her grandmother had died. It filled Charlie with joy to know that Jamila remembered her. Charlie waited patiently while Jamila examined the black-eyed Susan. When Jami was done, she picked the yellow flower and turned to her grandfather. "We can go now."

Jami went skipping down the towpath. Charlie took the opportunity to talk quietly with Zoya. He wanted to bring her up to date on his search.

"You were right."

"Of course I was. What exactly was I right about?"

"I took another look at the list of trustees. Spent all morning reading about the women on the list. About one woman in particular."

Zoya was only half listening, distracted by her granddaughter. "How I miss watching her grow up."

"Would you be surprised to find that one of the trustees is currently serving time in a federal penitentiary?"

"Really?" Charlie had gotten his wife's undivided attention.

"Abby Jackson. Serving four years for assaulting a Capitol police officer."

51

Charlie gathered his thoughts. "Apparently, Ms. Jackson rode a bus to Washington to take part in the insurrection. When she breached the Capitol Building, an officer tried to turn her back. She responded by throwing a brick at him."

"Four years? She got off easy." Zoya tried to picture the scene on January 6, as thousands descended on the nation's capital for the sole purpose of overturning the Presidential election.

"That's not all." Charlie held up a newspaper clipping. A photographer had caught the exact moment when Abby Jackson sent the brick flying toward the officer's head. In the photo, the man standing next to Ms. Jackson was wearing a distinctive plaid jacket.

"Omigod. Is that him?" asked Zoya.

"That's him. Tom Jackson."

"But how did he escape jail time?"

"He didn't." Charlie shook his head. "He's already out. The man served sixty days for impeding an official government proceeding."

They were approaching the bridge tender's house along the towpath. A crowd had gathered, dressed in camouflage pants and T-shirts emblazoned with Tom Jackson's face. A small cadre of police officers watched but made no effort to intervene.

"What's that all about?" asked Zoya.

"I don't know. It looks like they're protesting Mr. Jackson's disappearance. I guess they blame the police."

"They blame the police whenever it fits their narrative."

Charlie spotted Mr. Pisswater, nearly hidden in the crowd, wearing a Tom Jackson t-shirt and a second amendment ballcap, carrying a semi-automatic weapon.

For just a moment, he let go of Jamila's hand, and she rushed ahead, eager to show off her flower. Mr. Pisswater stepped out of the crowd. "We don't like her kind around here." He stared hard at Jamila and then at Charlie. "I warned you."

Off to the side, a tree branch snapped. Startled, one of the protesters squeezed the trigger. A bullet tore through the air. Mr. Pisswater jumped, but the bullet caught him in the arm.

Weapons at the ready, the police closed on the well-regulated militia, removing the shooter from the crowd. No one else in the crowd had the stomach for a shootout. They stood there, shuffling their feet, at a loss for what to do next.

One very large officer stepped out in front. Charlie recognized him immediately as Detective Warren. With his hand resting easily on his weapon, Detective Warren approached the crowd. "No little girl is gonna get kilt on my watch."

Despite the blood oozing from the bullet wound in his arm, Mr. Pisswater was determined to save face in front of the crowd. He puffed himself up. "She don't belong here."

Mr. Pisswater stood his ground. Detective Warren moved quickly, but calmly, and, in a moment, was standing next to the stranger, one huge hand on his weapon, the other on the stranger's arm. An ambulance arrived on the scene, along with additional police units.

"This is not over." Mr. Pisswater handed his weapon to Detective Warren. The EMTs checked his arm. He allowed himself to be cuffed and placed in the ambulance.

The detective turned his attention back to the mob. "You have a choice. You can go home, or you can go to jail." Detective Warren turned to the shooter, already in cuffs. "Obviously, you don't get that choice. As for the rest of you, I'd advise you to voluntarily turn over any weapons you're carrying. You can come by the station house, answer a few questions, and, if you're legal, we'll give them back."

The protesters grumbled, but they knew it was the best deal they were going to get. Whatever bravado they had started out with had dissolved at the sound of the gunshot. Only a few of the men were actually carrying. The rest were not about to go down for one man's stupidity.

Detective Warren strolled over to Jamila, knelt down, and smiled. "That's a very pretty flower."

Jamila handed the yellow flower to Detective Warren. "I picked it myself." She skipped back to Charlie and slipped her tiny hand into his.

The detective waited until the protesters were gone, one to the hospital, one to jail, the rest to their homes, before turning his attention to Charlie.

"What are you doing here?"

Charlie smiled. "Picking flowers."

"Yes. I know that. I have a few more questions to ask you." The detective pulled out a small pad and scribbled a note to himself. "If you would be so kind as to stop by the station house this afternoon." It was not a question.

Chapter Sixteen

1934

Abe retrieved a bottle of brandy from the cupboard and poured two glasses. Handing one to Otto, he explained, "It'll be good for our nerves." Abe was shaken by the encounter outside his home, and, from the looks of it, Otto was as well.

Otto drank the brandy in one gulp. Abe refilled the glass. "Sip, my friend, sip."

Otto refrained from gulping down the second glass. "It's going to get worse."

Ignoring his own advice, Abe downed his brandy in one long swallow. "Did you recognize the men?"

"I did." It took Otto a moment to recall, where it was he knew them from. "They do odd jobs for the canallers. I guess they're worried about how they'll survive now that the canal is closed." Otto took another sip of brandy. "I expect they blame you."

"They blame me? I don't have anything to do with the closing of the canal. I'm just a lock tender."

Otto put his glass down and looked closely at his friend. Did he really have to spell things out for Abe? "You're a Jew lock tender."

"That doesn't make sense!" But it did make sense. Abe knew that there were people who would always blame the Jews for every bad thing that might happen. He stared hard at Otto. Was his friend one of those people?

"Do you blame me?"

Abe's question hung in the air. Both men waited for Otto's answer.

"Of course not. You are my friend."

Abe smiled so that Otto would know that he appreciated their friendship. But Abe understood that their friendship had its limitations. This was not Otto's fight. If trouble came, Abe knew that his family would face that trouble alone.

"Am I your only Jewish friend?"

"You are the only Jewish family in the village."

Otto's answer was factually correct, but to Abe, it was inadequate. "Surely, I am not the only Jew you've ever known?"

"When I was a boy, in Germany, there were Jewish merchants."

"In Germany…" Abe sensed they were getting to the heart of the matter. "What was it like in Germany?"

Otto missed his family home in the Black Forest. "It was a magical place. Perhaps the best place on earth."

"What about the Jewish merchants and their families? Was it a magical place for them as well?"

Otto didn't have an answer. He never considered what life was like for the Jews. "I don't know. It was okay, I guess. They had it better than the Gypsies."

The two men fell silent, each lost in their own thoughts.

"When I was a child in Germany, my schoolteacher told me that Jews had horns."

Abe remembered the way Helmut had examined Miriam's head when she fell on the ice. Had he been looking for evidence of Miriam's horns?

"Why did you leave Germany?"

"I didn't leave Germany. Not really. I came to America."

"Is that why you have a picture in your home of the new Chancellor?"

"It's hard to explain."

"I have heard some of his speeches on the radio. He is an evil man."

"He is a politician. I tell myself not to take it seriously. It is only rhetoric, intended to appeal to his followers."

"No. It is a call to violence." Abe shook his head. "And I fear it will end badly for the Jewish people."

Otto pulled a handkerchief from his pocket and wiped his brow. "Why is it so easy to hate the other? Why do we so love to hate?"

"Life is hard, my German friend. Some men rise to the challenge. Some don't." Abe finished his brandy and put the glass down on the table. "The ones who don't, well, it seems to me that they can't admit their own shortcomings. It's convenient for them to place the blame on others. And then, a politician comes around who knows how to use those shortcomings to his own advantage."

"Are you referring to the new Chancellor?"

"Yes. You told me he was the future of Germany. You have his picture hanging on your wall."

"I'm sorry. I do not always express myself so good in English. When I said he was the future of Germany, I didn't mean that in a good way."

"But you have his picture on your wall."

"I put it there for Helmut."

Abe couldn't shake the feeling that Helmut was an evil man, capable of doing evil things. "Why do you care about him?"

"Because I need work."

Abe had nearly forgotten about work. "What kind of job can Helmut give you?"

"Helmut and his associates are planning to open a camp for German youth."

"And he has offered to give you a job at the camp?"

"I will be part of the construction crew."

The pieces were falling into place. "You have to support the new German Chancellor if you want the job?"

Otto nodded his head. "Helmut believes that German American youth are losing touch with their heritage. Having camps in America will restore their pride in the homeland."

"Do you believe what he's doing is right?"

"I believe in having a job. I believe in putting food on the table, having a roof over my head." Otto reached for the brandy and poured himself one more glass. "I don't think it's necessarily a bad thing for youth to take pride in their heritage."

"Even if they express that pride by attacking Jews."

"I guess that could become a problem in Germany," Otto said. "But that will never happen here in America."

"If tonight is any indication," Abe sighed, "it has already started here."

Chapter Seventeen

2023

Since moving into the lock tender's house, Charlie had explored the area by foot on the towpath and in his canoe, paddling up- and down-canal. His knowledge of the surrounding village was limited to a narrow vertical swatch of land that abutted the canal. His car had rarely left its spot in the bare patch alongside his home. Charlie plugged the address of the police station into the car's GPS. As he made his way through unfamiliar neighborhoods, he was disappointed to discover that farmland had given way to generic condo communities, and the supermarkets, pizza parlors, liquor stores, and convenience stores needed to support such communities.

He drove past an especially active strip mall and spotted the police station. It was, at least on the outside, one of the few older buildings remaining on the street, a two-story structure of concrete and brick with an imposing balustrade over the entrance. Charlie parked his car and climbed the wide steps that led to the entrance.

Inside, there was nothing old-fashioned about the building or the police force it housed. It looked as though the interior had been scrubbed clean and outfitted with the latest in high-tech police equipment. Charlie stopped to check in with a clerk sitting behind a computer screen.

"Can I help you?"

"I am here to see Detective Warren."

"Can I please see some ID?"

Charlie handed over his driver's license and waited while the clerk input his data. She handed Charlie a visitor's pass and pointed down a central hallway. "Third door on the left."

By the time Charlie walked down the hallway, the detective had stepped out to greet him. "Thank you for coming in, Mr. Levenson. Let's talk inside." He led Charlie to a small interview room. When they got to the room, Detective Warren pushed a button on the wall. Charlie didn't know what the button was connected to, but he had no doubt it activated some sort of surveillance. "You said you had a few questions?"

The detective ignored Charlie's question. "Would you like a cup of coffee?"

"Do you want my fingerprints?"

"Excuse me."

Charlie grinned at the detective. "I know how this works. You get me a cup of coffee. When I leave, you lift my prints off the cup."

"Well, yes, I could do that, but sometimes a cup of coffee is just a cup of coffee."

"In that case, thank you, yes. With milk and two sugars, if you don't mind." Charlie feigned nonchalance. "If you want my fingerprints, all you have to do is ask."

Detective Warren pulled out his cell phone and spoke quietly. Moments later, the desk clerk came in with a cup of coffee, a jar of creamer, two packets of sugar substitute, and one fingerprint kit. The detective waited while Charlie prepared his coffee.

"It's just a formality."

"Do I need an attorney, detective?"

"I don't know, Mr. Levenson, do you?"

"It's just, I'm starting to feel like you think I'm a suspect."

"Right now, as we sit here, you're a witness. Possibly, a very important witness." Detective Warren stood up and looked down at Charlie. "But if I come to believe that you're withholding information, well, let's just say, it's just a hop, skip, and a jump to suspect."

Charlie did his best to sound nonchalant. "I'm not withholding anything. I'm happy to help in any way that I can."

"This will just take a minute." Detective Warren opened the fingerprint kit. "And it will save us from playing games with your coffee."

Charlie considered his options. The detective had played him perfectly. Still, he had nothing to do with the disappearance of the man in the plaid jacket. It's not like they were going to find his prints on a murder weapon. "Okay."

"Thank you."

"I'm happy to help." But Charlie didn't look happy. "Anyway, I wanted to thank you for your assistance this morning. I don't know what might have happened to my granddaughter if you hadn't intervened."

"Protect and serve."

"Excuse me?"

"Protect and serve. That's what we're here for." Detective Warren pulled out a small notebook and reviewed his notes. "You have a knack for being at the bridge tender's house whenever there's trouble."

"Is that a question?"

"I guess my question is, what brought you to the bridge tender's house this morning?"

"I was taking a walk with my granddaughter." Charlie didn't want to become confrontational. "I live a half mile from the bridge tender's house. I can't go anywhere without passing by that building."

"Yes. I imagine that's so." The detective re-checked his notes. "Does the name Hank Morgan mean anything to you?"

"No. Should it?"

"He said, 'I warned you.' What did he mean by that?"

"I don't know."

This is not the time to hold back on information, Mr. Levenson."

"I'm not." Charlie tried as best he could to control his tell.

"I think you are." Detective Warren scowled. "Anyway, we can come back to that later. What I really wanted to talk about is the man who we found in the fire."

The detective took a photograph out of a folder and placed it on the table in front of Charlie. "The last time I showed you this photo, you told me you didn't know the man. Would you like to take another look?"

Charlie stared at the photo. "I don't remember."

"Would it help your memory if I told you that the forensic team found fingerprints inside the bridge tender's house?"

"I'm sure that there are many sets of prints in the bridge tender's house, judging by the beer cans and the ashtrays." Immediately, Charlie regretted his response.

Detective Warren leaned in close to Charlie. "How do you know about the beer cans and the ashtrays?"

"They line the windows. Hell, you can see them from the towpath."

"You're remarkably observant. I bet if I were to talk to every person who hikes the towpath, you'd be the only one who noticed the beer cans and ashtrays on the windowsill."

"Most people don't pay attention to their surroundings." Charlie grinned. "Surely, as a detective, you're familiar with the unreliability of witness testimony."

Detective Warren stood up, stretching his arms and unkinking his back. "I'm stepping outside for a moment. While I'm gone, I'd recommend that you re-consider your whole approach to this interview."

"Am I in any danger here?"

Detective Warren shrugged. He exited the interview room, shutting the door behind him.

Charlie broke out in a sweat. He wondered if the police had been messing with the thermostat.

Chapter Eighteen

1934

Gertrude was not a demonstrative woman, but she could not leave the Dubinski's home without giving Miriam a hug. "I'm so sorry." Miriam took a step back, startled by Gertrude's sudden show of affection. She hung limp in Gertrude's arms while she struggled to regain her composure. Miriam didn't know what to say. "It's not your fault."

Gertrude released Miriam from her embrace. "When did it become okay to hate people because they are different?"

"Are we different? Really?" She set her eyes on Gertrude. "If you prick us, do we not bleed?"

"I'm sorry that didn't come out right. I meant to say, *When did it become okay to hate people?*" Gertrude lowered her head. "We will keep you and your family in our prayers."

"As we will keep you and Otto in ours." The sentiment was fine, but in her heart, Miriam knew that prayer would not stop violence.

Gertrude and Otto took their exit and made the short walk along the towpath back to their home. Gertrude was the first to notice the broken window.

"What is this?"

Otto put an arm out, blocking Gertrude's path. "Please, mein Leibling, it may not be safe."

The front window had been shattered. Shards of glass were scattered across the front porch, and Otto could see, inside the house, the glint of broken glass in the parlor. That's when Otto spotted a star of David, painted blood-red on the parlor wall. Someone had been in the house. He turned to Gertrude. "I am going in. I will come out and get you when I know it is safe."

"Mein Barchen." Gertrude wasn't comfortable with her husband going inside alone, with no idea what he might find there. She grabbed him by the arm. "Perhaps we should get the police."

"No! Everything will be fine. I promise." Otto kissed his wife on her forehead. "I'll be right back."

Otto stepped into his home. He walked from room to room, checking inside the closets, under their bed, behind their curtains. No one was lurking in the house. Other than the broken window and the star of David, the house was as they left it.

"I don't understand." Gertrude was standing in the open doorway. "What does it mean?"

Otto knew immediately what the intruder's message meant. "Our friendship with the Dubinskis has been noted."

"Noted? What does that mean?"

"It means that we have to keep our distance from Abe and Miriam until things blow over."

"But they need our friendship, now more than ever." Gertrude stared at her husband.

"I will not put you in danger."

Gertrude glanced around the house, looking for the intruder. Otto stared through the broken window. The towpath was quiet, but it was not necessarily empty. Otto had the uncomfortable feeling that they were being watched. Someone was lurking in the shadows. "I need to board up this window."

Gertrude squeezed her husband's hand. "Let me clean up the broken glass first." She released her husband's hand and retrieved a broom and dustpan. "It will only take a moment."

While Gertrude swept the parlor floor, Otto went in search of wooden boards. He returned to the parlor, with the wood and with a pistol tucked in his pants. He didn't want to alarm his wife, but it was a husband's responsibility to defend his home. When Gertrude was satisfied that the floor was cleared of broken glass, Otto set to work, boarding up the window. The parlor would be darker in the daytime, and chillier, without the midday sun shining through the window, but the wooden boards were only intended to be a temporary fix. He would visit the glazier in the morning and make arrangements for a new window. Otto worried that the new glass would put a dent in their meager savings.

Gertrude disappeared into the kitchen, returning with a pile of rags and a bottle of vinegar. She poured vinegar onto one of the rags and began scrubbing the parlor wall. Without saying a word, Otto picked up a second rag and did the same. He scrubbed the wall until the pungent aroma of vinegar became unbearable. Greta refused to take a break as long as there was red paint visible on her parlor wall.

Otto stepped outside to breathe the fresh air. He knew every inch of the swing bridge. He knew its every creak and whine. He knew the grinding of its gears. And he knew, without seeing, that someone was on the bridge. On his bridge. Otto pulled the pistol from his pants and edged closer to the bridge. He spotted two shadows on the bridge and fired a warning shot. The shadows took off at full speed, off the bridge and down along the far side of the canal. Otto watched as the shadows disappeared into the night.

The warning shot drew Gertrude outside, carrying her vinegar-soaked rag like a weapon.

"Mein Barchen?"

"Everything is alright, mein Leibling. Go back inside."

Reluctantly, Gertrude obeyed her husband. Otto walked out onto the swing bridge, checking for damage. The canal might be closed, but he was still the bridge tender, no matter the business decision of the canal company. He stood on the bridge, daring the shadows to return. Otto figured that the shadows were attached to the men who had appeared earlier that evening at the lock tender's house. They were bullies, plain and simple. And in Otto's experience, bullies backed off when they were challenged. Satisfied that the danger had passed, Otto turned and walked back inside his home. Gertrude was still scrubbing the wall with vinegar.

Otto kissed his wife and picked up the second rag. By morning, the star of David was nearly gone, a faint pink reminder of the evening's ugliness.

"I will go see the glazier now."

"No mein Barchen, let me run you a bath."

"Are you sure?" For most of their married life, his wife's suggestion that she run him a bath had been a precursor to other, more intimate activities. Although they had never had children, they had never stopped trying.

Gertrude took him by the hand and led him upstairs. "I'm sure."

Chapter Nineteen

2023

Charlie had grown up with a healthy distrust of the boys in blue. He never gave it much thought. It had been that way since 1970 when Charlie's father had been arrested at an antiwar rally. Charlie grew up understanding that there were good cops and bad, but, on balance, he didn't like the odds.

Perhaps that had led him to lie to Detective Warren. To withhold the truth. It was not in his nature to be forthcoming with the police. But the detective seemed to be a decent fellow. And he had some sort of fingerprint evidence. Charlie sat in the interview room, waiting for the detective's re-appearance.

The door to the interview room swung open. The station clerk stepped into the room, carrying two cans of cola. "I figured you might be thirsty."

"Thanks." Charlie popped the top and took a quick gulp of lukewarm soda. "When is the detective coming back?"

"He's busy." The clerk sat down at the table. "He asked me to finish your interview."

Charlie frowned. "With all due respect, I would prefer to speak to a detective."

"I am Detective Massoud." The young woman smiled. "Let me give you a piece of advice. So far, you've only seen the friendly side of my gargantuan partner. Trust me on this, but you do not want to see his nasty side."

A million thoughts raced through Charlie's head. This woman had been sitting at the clerk's desk when Charlie arrived at the station house. Was that a deliberate bit of police deception? Did Detective Warren plan for the interview to go this way? Detective Warren had fingerprints. Charlie weighed his options. Perhaps it was time to get ahead of the trouble.

"One time, I was inside the bridge tender's house."

"Was that one time the day of the fire?"

"No!" Charlie put down his soda. He told Detective Massoud about the day he went looking for the Conservatorship for a Clean Canal. "I thought they could help me learn more about the history of my house."

Detective Massoud checked her notes. "That's right. You bought the old lock tender's house."

"I thought the Conservatorship had an office at the site of the bridge tender's house. Obviously, I was wrong. But the door was unlocked. I was curious."

"So you went inside. Was anyone there."

"Not at first. But after a few minutes, I heard voices outside. I hid on the second floor. I was able to see through a crack in the floor."

"What exactly did you see, Mr. Levenson?"

"I saw a plaid jacket. I believe it was the same plaid jacket worn by the man who was pulled out of the fire."

"I believe you may be correct. What happened next?"

"Mr. Plaid Jacket left. I waited a few minutes, and then I left as well."

"Mr. Plaid Jacket? That's a good one." Detective Massoud scowled. "And you were doing such a good job there, telling the truth. Then you had to go and spoil things."

"I'm telling the truth."

"Would it surprise you to learn that we have another witness who saw your Mr. Plaid Jacket walk out of the bridge tender's house that day in the presence of another man?" The detective's gaze was fixed on Charlie. "Are you sure you didn't leave with him?"

"I'm sure!"

Detective Massoud checked her notes. "Earlier, you said you heard voices outside. Voices. Plural."

"I didn't see the second man, but I did hear him speak. It was Hank Morgan."

"The thing is, Mr. Morgan doesn't exist." Detective Massoud stared hard at Charlie Levenson. "I mean, obviously, he exists. The man who calls himself Hank Morgan was standing right in front of us this morning. But he doesn't have a driver's license. He doesn't have a social security card. No address or phone number. He never registered for the draft. He's never voted in an election."

"Wow."

"That group today, they call themselves a well-regulated militia, but mostly they're beer-drinking white men harboring a grudge. They're harmless, or would be, except for our Mr. Morgan, who seems to be something of an enigma."

Chapter Twenty

1934

Manny ran home from school as fast as his legs could carry him. He was chasing a dream and would not allow his legs to delay his success. He burst into the house, calling out to his father.

"What is it?" asked Abe. But Manny was too winded to talk.

"Here. Sit down." He handed his son a glass of water. "Catch your breath."

Between sips, Manny rushed ahead. "I know what I'm going to do when I graduate."

"That is good." Abe smiled. "After all, graduation is only two months away."

Manny couldn't sit still in the chair. "I'm going to be Dr. Einstein's assistant."

Abe had so many questions, he hardly knew where to begin. "Doesn't Dr. Einstein live in Germany?"

"Actually, he lived in Switzerland." Manny was nearly jumping out of his skin with excitement. "But my science teacher announced that Albert Einstein has come to America. He has moved into a house in Princeton."

"Princeton is not far at all. But does he need an assistant? After all, he's Albert Einstein."

"I will transcribe his notes, doublecheck his calculations, catalog his manuscripts. It is a dream come true."

Abe shared his son's excitement, but not his unbridled optimism. "How do you plan to get this job with Dr. Einstein?"

"I'm going to ask him to hire me. Papa, can I borrow the Model T?"

"You're going to ask him now?"

"Never put off until tomorrow…"

"I know… what you can do today." Abe reached into his pocket and located one dime. "Here. This should be enough." He smiled. "Go, my son. Go get a job with Dr. Einstein."

* * *

Manny had to set the points, adjust the ignition timing, and crank the engine. He was more than a little jealous, remembering Helmut's Duesenberg Convertible with its starter button. He stopped at the gas pumps and bought one gallon of gas. He made a promise to himself to repay the dime out of his first paycheck. The drive was only six miles, but by the time Manny pulled up in front of the house in Princeton, the sun was low in the sky. Manny stared at the two-story home with the peaked roof. It was not unlike the other houses on the street, and yet, to Manny, somehow, it was different. It was home to the smartest man on the planet. Manny got as far as the front porch and froze. He could not bring himself to knock on the door.

He wasn't sure how long he could stand there, unable to move forward or to retreat, when the creaking of the front door brought him back to the moment. Standing in the doorway, underneath a mass of hair, there stood Albert Einstein.

"Please, young man, come in." Einstein scanned the front porch. "Did you bring your tools?"

Manny mumbled, "No…sir," and followed Einstein into the parlor.

"I have a small set of tools," Einstein said. "Perhaps they will be sufficient for the job."

Manny mumbled, "Yes… sir," and followed Einstein into his office.

"My desk wobbles."

It was true. Albert Einstein had shoved a book under the wobbly leg to provide a semblance of stability. "It is actually the floor that is uneven, but

71

it will be easier to adjust the leg of the desk."

Einstein removed the book *Im Kopf eines Geometrikers*, to give Manny a better look at the problem.

"Have you read it?"

Manny's face turned red. "My German is limited. I regret that I will have to wait until the day that it is available in English."

Einstein smiled and patted Manny on the head. "It is good that you are a carpenter by trade. If you were a scientist, you would not get far if you could not read German."

While they talked, Manny set to work adjusting the leg of Einstein's desk. Manny imagined Einstein sitting at the desk, working on his theories. He had no doubt that Einstein's thoughts would be even more insightful if he were not distracted by a wobble. Perhaps this would be Manny's contribution to science. If so, Manny decided, it would be enough. It might even earn a thank you in the acknowledgements for Dr. Einstein's next publication. But first, he had to try for more.

"I am not a carpenter, sir. I am a scientist... well, I am a high school student, but I hope one day to be a scientist. I came here tonight to apply to be your assistant. I can start the job in two months."

The whole time Manny talked, he stared at Einstein, looking without success for a clue in the great man's expression. Dr. Einstein handed Manny his copy of *Im Kopf eines Geometrikers*. "Bring this back in two months. If you can read it, you will be my Assistant."

"Thank you, thank you, sir. I will be back in two months."

"Then I should know your name."

"My name...my name," Manny stammered. "My name is Emmanuel Dubinski."

"It's good to meet you, Mr. Emmanuel Dubinski. Dr. Einstein broke out laughing, his tongue sticking out into space. "My name is Albert Einstein."

Chapter Twenty-One

2023

When Charlie got home, he was surprised to discover his son Ben waiting on the doorstep.

The sun was setting behind the house. Charlie was exhausted after a long and difficult day. He was grateful to see Ben. "What brings you by?"

"What brings me by?" Ben raised his voice. "What do you think brings me by?"

"Look, Ben, it's been a bad day." Charlie reached for his son, but Ben took a step back.

"Don't touch me!" Ben's fists were clenched, his face was red.

Charlie pulled back his arm. "Calm down. Just tell me what's bothering you."

"You nearly got Jami shot today!" Ben's voice rose an octave. "And you didn't even bother to tell me!"

Charlie couldn't make eye contact with Ben. "I was going to."

"When?"

"I don't want to have this conversation on the porch." He opened the front door. "Can't we at least go inside?"

Ben grumbled but followed his father inside the house.

In the kitchen, Charlie splashed some cold water on his face. He took his time toweling dry. "I meant to tell you when I dropped Jami off at your house, but you weren't home. I couldn't have that conversation with your wife."

"Her name is Olivia. For chrissake, she's Jami's mother."

"I know." Charlie hung his head. "I'm sorry."

"Sorry for what?"

"For putting Jami in harm's way. For not telling Olivia." Charlie paused. "For the death of your mother."

The third apology had Ben doubled over in pain. It took him several minutes to regain his breath. "This is not about Mom."

Charlie shook his head in disagreement. "Everything is about Zoya."

"Yes. I guess it is." Ben wiped a tear from his eye. In the six months since she had died, this was the closest Ben and his father had ever come to having an honest conversation about their anger and pain. "But at the moment, I'm more concerned about what Jami told me when I got home. She told me about a man with a gun."

"Jami asked me to take her for a walk on the towpath. She wanted to look for a flower."

"Get to the part about the gun."

So Charlie told his son about the men who had gathered at the bridge tender's house to protest the disappearance of Mr. Plaid Jacket. He told him about Mr. Pisswater's role in the protest and about the errant gunshot.

"Why do you care about any of that? It doesn't have anything to do with us."

Charlie patted the back of an empty chair. "Sit down, Ben. I guess I owe you an explanation."

"I guess you do." Ben took a seat. "What's this all about?"

"I'm looking for Mr. Plaid Jacket. I was getting close, and then he disappeared."

"You didn't have anything to do with the man's disappearance, did you?" Ben watched his father carefully, looking for a tell.

"I told you I'm trying to find the man."

"Why? I don't understand."

"It's about your mother."

"What about Mom?"

"I think Tom Jackson may know something about the temple massacre." Ben waited for his father to explain.

"I saw him in the crowd outside the temple."

"Are you sure?"

"I wasn't, at first. Then I saw him at the bridge tender's house."

"And you realized that you'd seen him before?"

"I recognized the plaid jacket."

"So what's your plan?"

"I don't have a plan. But if he knows anything about the murders, I intend to find out."

"We should make a plan!" Ben climbed out of the chair and began pacing as if pacing would help him think. "We need to do something."

"We don't need to do anything." Charlie stared at his son. "You have a life ahead of you. You, Olivia, and Jami. What I've got in mind could land me in jail. Maybe worse. I won't let you risk everything by getting involved. Go home. Be a loving husband and father. Leave me to do my thing."

"But if he knows something, I want answers too."

"I'm not looking for answers. I'm just hoping for the pain to go away."

Pain was the one thing Charlie and Ben had in common. But there was nothing Charlie could do to relieve his son's pain or his own. Not until he located Mr. Plaid Jacket.

* * *

It wasn't long after Ben said goodbye that Charlie fell into an uneasy nap on the sofa in his parlor, dreaming of a world where everyone dressed in plaid. In the dream, a man was banging on his door. Charlie awoke and slowly came to realize that the door banging was not part of the dream. The day just kept getting worse. He threw open the door to find Mr. Pisswater standing at the door, his left arm bandaged and in a sling. "Shouldn't you be in jail?"

"I didn't break any laws."

"The hell you didn't!"

"I was exercising my rights. My first amendment rights and my second amendment rights." Hank Morgan grinned. "You may not support my right to bear arms, but surely you support my right to free speech."

"I support my granddaughter's right to live." Charlie felt his blood pressure rising to dangerous levels. "Perhaps you should leave."

Hank Morgan patted his side, the universal symbol of *I'm packing*. "Perhaps we should continue this conversation inside."

"If you don't leave now, I'm going to call the police."

"No you're not. Look, I don't want to hurt your granddaughter." Hank Morgan's grin grew impossibly large. "But if she gets in the way, I can't be responsible for what happens."

Charlie had heard enough. Without any conscious control, he charged at Hank, barreling into the man's chest and sending them both sprawling. Under normal circumstances, he would have had no chance in a physical confrontation with the man. Hank Morgan was younger, fitter, and nastier. But Hank was limited by the gunshot wound in his left arm. Hank landed on his back on the front porch. Charlie slammed into the old stone wall, sending a shooting pain down his side and knocking the breath out of him. Before he could recover, Hank was on top of him. They rolled off the porch, through Charlie's flower bed, and onto the towpath. Hank struggled to his feet. From the ground, Charlie kicked his legs, landing a blow to Hank's stomach, knocking him backwards, toward the canal.

It appeared that Hank would regain his balance, and then, Charlie, back on his feet, rushed him one final time, sending them both into the canal. It had been a dry season. The water level was low enough that both men struggled to their feet, standing in the canal, swinging wildly at one another. A blow caught Hank on the side of his head. He collapsed in the water. For a moment, Charlie considered leaving him lying supine in the canal, his head partially submerged.

Charlie dragged Hank to the edge of the canal and pushed him up onto the bank, climbing up behind him. "If you ever threaten my granddaughter again, I will kill you!" He kicked the man's left arm for emphasis. Hank whimpered in pain. Charlie was surprised by his capacity for violence. But the whimper only made him angrier. Charlie kicked him again. It was, he assured himself, not in his nature. This man had threatened Jamila. He kicked the man one final time. What had Jamila ever done to deserve death threats? Nothing. Charlie's late wife, Jamila's grandmother, had been Muslim. Was that Jamila's crime? Jamila's parents were committed to making sure that she grew up with some knowledge of and connection to her grandmother's heritage. Did a three-year-old girl, one-quarter Iranian, pose such a threat to this man's way of life that she deserved to be threatened at gunpoint?

Charlie turned and walked back to his home, leaving Hank sprawled on the towpath, gasping for breath. Fifteen minutes later, Charlie looked out his window, confirming that Hank Morgan was gone.

"You look like crap."

"When did you get here?"

"I saw the whole thing." Zoya shook her head. "When did violence ever solve anything?"

Charlie didn't know what to say. When he attacked Hank Morgan, he hadn't been trying to solve anything. "He threatened Jami."

"I know what he did." Zoya shook her head again. "Is she safer now?"

"I think he got the message." Charlie could feel the adrenaline still surging in his system. "If it becomes necessary, I will kill the man."

Zoya gasped. "No!"

"If that's what it takes to keep Jami safe."

Zoya was at a loss for words. A deep, dark silence descended on the house, so deep and dark that Charlie questioned whether his dead wife had departed. Whether she would ever return. After ten minutes, she spoke up.

"You've changed."

Charlie wanted to argue, but he knew that she was right. "It's been difficult."

"You think living is difficult? Try dying. That's difficult."

Zoya's death had been especially difficult.

Chapter Twenty-Two

1934

"What are you reading, brother?"

Manny held up his copy of *Im Kopf eines Geometrikers*.

"*Im Kopf*... what?" Rachel stumbled, reading the title. "I'll bet you have a comic book hidden inside." She grabbed the book and rifled through the pages. "That is not a school assignment. And it doesn't seem like recreational reading... even for you. So why are you reading *Im Kopf eines Geometrikers*?"

Manny smiled. "Dr. Einstein gave it to me. He told me if I understand the book, I can have a job as his assistant."

Rachel was skeptical. "Do you understand it?"

"I'm struggling with the translation." Manny opened the book.

The mind of a something wants to something something, but the tendency toward something causes the *abstract* something in the something that is being studied. The tendency to something can become a something, as it were, which distracts the something from the meaning of something.

Rachel was determined to support her brother's effort, no matter what the results. "You've made a start."

"That's just the first paragraph... of the preface. And it's taken me all morning." Manny put the book down on the table. "At this rate, it will take me years," he jumped to the end of the book, "to read three hundred-ninety pages."

"You'll just have to read a little faster. I have faith in you." Rachel patted her brother on the arm. "So what does it mean?"

Manny groaned.

"Tell me, what was it like meeting Dr. Einstein?"

Manny perked up at the memory of his evening at the great man's home. "He thought I was a handyman."

"What?"

Manny told Rachel about Einstein mistaking him for the man who was supposed to repair his desk. He told her about the wobbly leg and about the book. He told her about their conversation. And he told her, now that he had started reading the book, that he despaired of ever becoming Einstein's assistant. "Dr. Einstein needs an assistant who can read the German texts. I fear that my grasp of the German language will never be good enough."

Rachel frowned. "I am sorry to hear that. I know it has always been your dream to become a scientist like Dr. Einstein."

"I have begun to understand that dreams are for little boys. Now that I am a man, I need to think about helping Papa with the bills. I need to finish high school and get a job."

"It is harder for a man." Rachel shook her head. "I don't need a diploma to be a good wife and mother."

"But you will get a diploma. You are fortunate to live at a time when a woman can be anything she wants to be. Especially if she is bright and beautiful, like you. Women are working in shops and in offices now. I even heard that there's a woman doctor at the hospital in Princeton. You can be a wife and mother and also be whatever else you want to be." Manny was surprised to realize he had no idea what his sister dreamed of. "What do you want to do after high school?"

"I have been hesitant to say anything, but since we are having this conversation, would you be angry if I became Dr. Einstein's assistant?"

"You?" Manny was stunned. "You are very smart for a girl, probably the smartest girl I know, but if I can't understand *Im Kopf eines Geometrikers*, I'm afraid you would embarrass yourself."

"Nevertheless, I would like to try."

"I won't get angry. And I promise I won't say I told you so." Manny didn't want to hurt his sister's feelings. "What he needs is a housekeeper. Dr. Einstein is so busy with his theories, he doesn't seem to notice the mess."

An idea began to take shape in Rachel's head. "I could be his housekeeper."

"I think that is a sensible plan." Manny nodded his head in agreement. Perhaps, after she established herself as the Einsteins' housekeeper, she might put in a good word on Manny's behalf.

Chapter Twenty-Three

1979

Z oya Aziz was fourteen when she knocked on the door of an unfamiliar house in a strange new land. A woman answered the door. For a moment, she stared at the girl, wondering who she was and why she was standing on the doorstep. Then she let out a yell and scooped the girl up in her arms.

Zoya didn't know what to say. Nothing in her short life had prepared her for such a greeting. "I'm Zoya."

"And you're alive! Come in! Come in!"

It was the spring of 1979, on the cusp of the Iranian Revolution. Zoya's parents, in a last, desperate act, had sent their daughter to America.

Zoya's parents were academics, with appointments on the faculty at the University of Tehran. Her father, Karim Aziz, was an economist. Her mother, Leila, a pediatrician. Early in their careers, they had admired the Shah. He seemed to understand the modern world and wanted Iran to be a part of it. They liked his policies on education and were especially impressed by his support for women's rights. But, over time, things changed. The government under the Shah became increasingly oppressive and anti-democratic. There were things about the Shah they admired, but they could not abide a dictatorship. They recognized that Iran needed to change. When the protests began, Karim and Leila were cautiously optimistic about the return of democratic principles. But they could not accept the fundamentalists' version of Islam. From the safety of their university classrooms, they spoke out against both sides.

Leila was lecturing when a pipe bomb exploded in the hallway. Thirteen students were injured. Two died. The university was no longer a safe place from which to voice an opinion. Quietly, they made plans to get out of Iran.

But they had waited too long. They would not be able to leave the country. In the end, they managed to pay an extraction team to get their daughter safely out of Iran. Leila Aziz had a colleague in America, a Jewish woman with no children of her own. Leila had met Dr. Shira Barookhian at an international medical conference. Karim and Leila hoped their daughter would understand. For her part, Zoya understood nothing, only that the world, as she knew it, was gone forever.

The last time she saw her parents, Zoya was being lowered into a crate in the false bottom of a truck. When the extraction team began piling crates of rice onto the back of the truck, obscuring the false bottom, Leila lost control. It was as though she was watching her baby being buried alive. Karim held his wife close. They cried until they ran out of tears. When the truck pulled away, they drove back to their home in Tehran. Their lives were over. They prayed to Allah that their daughter might have a life in New Jersey.

Inside the crate, in the false bottom of the truck, Zoya's world had grown small, dark, and exceedingly hot. As the truck made its way through the desert, Zoya felt every bump in the road. The pain was excruciating, but at least she was alive. If the pain stopped, it would mean that she was dead. Zoya prayed to Allah for the pain to stop.

Suddenly, the driver hit the brakes. Zoya's head smashed against the inside of the wooden crate. She bit her tongue, to stop from crying out. She didn't know if anyone could hear her, buried under a thousand pounds of rice, but she wasn't eager to find out.

She didn't see what happened next, only saw the outcome; sometime later the same day. Three men had stopped the truck at gunpoint. Were they revolutionaries? Members of the Shah's guard? Were the men looking for Zoya? Or was this perhaps a simple case of attempted robbery? Zoya would never know.

She waited, what felt like hours before pushing the top off the crate and struggling to move the wooden boards that hid the false bottom. Apparently, the men, whoever they were, had rummaged through the crates of rice. Again, Zoya didn't know what they had been looking for, but she realized, if they hadn't been looking for something, she never would have had the strength to push the heavy crates aside.

Zoya stood on the back of the truck and surveyed the surroundings. Both members of the extraction team were now lying on the ground, dead of multiple gunshot wounds. The attackers, three men, also lay dead on the ground. Zoya tried to drive off in the truck, but she couldn't get the engine to turn over, and, in any event, the tires were riddled with bullet holes.

With no other options, Zoya set out on foot. This was the worst part of the journey. Alone, with limited resources, and no way to judge friend or foe, she slept during the heat of the day and walked at night. At some point, in the dead of night, at some unmanned stretch of border, Zoya crossed into Turkey. She made her way across Turkey, and, using what little money she had, travelled by bus to Greece. In Greece, she came to the attention of a refugee organization. Two months later, she was knocking on a door in New Jersey.

Charlie's grandfather had left Eastern Europe at the age of fourteen, dreaming of America, where the streets were paved with gold. His grandfather had worked his way to England, finally stowing away on a steamer heading for America.

Charlie liked to believe that Zoya's journey was not so very different than his grandfather's had been. It was, he told himself, a harmless bit of self-deceit.

In any event, she had made it to America, and within that huge expanse of land, she made her way to West Covington, New Jersey. She stood on the doorstep, taking in the two-story suburban house with the well-maintained lawn.

She knocked on the door. A strange woman opened the door and hugged her tight. They stepped inside like that, still hugging, the woman still yelling.

Zoya was starting a new life in America.

Chapter Twenty-Four

1934

"Do you think Helmut will come back?" Rachel and Manny were upstairs, in Rachel's bedroom, where they could speak privately. Rachel wasn't sure why she bothered asking the question. She knew what her brother's answer would be.

"I hope not."

Rachel said nothing until Manny asked a question of his own. "Why do you care?"

She smiled shyly. "I think I like him."

"He's a Nazi." Manny spit the words out. "You do know what that means, don't you?"

"I know what you think it means." Rachel frowned. "You think that Nazis hate Jews."

Manny shook his head. "They do."

"If Helmut hates Jews, tell me this, smarty pants…" Rachel stared at her brother, a challenge in her eyes and in her voice, "Why did he help Mama that day on the ice?"

"That was before he knew that we were Jewish." Manny stood up and walked around the bedroom before continuing. "Think about it, Rachel. We're the only Jewish family in the village. We dress like the villagers. We talk, at least in public, like the villagers. We don't keep a kosher home, don't go to temple. Except for lighting the Shabbos candles, what do we do that would alert a stranger, on first meeting, that we're Jewish?"

"But he was nice to me, even after he found out."

"That is what makes him so dangerous."

"I don't understand."

Manny sat down on the bed next to his sister and held her hand. "He wants something from you."

Rachel smiled. "He wants to take me to the movie theater."

"No, my sweet, innocent sister. I fear he wants something more from you." Manny picked his words carefully. He was navigating through a minefield. If he said the wrong thing, his dear sister was likely to explode. "He wants something that you should be saving for your husband."

"Oh, that!" Rachel picked up her pillow, hit her brother across the head, and burst out laughing. "I know how to handle myself around boys!"

Manny backed away from the bed lest his sister hit him again with her pillow. "You haven't..." but Manny couldn't bring himself to finish the question.

"I haven't." Rachel grinned. "But I'd like to."

"Not with a Nazi!" Manny didn't bother hiding his anger. "I forbid it!"

"You are a silly boy." Rachel laughed and picked up the pillow. "Don't make me hit you again."

"But—"

"I will explain this to you one time because you are my brother, and I love you. You cannot tell me what to do. You do not have the authority."

"Then I will talk to Papa."

"That will only make Papa sad. It will not change what I do."

"So, you've made up your mind." Manny didn't want to believe he was powerless to protect his sister. But he was.

"If he returns, I will let him take me to the movie theater."

"And?"

"And nothing." Rachel was clear on this final point. "I know how to handle myself around boys."

Chapter Twenty-Five

1980

"I don't want you to feel like you're an outsider," Shira Barookhian said to Zoya, even as she recognized that Zoya was, in every respect, an outsider. "It's a delicate balance, and I'll probably get it wrong sometimes, but I want you to know that you and I are family now. I hope that the things that are important to me will become important to you." Dr. Barookhian saw a frightened look on Zoya's face. She realized that she might have overstepped. "Of course, you don't have to. Do you understand?"

Zoya said nothing but nodded her head in agreement.

"I go to temple most Friday nights. Would you be willing to go with me?" Dr. Barookhian gathered her thoughts before continuing. "I don't expect you to abandon your faith, but I…" She cleared her throat.

Zoya just wanted this awkward conversation to be over. "I think I'd like that."

As things turned out, she did like it. The congregation accepted her for who she was. She liked the music and the stories. She liked the feeling of community.

Mostly what Zoya liked was meeting the rest of the Barookhian clan, Shira's brother Solayman ("Call me Sol"), her sister-in-law Dana, and their daughter Sarah. The Barookhians were Iranian Jews. Zoya felt an immediate connection with these Barookhians. Notwithstanding the religious difference, they spoke the same language, ate the same foods, and listened to the same music. These Barookhians would be Zoya's bridge to America. She looked forward to going to school in the fall with Sarah. It would be good to start the school year with one friend. It didn't occur to Zoya that these Barookhians might not live in the same town, that Sarah might not go to the same high school.

In September 1979, Zoya learned that she was a West Covington High School Owl and Sarah was an East Covington Eagle. She didn't understand what it meant to be an owl. It wasn't like being a Sunni or a Sufi, but everyone at her high school was an owl, so Zoya was too. She was confused by the banner at the main entrance welcoming the newest owls, the Class of '83, but she was also proud. She flapped her arms as she imagined an owl must flap its wings, and she screeched "Howt!" as she walked under the banner and into the building.

It was not an auspicious start to her high school career, kids pointing at her in the hallways, laughing and screeching, "Howt!" From there, things went downhill.

High school was difficult for Zoya. Not the academics. She knew enough English to understand her teachers, and anyway, her assignments were far less rigorous than they had been in Tehran. But nothing had prepared her for the peer pressure of an American public school. She told everyone that she was Persian. Most of the comments she heard in the hallway made reference to genies and flying carpets. Then, fundamentalist revolutionaries in Iran attacked the US embassy, taking fifty-two Americans hostage.

Zoya tried to explain that not all Muslims were the same, that not all Muslims wore hijabs and hated America. But America was at war with Muslims in Iran. Zoya was a Muslim from Iran. So Zoya was the enemy. When her locker was jimmied open and her possessions ransacked, the hall monitors looked the other way. Outside, on school grounds, when she was pelted with rotten eggs, her teachers looked away. Students in art class designed a life-sized Zoya doll dressed in a hijab. They got an "A" for the assignment. That afternoon, the school had a pep rally. Zoya was burned in effigy.

She longed for the days when she was the girl who didn't know how to pronounce "Hoot."

She ate lunch alone, too scared to sit down with her classmates, too shy to sit down with strangers. The day after the pep rally, a boy sat down next to her in the cafeteria. She was so nervous that her hands shook. She nearly dropped her glass of iced tea. The boy sat there, impassive, eating a grilled cheese sandwich and a cup of tomato soup. He said nothing. When lunch period was over, he stood up and left.

He returned the next day and the day after that. He had lunch with her every day for the remainder of the school year. They never spoke. But it was enough to get Zoya through her freshman year at West Covington High School. On the last day of school, he looked at Zoya. "I'll miss having lunch with you." The boy smiled. "I'll see you next year."

It would be ten years before Zoya would see Charlie again.

Chapter Twenty-Six

1934

Rachel was helping her mother in the kitchen when Miriam stumbled and grabbed for the back of a chair. She stood there for a minute, swaying slightly, before shaking her head, as if to clear the cobwebs. She sat down awkwardly.

"Mama, are you alright?"

Miriam was slow to respond. "Yes, child. I'm fine."

"You don't look fine, Mama."

"Come here, my child."

Rachel walked over to her mother. Miriam took her daughter's face in her hands and held it tenderly.

"Do you need anything, Mama?"

Miriam thought for a moment. "Please bring me your father's bottle of brandy."

"Brandy Mama? Are you sure?"

"Yes, child." She swatted playfully at her daughter. "Now go."

Rachel went off in search of the bottle. When she returned, Miriam was standing at the stove, stirring the soup.

"I can do that for you, Mama."

"Yes, thank you." Miriam poured herself a small glass of brandy, spilling just a bit as she poured.

Rachel was surprised when her mother didn't immediately wipe up the spill. "I'll get that for you." Rachel grabbed a towel and wiped up the small spill.

"Thank you, my child. There is one more thing." Miriam smiled. "Please ask your father to come talk to me."

"Of course, Mama." Rachel rushed outside, where her father was fiddling with the Model T.

"Papa, come quickly."

"What is it?"

"I fear Mama is unwell."

Abe dropped his tools, wiped the grease from his hands, and rushed inside.

In the kitchen, Abe and Miriam spoke quietly so that Rachel wouldn't hear their conversation. When they were done talking, Abe gestured for Rachel to join them.

"Where is your brother?"

"He stayed late at school today. I think he's eager to complete all of his requirements in time for graduation. I expect he'll be home soon."

"Then you're in charge until we get back."

"Where are you going?" Rachel was worried by this sudden change in plans.

"I'm going to get Dr. Benjamin."

Rachel gasped. *How sick was she?* No one in the Dubinski family had the habit of seeing a doctor.

"No child. Your mother is fine. It is just a precaution."

Rachel didn't know whether or not to believe her father. She had only recently come to understand that her father would shield her from bad news.

"Please help your mother get into bed. And keep an eye on the soup. When your brother gets home, tell him that everything is alright."

Rachel kissed her father goodbye and helped her mother climb the stairs. Miriam objected to Rachel's help, but followed her daughter's directions and, before long, she was resting comfortably in bed. Rachel went back down to the kitchen. The soup was bubbling gently on the stovetop.

If there was one thing Rachel had learned from her mother, it was the medicinal benefits of homemade chicken soup. She stirred the soup, inhaling deeply. Perhaps all her mother needed to feel better was a bowl of soup. She ladled a small serving into a bowl, put the bowl on a tray, and carried the tray carefully up to her mother's bedroom.

When she opened the bedroom door, Miriam was sleeping fitfully, bathed in sweat.

"Mama?" Rachel touched her mother's arm. It was hot to the touch.

Miriam opened her eyes and smiled weakly. "Yes, my love?"

"I brought you a bowl of chicken soup."

"Thank you."

Rachel offered her mother a spoonful of the soup.

Miriam shook her head. "I think I should wait for the doctor."

Rachel had never known her mother to pass on a bowl of chicken soup. "As you wish."

From the window in her parents' bedroom, Rachel spotted the Model T pulling up alongside their house. Dr. Benjamin climbed down with his medicine bag. He didn't wait for Abe and hurried inside.

Rachel was still standing by the window when the doctor entered the bedroom. He shooed Rachel out of the room. "Wait downstairs with your father."

"Is she going to be okay?"

"Let me examine her first." Dr. Benjamin was already taking a variety of medical instruments from his bag. He paused, looked at Rachel, standing there worrying about her mother. He softened his tone. "I'm sure it's nothing serious."

While Rachel and Abe waited downstairs, Dr. Benjamin conducted a thorough examination. Meanwhile, Abe was explaining to his daughter how lucky they were to have a doctor like Dr. Benjamin. He was young, by doctor's standards, having recently completed his training at the brand-new hospital in Princeton. "But what he lacks in age, he more than makes up for in training in the most modern medical procedures."

Abe had heard rumors that Dr. Benjamin had a Jewish grandparent. He looked at his daughter and smiled. "Mrs. Dr. Benjamin."

"What was that, Papa?"

Abe's cheeks reddened. He was rescued by the good doctor himself, walking down the staircase.

"Doctor, how is my wife?" Abe couldn't hide the worry in his voice.

Dr. Benjamin spoke quietly, but firmly. "I would like to take her to the hospital."

"What is it?"

"I'm sure it's nothing." Dr. Benjamin frowned. "But I can run more sophisticated tests at the hospital."

Chapter Twenty-Seven

1990

Zoya found her refuge in books. She loved reading books that helped her understand what life was like in America. She was determined to make a life in America. She also read stories that reminded her of the home she would never see again. She especially enjoyed books that transported her to places that only existed in her imagination. She made friends with her favorite characters, sharing secrets and going on adventures. At a time when she had few real friends, fictional characters became her closest confidantes. She spent most evenings at home, reading and then chatting well into the night with the book's characters. One night each month, she went to a meeting of the library book club.

Zoya volunteered at the public library, eventually becoming a part-time employee. She went to college at night, with a major in library science. She joined a local mosque and worshiped there from time-to-time, but continued to attend Jewish services with the Barookhians. Gradually, and without being able to pinpoint a specific moment in time, Zoya realized that she thought of America as her home. Teheran would always inspire her imagination, but she had made a life in West Covington.

At the library book club, Zoya discovered a community of like-minded individuals. She read the book club selection without fail, and for nearly a decade, she showed up religiously for the monthly meetings. She considered the other members to be her friends, even though she rarely saw them outside of the meetings.

Zoya claimed a vacant chair and waited for the discussion to begin. Just as the meeting was getting started, a newcomer joined the group, taking a seat next to Zoya. He mumbled a greeting to no one in particular and sat down. As Zoya expected, the discussion that evening was spirited, with members debating whether Howard W. Campbell Jr. was a patriot or a traitor. Zoya's opinion was that Campbell could very well be both. "Be careful who you pretend to be," was the way she explained it to the group.

The newcomer didn't contribute to the discussion, but it was obvious that he was listening. Zoya could tell that some of the regular members were made uncomfortable by the newcomer's silence. Zoya, however, found his silence to be comfortable and oddly familiar.

Something tugged at her memory. When the meeting came to a close, Zoya took the initiative.

"Do I know you?"

The shy newcomer shook his head no. But Zoya saw something familiar in his eyes. She was not going to let him walk out on her again.

"Charlie?"

The newcomer fidgeted in his seat. Then he jumped up and ran around the library, flapping his arms like a wild man. The librarian jumped up and attempted, without success, to curtail the newcomer's antics. Members of the book club looked on in silent astonishment. But Zoya grinned and flew from her seat, flapping her arms, shouting "Howt!"

The librarian didn't know what to do. This was not the same Zoya who had been coming to the library for a decade. She put her finger to her lips and said, "Shush!"

Zoya looked at the librarian, at the newcomer, and then back at the librarian. She sat down in her chair and whispered, "Howt!"

For ten years, Charlie had never doubted that their paths would cross and he would see Zoya again. He had imagined elaborate scenarios and rehearsed multiple scripts. But when the moment arrived, he didn't know what to say. So he flapped his way around the library. Embarrassed, he sat back down in the chair next to Zoya and whispered, "Howt."

Zoya started to giggle and couldn't stop.

Charlie took her by the arm and walked toward the exit. "We should go, before we get kicked out." They stopped at the reference desk and apologized to the librarian for their behavior. "We'll be better next time." Charlie grinned. "I promise."

He turned his attention back to Zoya. "Can I buy you a cup of coffee?"

"I prefer tea." She flapped her arms lazily. "There's a place nearby."

Zoya took him by the hand, as if he might otherwise disappear, and together they walked two blocks to *Sarah's Persian Tea Room*. The tearoom was tiny, fragrant, and filled to overflowing with Iranian relics. Zoya waved hello to the proprietor, Sarah Barookhian. Sarah, for her part, seeing Zoya enter the tearoom with a man, came out from behind the counter with a huge grin spilling out all over her face.

Sarah turned her attention to the man holding Zoya's hand. "I'm Zoya's cousin. And you are?"

Charlie blushed. "I'm a friend of Zoya's from high school."

"Really! I didn't know Zoya had any high school friends."

Charlie grinned. "I didn't know she had any cousins."

They sat down at a small table at the rear of the tearoom. Zoya struggled to orchestrate the conversation. Eventually, she managed to make proper introductions.

Sarah smiled. "I'll bring you a pot of tea, then." She hurried off to brew a fresh pot of Persian tea.

Silence enveloped them at the table. To Zoya, it felt like the high school cafeteria all over again. "How come you never spoke to me?"

Charlie blushed. "I'm not very good at small talk."

Zoya was reminded of her parents, scholars who loved to engage in big talk with their academic friends. No topic was too big. They could spend hours debating the latest journal article. But simple social interaction was too small for them to grasp. "My parents were like that."

"Do you miss them?"

"Do I miss them?" Zoya allowed herself a moment before continuing. "Of course."

"Do you know what happened to them after you left?"

"The first year, I got an occasional letter. The Barookhians must have had some contact with them because the letters included a few details about my life in America."

"And then?"

Sarah returned with a tray of assorted pastries, a bowl of sugar cubes, and two cups of black tea seasoned with cardamom. Zoya was relieved she didn't have to answer Charlie's question. She took a sugar cube from the bowl and held it between her teeth. She sipped her tea.

"Is that how it's done?" Charlie took a sugar cube and held it in his teeth. Sipping the tea, he nearly choked on the sugar cube. He coughed and successfully dislodged what remained of the sugar cube, wrapping it discretely in a napkin.

Zoya chuckled. "It's an acquired taste."

Charlie blushed. "I hope I'll have more opportunities to acquire it."

"You didn't come back after summer break." It was Zoya's turn to blush. "What happened?"

"My father got transferred to Cleveland."

Zoya remembered how empty her lunch table was without Charlie. "I missed you."

Charlie remembered how empty Cleveland was without Zoya. "I missed you too."

"Do you still live in Cleveland? Are you in town on a visit?" Zoya held her breath, praying for the right answer.

"I came back to pursue a business opportunity. I live here now." Charlie wasn't ready to share the details. Zoya, for the moment, didn't care about the details. She exhaled.

"Will you come to the next meeting of the book club?"

"I will. If they let me in after tonight's performance."

"I'll put in a good word." She leaned across the table and kissed Charlie lightly on his cheek.

From her spot behind the counter, Sarah Barookhian looked on and nodded her head approvingly.

Chapter Twenty-Eight

1934

Abe held Miriam's arm tenderly and steadied her as they walked out to the automobile. He helped her climb into the seat. The Model T was getting finicky in its old age, but Abe managed to crank the engine. It rattled but started on the third attempt.

Abe drove as quickly as the Model T could manage. With each bump in the unpaved road, the car clanked in protest, and Miriam cried out in pain. Abe slowed the Model T, offering up a silent prayer for Miriam's safe arrival at the hospital.

It wasn't a long ride to Princeton, but it felt like they spent an eternity on the old country road that led to town. Abe pulled up to the circular drive that marked the front of the impressive two-story building on Witherspoon Street. It was the first time, and he prayed, the only time, his family would have need of such a place. Still, he was grateful it was available. The hospital was only five years old. It had fifty-six beds and a delivery room with twelve bassinets. Everything about the hospital was modern. They even had one female physician on staff. Perhaps, in some respects, the hospital was too modern. He was glad to have Dr. Benjamin handling the case.

The nursing staff got Miriam settled in a bed while Abe took care of the paperwork. If she needed to stay overnight, the bed would likely cost him as much as $7.00. That was on top of the house call, which had already cost him $2.39. He stopped reading before he got to the rest of the medical costs.

He didn't want to think about his wife's health care in economic terms. He just wanted her to get well. Dr. Benjamin would tell him what he needed to know. He would figure out later how to pay for it.

Abe sat with Miriam until Dr. Benjamin began his examination. The doctor walked Abe to the exit. "The nurse will show you to the waiting room. I'll come find you when I've completed my examination."

The waiting room was comfortable or would have been under other circumstances. Abe settled into an overstuffed chair. He didn't want to dwell on his sick wife in the room down the hall. He let his mind drift to another Miriam, a younger Miriam, the girl that Abe had fallen in love with when they still lived with their parents in Manhattan. Abe's mother had entered into a contract with the neighborhood matchmaker to find him a wife. The matchmaker recommended Miriam's older sister. Bertha was a perfectly appropriate candidate. Abe's mother gladly paid the matchmaker for her services. Abe might have married Bertha, accepted a job at his father-in-law's textile business in the Garment District, and lived happily ever after surrounded by Jewish family and friends. Instead, he fell for Bertha's younger sister. He couldn't articulate what it was that he wanted in a wife, but whatever it was, he recognized it in Miriam. They got married without the approval of either family, left New York forever, and started a new life together in New Jersey. He never regretted his decision.

Dr. Benjamin interrupted his memories. "Excuse me, Mr. Dubinski."

Abe jumped to his feet. "Yes, doctor?"

Dr. Benjamin patted Abe on the shoulder. "Sit."

The two men sat down in the overstuffed chairs in the hospital waiting room.

"A woman's body is an amazing thing." Dr. Benjamin began.

"Yes," Abe smiled. "It is."

"No...yes...what I mean is, there is a lot we don't know about a woman's body. What makes it work." Dr. Benjamin stammered. "What makes it stop working."

"Are you saying my wife's body isn't working properly?" Abe was alarmed by the doctor's explanation. "I don't understand."

"To be blunt, Mr. Dubinski, women's bodies don't seem to obey what we know to be true about the human body. If I didn't know better, I'd say that women require a different kind of medical care." Dr. Benjamin patted Abe's arm. "Of course, that's just the ramblings of a very tired doctor. I'll run more tests. I'm confident that things will be better in the morning."

* * *

Rachel watched her parents drive off, before going back inside the house. It was not a large home, but it always felt huge to Rachel when she was the only one at home.

Rachel retrieved her French book. Ever since deciding that she would go to work for Dr. Einstein, Rachel had been uninterested in her homework, even Proust. She put down her French and rummaged through her brother's things, until she located the copy of *Im Kopf eines Geometrikers*.

She flipped through the pages. The book was written in formal, academic German, not the conversational German she had picked up over the years, chatting with Gertrude Becker. Nevertheless, Rachel had absorbed enough vocabulary that she discovered she could understand bits and pieces of the tome. The illustrations were a tremendous help. Rachel managed to make her way through a discussion of the eleven properties of the sphere. She didn't really understand all of the properties, but at least she could name them. Her brother could barely keep straight the difference between antipodal points and umbilical points. Try making that mistake in front of Dr. Einstein.

She might have read more, but her reading was interrupted by the toot of a car horn. Were her parents home from the hospital already? She realized it was not the toot of their Model T. But Rachel had heard the toot once before. She ran to the window in time to see a Duesenberg Model J Convertible coming to a stop just a few hundred feet down the road. Helmut had returned. She did a little dance in front of the mirror. Rachel spent a moment fixing her face before racing downstairs. She was heading for the door when she remembered the soup.

Rachel never resorted to indecent language, but it's possible that a certain expression associated with sailors and stevedores slipped from her lips. She rushed into the kitchen, stirred the soup, and turned the gas off. She would have a hard enough time explaining what she was about to do without having to explain a kitchen fire.

She smelled of schmaltz as she ran down the road to the Duesenberg.

Chapter Twenty-Nine

1990

For three months, Charlie attended the book club meetings religiously. He sat next to Zoya and held her hand while they talked about books. After each meeting, they repaired to *Sarah's Persian Tea Room* for a cup of black tea with cardamom and a platter of assorted pastries. He enjoyed the book discussions, but, if he were being honest, the books were merely an excuse to spend time with Zoya. He was working up the courage to ask Zoya out on a date. Without the entire book club acting as chaperones.

The leader of the book club had announced the next month's book, *An Imaginary Geometrician.* Charlie would never complain in front of the group, but privately, between bites of nazook, he shared his reluctance with Zoya.

"A math book?" Charlie snorted. "I haven't looked at a math book since high school."

Zoya put down her tea and smiled. "It's not a math book. It's the memoir of a famous mathematician."

"I can't." Charlie gulped down a swallow of hot tea and forged ahead. "Are you familiar with *Gitane?*"

Zoya shook her head no.

"It's a new jazz club, just opened last month. I've heard good things about it." Charlie wasn't ready to tell her *Gitane* was his new jazz club. There would be time enough for that if their relationship developed.

Zoya was ready to say yes. She just needed Charlie to get around to asking.

Charlie asked. "Would you go with me... next Friday?"

"Next Friday?" Zoya was torn. "I go to temple on Friday."

"Temple? Don't you mean mosque?"

"If I meant mosque, I would have said mosque." Zoya chuckled to let Charlie know she wasn't angry. "The Barookhians are Jewish. Don't you think it's a good thing when a Muslim woman is welcome in a Jewish temple?"

"Yes. I guess that must be a very good thing."

They sat at the corner table, sipping tea, each of them considering what to say next.

Zoya's face brightened. "So, why don't you go to temple with me? And then we can go to the club, what did you call it, *Gitane*, another night."

"It's a date." Charlie was beaming. "Two dates, actually."

* * *

Friday evening, Charlie pulled into the parking lot that abutted Zoya's apartment. It was a warm spring evening. Zoya was waiting for him out front. He hopped out of the car and held the car door open. Zoya gave him a peck on the cheek and slid into the passenger seat. Zoya told him to turn left onto Mulberry Street. He knew the way to temple, but he allowed Zoya to give him directions. She pointed out the half dozen turns that would lead them to the temple. He missed the last turn, sliding through the intersection, but turned at the next block and made the circuit back to Cypress Lane and the entrance to B'nai Shalom.

Charlie had not been to temple since his Bar Mitzvah. When he was a child, temple had been an expectation, an obligation, and perhaps because of that expectation, he never appreciated it as a spiritual experience. Once the obligation had been fulfilled, he stopped attending services. Zoya, on the other hand, had been going to temple religiously since Shira Barookhian, her surrogate mother, had taken her in. Charlie recognized the irony, that Zoya, a Muslim woman from Iran, was an integral part of this Jewish community, and he, a secular Jew who was Bar Mitzvah in this very synagogue, was now the outsider. But he recognized the prayers and remembered the words. Once learned, never forgotten. Being Jewish was like riding a bicycle. He told himself to be careful lest his pants' legs get caught in the bicycle gears.

When the service was over, Zoya told Charlie that she wanted to stay for the Oneg Shabbat. They got on line for a cup of coffee and a bit of pastry and found seats at an empty table. Charlie took a nibble of pastry. He turned to Sarah and grinned. "Not as good as your nazook."

"Thank you."

Zoya chuckled. "No one makes pastries like my Sarah."

While they ate, Zoya told Charlie about her arrival in New Jersey, how Shira Barookhian, an Iranian American Jewish woman, had taken her in and raised her as her own, how it was at temple that Zoya met the rest of the Barookhians and how this temple was the only place where she felt truly welcome during those first difficult years. Zoya reached over and hugged Sarah, spilling a bit of coffee in the effort. Sarah grabbed a napkin and wiped up the coffee before it spilled onto the floor. Sarah grinned, "I am, after all, a trained barista."

"You are way more than a trained barista," said Zoya. "You are the sole proprietor of the finest Persian Tea Room, this side of Manhattan."

"Do you mind if I join you?" Without waiting for a reply, the rabbi sat down at the table. "Shabat Shalom."

Zoya and Sarah replied, in unison, "Shabat Shalom."

Charlie was a beat behind in his Sabbath greeting.

Zoya took the opportunity to make introductions. "Charlie Levenson, meet Rabbi Harry Cohen. Rabbi, Charlie Levenson."

"It's a pleasure, Rabbi Cohen." Charlie extended his hand.

"Please, call me Rabbi Harry." Rabbi took Charlie's hand and gave it a vigorous shake. "Levenson? That's a familiar name, is it not?"

"My parents were members."

"And you?"

Charlie blushed. "It has been many years."

"Welcome back." Rabbi dismissed Charlie's embarrassment. "What is time, after all?"

* * *

Charlie and Zoya sat in the car, waiting for the light to change. There were no other cars at the intersection. Charlie felt like the traffic light was mocking him.

"Maybe I should just go. Maybe it's broken. Maybe we'll be here forever."

"Maybe we will." Zoya grinned. "What is time, after all?"

Charlie checked his phone. "We can still catch the second set at *Gitane*."

"Our second date! I would like that. This way, I don't have to sit home waiting for you to call."

It was a short drive to the jazz club. Charlie pulled into the crowded lot and parked his car in a reserved spot.

Zoya was surprised, but made no comment. She hoped the club wouldn't tow Charlie's car.

Inside, the manager greeted Charlie and Zoya warmly. There was a table set discretely along a side wall, affording a surprisingly good view of the stage and spacious seating in the otherwise crowded club.

The waiter came over, carrying a bottle of red wine as well as a bottle of white. He asked Zoya if she had a preference. Zoya declined the wine, asking instead for a glass of sparkling water. Without asking, the waiter poured Charlie a merlot.

"It seems like everyone on the staff knows you. Do you come here often?"

Charlie blushed. "I'm a part owner."

"Which part?"

Before Charlie could answer, a trio came out on stage. They launched into their version of the Cole Porter classic, *Could It Be You?*

When the set was done, Zoya took the opportunity to respond to a comment Charlie had made in the car.

"All that trouble in high school? It wasn't because I was Muslim, not really. It was because I was the Other. In 1979, it was Muslims. Other times, it's been Jews. Gypsies. Persons of color. Hippies. Homosexuals. The Other."

At temple with Zoya, it was Charlie who felt like he had a label on his forehead. Lapsed Jew, the label said. The Other.

Chapter Thirty

1934

Rachel knew how to manage boys. The last thing she wanted was to appear to be overeager. She slowed to a walk, stopping halfway to the Duesenberg. She struck a pose much like the sexy French woman standing on a pile of gold coins on the cover of the February issue of *Life*, promising *I can't give you anything but love.* She didn't have the lady's red hair and lips, she most certainly didn't have her bosom, but she had the come hither look. She would leave the rest to Helmut's imagination.

Rachel could hear the ignition turn over as Helmut started the car and pulled up next to her. "Hallo, mein Rachel."

Rachel did her best to smile coyly. "You're back."

"I am."

"Did you come back to see me?"

"I came back on business." Helmut smiled. "And perhaps for a bit of fun."

Rachel leaned in toward Helmut.

Helmut stepped out of the Duesenberg. He took Rachel in his arms and kissed her. It was a rough-and-tumble sort of kiss. Rachel knew how to manage boys, but in that moment, she came to understand that Helmut was not a boy. Helmut was a man. It was exciting. And also scary. She backed away.

"What do you have in mind?"

"King Kong."

"I don't understand."

"You said you would let me take you to a movie. King Kong is playing tonight at the theater in Princeton."

"I can't. Not tonight." Rachel felt herself being tugged in two competing directions. "Perhaps we could sit here in your car and talk."

"Won't your father see us? You made it clear to me that your father would not approve of our liaison."

"He's not home. Papa had to take Mama to the hospital."

"He's not home?" Helmut directed Rachel toward the house. "Perhaps we could sit inside and talk."

Rachel dug her feet in the dirt. "No!"

Helmut smiled a conciliatory smile. "Then we shall sit outside in the automobile." He helped Rachel into the Duesenberg.

"So tell me, where have you been?"

"I have been travelling the countryside, looking for a suitable property for my business."

"Your business?"

"Yes, my youth camp. After looking at an endless array of properties, I have come to the conclusion that the site here is perfect. I will open camp this summer on the land between your home and Herr Becker's."

Talking about the camp made Helmut excited. His breathing quickened, his cheeks reddened, his posture grew erect. Rachel liked Helmut's enthusiasm. Then she remembered what her brother Manny had told her about Helmut's business. It didn't seem possible that Helmut was a Nazi. Why would a Nazi care about providing American youth with a camp experience on the banks of the canal?

Helmut leaned over and gave Rachel another kiss. This one, rougher than the first. Why would a Nazi want to kiss her?" Manny was surely mistaken.

Helmut took her hand and placed it on him. She had often wondered what a man might feel like. She had not imagined it could be so hard. She didn't know what to do. She didn't know what she wanted to do. It was all happening too fast. She knew she should pull her hand away, but she didn't want to make Helmut angry. She was beginning to understand that

Helmut might not be a nice man when he was angry. Nervously, she rubbed her finger one time and then moved as far from Helmut as she could in the front seat of the Duesenberg.

"I think it's time for me to go inside. Until Mama gets healthy, I'm responsible for the house."

Helmut started to drive off, with Rachel still sitting in the passenger seat of the Duesenberg.

"Where are we going?"

"On our date." Helmut grinned. Rachel, for the first time, recognized that Helmut had the teeth of a predator. "We don't want to be late for the main feature."

Helmut drove in silence, staring at the road that led to Princeton. Rachel, for her part, spoke incessantly. No matter the topic, she could not engage Helmut in conversation. Rachel thought Helmut's silence was a sign of bad things to come. She was grateful when she stumbled into a topic that seemed to interest Helmut.

"My brother is studying geometry. But the book is written in German, and Manny's command of the German language is greatly limited."

"Soon, everyone in the world will learn to speak German." Helmut chuckled. "Heil Hitler."

Helmut turned the Duesenberg onto Nassau Street and found a place to park the car. He purchased two tickets at the theater. For an additional nickel, he purchased a bag of popcorn with melted butter. With the popcorn in one hand and Rachel in the other, Helmut made his way to the balcony. They had missed the cartoon but were settled in their seats in time to watch the newsreel. A dirigible, "Akron" crashed off the coast of New Jersey. Tornadoes ravaged Arkansas. Theatergoers were visibly upset by the footage, but Helmut appeared to enjoy the death and destruction.

The audience cheered when the title sequence came on the giant screen. Radio Pictures Presents KING KONG David O. Selznick Executive Producer. Rachel was fascinated by the movie. The film crew had figured out ways to make the giant ape appear to be real. Helmut put an arm around her. "I'll protect you."

Helmut kept his word. He protected Rachel from the giant ape. But who would protect her from the Nazi? Helmut's hand rested on Rachel's shoulder. Two fingers slid inside her blouse. Buttons popped. Her eyes scanned the balcony. There were other theatergoers in the balcony, but none were sitting close enough to be of any assistance. Rachel spotted three men, each of them sitting alone in ostensibly random seats. The three men were paying scant attention to the movie. Their eyes were trained on Helmut and Rachel. They were bodyguards, in Helmut's employ. Helmut had established a safe zone within which to violate his date.

On the screen, King Kong was ascending the Empire State Building. In the balcony, Helmut's fingers freely explored Rachel's bosom. His fingertips burned like ice pressed against her skin. She needed to act and act quickly lest her virtue be irrevocably soiled. She hoped that Helmut's ego was as inflated as his manhood. She needed him to believe she was enjoying his attention.

King Kong reached for Fay Wray. Rachel reached for Helmut, bumping his arm. Hot buttered popcorn flew in all directions, arcing in the air and descending in a shower on the two of them. Helmut jumped out of his seat. Rachel screamed. All eyes turned toward the commotion in the balcony. She scurried to the ladies' room.

Rachel considered her next move. She couldn't stay in the restroom forever. At some point, she would have to step out, and when she did, she expected Helmut would be waiting. There was no way for her to summon help. Perhaps she could slip out when the movie ended, hidden in the throng of moviegoers. She opened the door a crack and peeked out. Helmut was nowhere in sight. She breathed a sigh of relief. Rachel stepped into the hallway leading toward the stairs, and ultimately, the exit.

At the bottom of the stairs, Rachel spotted the three young men. There was no place else to go. Squaring her shoulders, head held high, Rachel walked down the stairs. One of the men hissed, "Jewess," and took her firmly in hand. They walked out to the street like a couple, with the other two men trailing behind.

Helmut was waiting in the Duesenberg. His voice was calm, but his eyes revealed his anger. "We should be on our way."

The man who had walked her to the car picked her up like a burlap sack.

"How dare you? Put me down!"

The man laughed, depositing her in the seat of the Duesenberg.

Helmut laughed. "I'm taking you home."

"Really?" Rachel was trembling.

"Are you chilly?" Helmut snapped his fingers. From out of nowhere, one of Helmut's henchmen produced a woolen blanket. The man tried to wrap it around Rachel, but she grabbed it out of his hands. "I'll do it myself, thank you."

She pulled the blanket tightly around her. "This isn't the way home!"

Helmut pulled Rachel toward him. "I have to make one stop before we head back to the village."

"At this hour?"

"Yes, mein Rachel. Especially at this hour."

They were driving through a wooded area on the edge of the borough. Helmut stopped the car on a dark, unpaved street. "I'm told that the locals call this Lovers' Lane."

"Don't be ridiculous." Rachel snorted. "We're not lovers!" She held the blanket like a shield.

"Jewess, I am going to have you tonight and you are going to enjoy it." Helmut snarled. "Or perhaps you won't enjoy it. That is of no concern to me." He grabbed Rachel and the blanket and pulled her from the car. He dragged her into the woods. They walked until they came to a clearing. Helmut threw Rachel and the blanket to the ground. Rachel saw the anger in his eyes. She scanned the woods, looking for anything that she might use in defense of her virtue. All she saw were trees – oak, pine, sweetgum, birch—and between the trees, establishing another perimeter, Helmut's three henchmen.

He ripped at Rachel's skirt. She screamed.

"Scream all you want. No one will hear you." He undid his trousers. "And, as you can see, your screams excite me." He stroked himself and then grabbed her right hand. He closed her hand around him. She wouldn't give him any pleasure. She squeezed as hard as she was able.

"You bitch!" Helmut signaled to his henchmen. "Hold her down."

Rachel sent her mind to a safe place. To Proust. Silently, she recited from the French masterpiece. It was all over quickly.

Helmut fixed his trousers and stalked off. When Rachel was certain it was truly over, she stopped her silent recitation. Her mind reconnected with her body. She sat in the woods and cried. Her life, as she knew it, was over.

Chapter Thirty-One

2023

Charlie sat on the front porch, enjoying the lovely spring weather, daydreaming about the life he had built, and then lost, with Zoya. It's funny, he thought, how the simple act of sitting with her at the high school lunch table had set forces in motion that changed the arc of his life.

Charlie was a secular Jew, proud of his heritage, but not especially religious. To the extent that he observed any of the rituals, it was a matter of habit, rather than faith. Zoya didn't pressure him to go with her to temple, and he made the choice to stay away. He told her that he had obligations at *Gitane* on the weekends, and that was true, although misleading.

Zoya was a proud Iranian woman. She had deep roots in Muslim culture, but was no more observant of the Muslim rites than Charlie was of the Jewish rituals. She identified a mosque in the neighborhood and enjoyed the cultural connections, but she was not devout. She had no intention of converting to Judaism, but she enjoyed the community she found with the Barookhians.

Charlie told himself he hadn't lost everything. He still had Ben and Olivia and, of course, his darling granddaughter Jamila, but, without Zoya, life had no meaning. He was treading water.

Thank God for Jamila. She alone could make him smile. And thank God that his son Ben had forgiven him for the incident at the bridge tender's.

Ben and Olivia were going out of town. They agreed to let Jami spend the days with her Grampa. Charlie promised he would keep her safe. At the moment, Jami was sitting at the edge of the canal, deep in conversation with the snapping turtles. It was a one-sided conversation, but neither Jami nor the turtles seemed to mind. Jami asked the turtles whether they were a family.

"Yes, we are." From out of nowhere, someone had answered Jamila's question. Had Charlie nodded off? He jumped to his feet. Mr. Pisswater was crouched down, next to Jami, a smile on his face.

"Get the fuck away from her!"

Mr. Pisswater raised his hands, as if in surrender, and turned toward Charlie, who was still on the front porch. "I come in peace."

"And you'll go that way, if you know what's good for you!"

"Take it easy. I just want to talk."

Charlie stepped down off the porch. "If you don't step away from my granddaughter, I'll beat the crap out of you... again."

"It's possible I underestimated your capacity for violence. I won't make that mistake again." Mr. Pisswater took a step back. "Or perhaps you underestimated how much the bullet limited my own. The result might be very different if we go at it again."

"That bullet could have killed my granddaughter. Thankfully, you didn't get out of the way in time."

"Is that what you think I was doing? Trying to get out of the path of the bullet?"

Charlie approached Mr. Pisswater. They were nose to nose now. "I was there. I know exactly what you were trying to do."

"Is that so? Think back. What direction was I moving?"

Charlie didn't bother to respond. He knew what he knew.

"I put myself between your granddaughter and the bullet. Thank God I got there in time."

Charlie replayed the scene in his memory. Jamila had been rushing toward trouble, eager to show off her flower. Mr. Pisswater stepped out of the crowd. A tree branch snapped. One of the protesters discharged his weapon.

Mr. Pisswater jumped. But which direction had he jumped?

The scene played in Charlie's memory like it was on a tape loop. Flower, tree branch, gunshot, jump. Flower, tree branch, gunshot, jump. Flower, tree branch, gunshot, jump. How had he not seen it before? Mr. Pisswater had jumped into the path of the bullet. "I don't understand."

"Perhaps we can have that talk now."

Charlie motioned to the chairs on his front porch. "Have a seat." He turned toward his granddaughter. "Jami, please get a cold glass of water for our guest."

The two men sat down. Neither one spoke. Jami returned, clutching a glass of water in her two hands. She gave the glass to their guest. "This is for you, Mr. Pisswater." With that, Jami returned to her unfinished conversation with the turtles.

Mr. Pisswater frowned. "Now I'm the one who doesn't understand."

Charlie chuckled. "We should never forget that children pay more attention to what we say than we realize. Our first encounter, I offered you a beer. You said you didn't drink that pisswater. I've been calling you Mr. Pisswater ever since."

It was Mr. Pisswater's turn to chuckle. "I've been called worse."

"I've called you worse, myself." Charlie took a closer look at the man sitting on his front porch. He was wearing camo pants and a Second Amendment t-shirt, mirrored sunglasses, and a hunter's cap pulled low over his forehead. It all looked just a little too deliberate. "So you're not the right-wing, gun-toting asshole you appear to be?"

"I'm not a right-wing gun nut, if that's what you mean." Mr. Pisswater grinned. "Asshole is a matter of opinion."

"Are you law enforcement?"

Mr. Pisswater ignored Charlie's question. "Here's the thing, Mr. Levenson. I don't think you moved here because you love the canal. And I don't think it's a coincidence that you were hiding on the second floor of the old bridge tender's house the day I was there with Tom Jackson."

"What makes you think I was there?"

Mr. Pisswater rubbed his forehead. "Please, save the bullshit for someone else. It's my job to know stuff."

"Okay, I was there."

"Did you find what you were looking for?"

"Yes…and no."

"Were you looking for Tom Jackson?"

Charlie didn't answer.

"You think Mr. Jackson had something to do with the death of your wife."

Chapter Thirty-Two

1934

Rachel wrapped herself in her arms, alone in the woods, rocking and crying softly. What was she to do? Where was she to go? She couldn't bring this shame on her family, even if she had a way to get home. She would have to bear the shame alone.

It was, she calculated, sometime after midnight. She had no plan, no money, no destination, and, worst of all, no virtue. Rachel knew what happened to such women. She would see them on the streets and in the taverns, offering themselves to men and, more shocking, to other women. They would do anything for a hot meal and a warm place to sleep. Was she one of those women now? Rachel was shocked at how quickly a woman's fortune could change. Society would excuse Helmut. It was, after all, in a man's nature. If only she had refused to get in the Duesenberg. It was her fault. She held herself tight, waiting for morning.

At some point, the sun peeked through the birch trees. Sunrise had always brought with it the promise of a new day. This day, for Rachel, there was no hope, no promise. Still, she couldn't hide in the woods forever. Rachel stood up, brushed the dirt off her clothes, and located an unmarked trail. From the sun's position, she was able to calculate her direction. It was the smallest of victories, but it buoyed her spirits. At least she could control her direction. She made her way south. In fifteen minutes, she had reached the edge of the woods and looked out on a neighborhood of well-maintained

Tudor houses.

Rachel's skirt and blouse had been torn in the scuffle with Helmut. They were caked in dirt and leaves. She was grateful that no one was out and about so early in the morning. She spotted a clothesline. I am the Lord thy God. Thou shalt have no other Gods before me. Thou shalt not make unto thee any graven images. She recited the commandments, making her way to the clothesline. Remember the sabbath day to keep it holy. Honor thy father and thy mother. Thou shalt not kill. Thou shalt not commit adultery. Rachel unpinned a woman's shift from the clothesline. Thou shalt not steal. Rachel hurried back under the cover of the woods. Thou shalt not bear false witness against thy neighbor. She disrobed and pulled the clean shift over her head. She left her filthy clothes in a small bundle at the foot of a sweetgum. Thou shalt not covet.

Chapter Thirty-Three

2023

Temple was the first place where Zoya had felt welcome in America. Over time, there were others—the book club, the mosque, Sarah's Persian Tea Room, Gitane. She only attended services on a sporadic basis, but she had penciled in one very special date on her calendar: May 5, 2023. Temple had announced plans to honor the Barookhian family for fifty years of service to the congregation. Sarah would be there along with her parents Solaymon (call me Sol) and Dana. Zoya wished that her American mother, Shira Barookhian was still alive, but Zoya would be there in her stead.

The day started early with a phone call from Sol Barookhian. He was in a contemplative mood. "We met at temple. Do you remember?"

"Uncle Sol, how nice of you to call," Zoya peeked at the clock, "at 6:30 in the morning."

"Is it too early? I'm sorry, I've been up for an hour. I'll call later."

"No. It's okay. I have to get up anyway." Zoya cancelled the wake-up alarm she had set for 9:45. "What is it?"

"I guess I'm just feeling sentimental. You know when my sister took you in, a Muslim girl from Tehran? When was that?"

"1979."

"Yes, when my sister took you in in 1979, well, I thought she was crazy."

"Maybe she was. But I never would have survived in America without

118

her." Zoya smiled, remembering. "And, of course, you and Aunt Dana."

"And Sarah."

"Sarah, most of all. She taught me how to dress, how to comb my hair, how to shop, what music to listen to. Madonna. Michael Jackson. She taught me how to be a teenager in America."

Someone at temple had the clever idea to surprise the Barookhians by serving Iranian pastries at the Oneg Shabat. It would have been a wonderful surprise, except that the only Iranian bakery in the neighborhood belonged to Sarah. They placed the order at Sarah's Persian Tea Room. Zoya volunteered to help Sarah bake three hundred assorted pastries.

Zoya was not a baker, but she knew how to follow instructions, and she could be precise when circumstances demanded. Sarah gave her a crash course on how to prepare Persian almond cookies. An hour later, the first batch was ready. They had a lovely, sweet flavor, but Sarah judged them to be too chewy.

Zoya was disheartened. "I thought they were supposed to be chewy."

Sarah smiled. "There's chewy, and then there's *chewy*." Sarah emphasized the second chewy, and Zoya knew which chewy described her effort.

"I'll try again."

Sarah pronounced the second batch perfect. While Zoya labored over the almond cookies, Sarah got started on the chickpea cookies. "These will satisfy the gluten-free and dairy-free members of the congregation.

"But will they taste like food?"

Sarah laughed. She made her chickpea cookies with rosewater and pistachios. They were surprisingly full of flavor.

Working together, they made short work of the cookies. Zoya cleaned up while Sarah boxed the order. "I've made arrangements to have a car service deliver the boxes to temple. Tonight, we can pretend to be surprised."

When Zoya got home from the Persian Tea Room, she made one last attempt to convince Charlie to go with her to temple. For Zoya, it was a simple matter. The Barookhians were being honored. She was a Barookhian, if not by blood or marriage, then by action. For Zoya, going to temple had never been a religious act. In all the years she had been attending services, she never once felt like that made her a Jew. She was a proud Muslim woman, sending a message to anyone who cared to listen. Jews and Muslims did not have to be enemies. Even if just this once, Charlie should be there with her.

For Charlie, it was more complicated. He was proud of his wife. He respected her decision to attend temple with the Barookhians. But he was Jewish. If he went to temple, it meant he was fulfilling some sort of religious obligation. It was the very notion of obligation that had driven him away from temple in the first place. Charlie would not allow himself to become obligated to God. To any God.

They argued. Charlie used *Gitane* as an excuse. "I'm needed at the club tonight."

"It's alright, Charlie. I understand." Zoya didn't understand, not really, but there was nothing to be gained by continuing the argument.

"What time will you be home?"

"I don't know." She pulled the door closed behind her. It closed with a thud.

It didn't take long for Charlie to regret his pigheadedness. Zoya was right. He promised himself he would apologize when she got home.

* * *

Bobby Ray checked the calendar every day for a month. This was the day he'd been waiting for, the day he would finally earn the respect of his stepfather. With the help of a man he'd met in drug rehab, he planned the day down to the minute. He practiced the drive repeatedly, taking into account the possibilities of traffic jams, roadwork, storms, anything really that might require him to make a change en route. He examined the building's blueprints and committed every square inch to memory. He copied the key to his stepfather's gun box, not that the man ever kept the thing locked up.

Bobby Ray stared at himself in the bathroom mirror. He wanted to make a statement. He rummaged in the bathroom vanity and pulled out the electric shaver. He started to carve a design in the side of his head but couldn't do it as well as a professional. Bobby Ray wanted to look his best. When he first suggested the design, his accomplice objected. Bobby Ray would be too easily identifiable. But Bobby Ray wanted to be recognized. That was the whole point.

Not just any barber could or would do what Bobby Ray wanted. Fortunately, he had studied every piece of the plan, down to scouting barber shops. He had found what he was looking for less than an hour from his stepfather's house. Bobby Ray checked his phone. He had plenty of time.

An hour later, he pulled into a trailer park just off the parkway. It didn't take long for him to locate the barbershop. If he hadn't seen the barber pole, the Nazi flag would have been a dead giveaway. Thirty minutes later, the barber was finished. Bobby Ray paid the bill with the last of his cash. He couldn't afford to tip the barber. Instead, he advised the man to watch the news that night. Bobby Ray would make the barbershop famous. He stepped out of the shop and climbed into his car. Bobby Ray adjusted the rearview mirror and examined the finished look. The barber had shaved a swastika into the side of Bobby Ray's head. He peeled out of the trailer park and made it home ahead of schedule.

* * *

Zoya pulled into the temple parking lot at 6:00. She was surprised by how full the lot was thirty minutes before the start of the Friday evening service. Inside, in the lobby, she was greeted warmly by long-time members of the congregation. Rabbi stepped out of his study and gave her a hug. Sarah spotted Zoya and pulled her aside.

"Charlie?" she asked, looking around.

Zoya shook her head no.

"I'm sorry, Zoya." But Sarah understood that temple was not part of Charlie's life. "He's a good man. You need to cut him some slack."

"I know. I just wanted him to be here tonight." She sighed. "Anyway, I'm sure we'll work it out when I get home."

Sarah was ready to change the subject. "I managed to peek into the kitchen," she said in her best conspiratorial tone. "The cookies arrived safely."

"Excellent!" Zoya looked around the crowded lobby. "Are your parents here yet?"

"I just got a text from my Dad. They're running late."

As 6:30 approached, everyone made their way into the synagogue. The latest text from Sol and Dana Barookhian announced that they were on their way.

It was a lovely service. Rabbi's sermon spoke to the nature of God.

"Why is it that man once believed in a multiplicity of Gods—a God of Thunder, a God of the Ocean, a God of Fertility, for so many things, man had a specialized God? I would suggest that everything in the world fits into one of two categories. The knowable and the unknowable. The knowable is the realm of man, and the unknowable is the realm of God. When man didn't have knowledge of the oceans, he needed a God of Oceans to keep him safe. For every unknowable, man needed the safety that came from believing a God was on the job. When scientists explained thunder and lightning, Zeus was out of a job."

Zoya listened intently to the rabbi's message.

"No matter how great man's knowledge, no matter how many things that were once unknowable are now easily understood, there is one great unknowable. The miracle of life and death. Who were we before we were born? Who are we after we are dead? These are the great unknowable questions that have always been the realm of the Lord our God."

* * *

Bobby Ray's accomplice was waiting for him outside his garden apartment. He took one look at Bobby Ray's head and saluted. "I was wrong, dude. That looks awesome."

Bobby Ray didn't answer. There was no time in their plan for idle conversation. At 7:15, he pulled into the alley behind the temple. His accomplice climbed out of the car, carrying a small Army surplus duffel bag. Bobby Ray drove around to the front of the building and pulled into the only vacant space in the lot. The area out front was empty. The synagogue would be crowded.

Bobby Ray checked his watch and waited. His accomplice needed ten minutes to set the incendiary device. It was the longest ten minutes in Bobby Ray's life. At 7:25, he hurried up the steps, cradling his stepfather's semiautomatic weapon. He pulled open the front door. The lobby was empty. He pulled open the door to the sanctuary. The Rabbi was speaking.

"Who were we before we were born? Who are we after we are dead? These are the great unknowable questions that have always been the realm of the Lord our God."

Bobby Ray opened fire, shooting above the heads of the Jews. His first shots were intended to create widespread panic. Where is the fun in killing, they had agreed, if the victims don't have the time to contemplate their death?

Some people hit the floor, climbing under the pews, hoping against hope to be safe. But most stampeded for the rear exit, anything to get away from the gunfire. Bobby Ray loved it when a plan came together. If they made it to the rear exit, the Jews would be funneled into a hallway that led to the rear event space. That's where the real fun would begin. His accomplice had set the incendiary device at the other end of the rear hallway. When Bobby Ray heard the explosion, he would point his weapon at the crowd. Kill as many Jews as possible. Bobby Ray grinned. As easy as shooting fish in a barrel. Only after today, there would be a new expression. As easy as shooting Jews in a funnel.

Bobby Ray watched the surging crowd and waited for the explosion. It should have happened by now. Where was the explosion? The fire? The smoke? The burning bodies? Bobby Ray didn't know what to do.

He opened fire.

Zoya spotted Sarah in the line of fire. She pushed Sarah to the floor and climbed on top of her. Bullets ripped through her body. Blood seeped out, pooling on Sarah, lying beneath her.

* * *

The closer Charlie got to *Gitane*, the worse he felt about their argument. It didn't matter whether or not he was needed at the club. He belonged at temple. Not because he was a Jew. Not because it was Sabbath. He belonged at temple on this particular night because it mattered to Zoya.

Charlie turned the car around. Immediately, he began to feel better. He couldn't wait to see Zoya's reaction when she saw him enter the synagogue. He pushed the speed limit as he made his way across town.

Two blocks from the temple, Charlie was stopped in a line of traffic. *Not now*, he thought, *not when I'm almost there*. He couldn't see to the front of the line. He didn't know the cause of the delay. As he crept closer, Charlie spotted a police barricade. They weren't letting anyone through. They didn't appear to be traffic cops. The officers standing behind the barricade were on high alert. Charlie thought they looked like a SWAT team. He managed to pull his car to the side of the road and into a convenience store parking lot. A crowd of people were standing around. No one seemed to know what was happening, but that didn't stop them from having an opinion.

Charlie didn't care what was happening, except that it was delaying his arrival at the temple. The temple! Charlie felt like he was going to throw up. He ran ahead but was stopped by the police.

"I need to get to the temple."

"I'm sorry, sir, but that's not possible."

"You don't understand." Charlie wanted to tell the officer about the event honoring the Barookhians. "I'm supposed to be there."

"Do you know people at the temple?" The officer softened his tone. "There's been an incident."

"An incident?"

"I'm sorry, sir. That's all I know."

Charlie stepped back and considered his next move. He turned and walked back the way he came. He ducked down a side street and slipped inside the police perimeter. The area in front of the temple was a mob scene. Dozens of police officers dressed in tactical gear. EMTs tending to members of the congregation, dazed, wounded, crying out in anguish, some hysterical.

Charlie's first reaction was that, at least, they were alive. He looked frantically for Zoya. He spotted Sarah Barookhian, covered in blood, her head in her hands, crying, being comforted by a stranger. He rushed over.

"Omigod, Sarah. What happened? Are you alright?"

"Do you know this woman?"

"Yes, of course, this is my friend Sarah."

"Were you inside when the shooting started?"

"The shooting? Omigod. Did Zoya get out?"

"Zoya?"

"I need to go inside."

"I don't think you can."

Charlie pushed his way through. Everywhere he looked, he saw bodies, some dead, some dying, all of them drenched in blood, bodies ripped apart by multiple bullets. The smell of death was overpowering. Charlie wandered through the synagogue, praying to a God he didn't worship.

"I'm sorry, Zoya. I should have been here with you. We should have faced this together." Charlie collapsed on the floor. Zoya was dead. Charlie would have to find a way to keep living.

Chapter Thirty-Four

1934

Manny was beside himself with worry. He had stayed late at school, studying for exams. When he got home, the smell of chicken soup drew him into the kitchen. As he expected, there was a pot of soup sitting on the stovetop, but the fire was turned off. The soup was ice-cold. He called out for his mother, but she didn't answer. No one answered. The house was empty.

In all of his seventeen years, he had never known the house to be empty. Manny stepped outside and looked around. How had he not noticed? The car was absent. His family had gone for a drive. This was certainly out of the ordinary. They didn't have money to waste on gasoline, driving around the countryside. Still, it made him feel better, believing he had found an answer to the empty house. He was confident that it would only be a matter of moments before his family would pull up in front of the house in the Model T. They would have a fabulous tale to tell. Manny was sure he had missed out on the adventure of a lifetime.

He was too hungry to wait for them to return. He heated up the soup and served himself a large bowl. As always, his mother's chicken soup warmed his body and soul. He picked up his copy of *Im Kopf eines Geometrikers,* eager to take another shot at deciphering the indecipherable. When he put the book down, he had translated parts of four pages. He was making progress. It had only taken him four hours.

Four hours! Manny hadn't noticed the passage of time. His family had not returned. The house was still empty. Manny didn't know what to do. He started walking to the Becker's house to ask if they knew his family's whereabouts. If it turned out that everything was okay, his Papa would be angry at him for bothering the Beckers. And if everything was not okay, that would be even worse. His Papa would not want the Beckers dragged into their troubles. Manny turned and walked home.

For the first time in his life, Manny slept alone in the house. He heard every noise: the creaking of the floorboards, the groaning of the roof, the scraping of the tree limbs, the whispers of the wind. In the middle of the night, he heard, or at least he thought he heard, the sound of voices coming from the towpath. It was uncommon for someone to be out on the towpath in the middle of the night. Manny looked out the window but saw nothing unusual. He stepped outside. The air was crisp. The sky teemed with constellations. Manny knew most of the stars. He located the Big Dipper and followed the handle until he spotted Arcturus, the bright star in the Bootes constellation. From there, he continued looking down to the right until he identified another bright star, Spica, in Virgo. He tried to make out the rest of the constellation Virgo, but the remaining stars were too dim.

The towpath was empty. And the Model T was still absent. Manny headed back inside. He slept fitfully and woke early in the morning. He made himself a bowl of kasha and picked at his breakfast. Manny no longer imagined that his family was out on some grand adventure. It was time to contact the sheriff.

* * *

The Sheriff didn't seem especially worried about the missing Dubinskis. "I'm sure there's an innocent explanation." But he promised to conduct a search for Manny's family. Manny got the impression that the sheriff's idea of mounting a search amounted to little more than sitting at his desk, waiting for news to trickle in.

Manny walked home. The spring flowers were in full bloom. He barely noticed. When he got to the house, he couldn't make himself go inside. He had already spent too much time alone in the empty home. He sat outside, keeping an eye out for any missing Dubinskis. Manny said a prayer, and much to his surprise and delight, his prayer was answered. He could see the Model T in the distance.

Abe pulled the car to a stop beside the house and helped Miriam step down. He tried to help her walk, but she pushed him away.

"I'm fine," she insisted. "Didn't you hear the doctor say I was fine?"

"Yes, dear," Abe replied, but in truth, he hadn't heard the doctor say she was fine. What he'd said was, *Hopefully, you'll be fine.* Hope was a precious commodity, best recognized, according to Abe, by its absence.

Manny had never been so excited to see his parents. "Where have you been?"

"First, let me get your mother settled in the house." Abe kept a nervous eye on Miriam. She walked slowly to the front door, opened the door, and smiled. "It's good to be home."

Manny tried, without success, to make sense of the situation. "Where were you?"

"Didn't your sister tell you?"

"I thought she was with you!"

"With us?" Abe was more confused than Manny. "Your sister was home when I took your Mama to the hospital."

"The hospital!" Manny was beginning to doubt that any of this would ever make sense. "Is Mama okay?"

Miriam pushed her way into the conversation. "The doctor said I was fine."

Abe wished that were true. "The doctor said *Hopefully, you'll be fine.*"

Miriam smiled weakly. "Hope is a good thing."

Abe hoped that Miriam's doctor was correct. In the meantime, he had a new problem. "Your sister's not here?"

"No, Papa, that's what I'm trying to tell you. I've been alone here since last night."

Abe tried to process the latest information. His teenage daughter had been out all night. "I need to make a report to the sheriff."

"Papa, I've already spoken to the sheriff."

"Yes. But things have changed. He's no longer looking for a family. He's looking for a missing girl. Our Rachel is in trouble."

"We don't know that Abe." Miriam struggled to sit up in bed. "Hopefully, she will be fine."

"Hopefully, she will be fine. Hopefully, you will be healthy. Hopefully, the Messiah will come soon. We cannot leave everything to hope."

"You're right, Papa." Manny headed for the door. "There's something I need to do."

"Where are you going?"

"I won't be long." Manny rushed out the door before his father could stop him. He ran the half-mile to the Becker's house and pounded on the door.

In her kitchen, Mrs. Becker was startled by the pounding. Who would be banging on her front door like that? She peeked out the window. Manny Dubinski was standing on her porch, trying to catch his breath. She opened the door and before she could say anything, he pushed past her into the house.

"Mrs. Becker, I need to talk to Mr. Becker. It's important!"

"I'm sure it is. Otherwise, a young man like yourself would not be forgetting his manners."

"I'm sorry."

"Can I offer you a glass of lemonade?"

"No, thank you, Mrs. Becker." Manny asked again, "Is Mr. Becker here?"

"He's working on the bridge. I'm surprised you didn't see him." Gertrude Becker sighed. "I don't know why he's working on the bridge. It's no longer his responsibility."

Manny barely waited for Mrs. Becker to finish speaking before he stepped outside. He called out to Mr. Becker.

"What is it, Manny?"

"Did your friend Helmut come back?"

"I don't think so. I haven't seen him." Otto put down his tools. "What is this about?"

"If you see Helmut, please tell him I need to speak to him."
Manny turned and headed for home.

Chapter Thirty-Five

2023

"People tell me there would have been more casualties if Bobby Ray's partner had stuck to the plan," Charlie began. "Some of them sound almost disappointed when they start to explain what they mean. But when the incendiary device failed to ignite, his partner hightailed it out the back alley and disappeared into the night. Some people say that all things considered, the Jews in the temple were lucky. So many more of them might have died that night."

Mr. Pisswater had his own explanation. "People are assholes."

"True that." Charlie made eye contact with Mr. Pisswater. "I know I can be an asshole. The jury's still out about you." He went inside and returned with a bottle of rye and two glasses. "I'm parched."

Charlie knocked down his first rye and poured himself another. "I wonder how lucky Zoya felt when the bullets ripped through her chest."

Mr. Pisswater poured himself a tall glass of rye. "I'm sorry about your wife."

"Zoya died before the police took out the shooter. She was neither the first nor the last casualty of the temple massacre. But she was the only Muslim. News outlets grabbed that detail and ran with it. Let's be honest, fourteen dead and twenty-seven wounded, is part of the daily landscape of America. It's enough to make the news, but not enough to make a difference. Normally, that story will get two, maybe three days of coverage, before it is supplanted by the next mass casualty event."

"But when you discover one dead Muslim in a Jewish temple, among the fourteen Jews killed, that's the sort of human interest story the news outlets love. Zoya was interesting. A Muslim from Iran who escaped on the eve of the Iranian Revolution, raised by an Iranian American Jew in New Jersey. That got the story an additional day in the news cycle. And then the coverage disappeared. Zoya was forgotten. I like to think she died knowing that she saved Sarah's life."

Mr. Pisswater thought back to the news coverage. "The case never went to trial. Bobby Ray was killed at the scene. They never identified his accomplice."

"That's right."

"I think perhaps we can help one another."

Charlie leaned forward, the better to hear Mr. Pisswater's proposal. "I'm listening."

"You're looking for Tom Jackson."

"Yes, I am."

"Would you care to explain why?"

"There may come a day when I trust you enough to answer that question. For now, it's enough for you to know that I'm looking." Charlie took a long, slow sip of rye. "And that I intend to find him."

"I assume you already know that Tom Jackson is a member of the Conservatorship for a Clean Canal?"

"The CCC." Charlie nodded in agreement. "But I can't figure why Tom Jackson, and his wife, for that matter, are so involved with a canal environmental group."

"When they talk about cleaning up the canal, they're not talking about litter. They're referring to ethnic cleansing."

"The CCC?"

"It's spelled CCC, but they pronounce it KKK." Mr. Pisswater drained his glass of rye. "I'll be in touch."

Chapter Thirty-Six

1934

Rachel didn't consider herself to be an expert problem-solver. In her seventeen years, she had rarely found it necessary to try. Solving problems was the responsibility of her father, and, more recently, her brother. Her only responsibility was to be a respectable Jewish daughter and sister. And, one day, a fine Jewish wife and mother. But her circumstances had changed. Her responsibility was to survive. Faced with the problem of having nothing but her filthy, ripped clothing, Rachel had solved that problem all by herself. It made her feel good, realizing she was capable, even if her solution required her to violate a commandment.

Was that what life now held in store for her? Sin? Rachel again was startled by how quickly a woman's life can be turned on its head. She had no time for self-pity. She had too many problems yet to solve. The most pressing, she quickly decided, was food. She craved a bowl of her mother's soup. Perhaps a slice of kugel. Flanken in the pot.

Rachel roused herself. Daydreaming was not problem-solving. She needed to find something to eat. She set out on foot, hoping she was heading for the downtown section of Princeton. She passed a small farm with a stand of apple trees. She was ashamed to admit even to herself that her plan was to steal an apple. But the farmer's wife had one eye on her apple trees and her other eye on Rachel.

"Can I help you with something?"

133

"I haven't had anything to eat today."

"A basket of apples will cost you ten cents. I picked them this morning."

"I'm sure they're wonderful. But I don't have ten cents."

"How much do you have?"

Rachel told the lady that she had no money at all.

"Fallen on hard times?" The farmer's wife smiled kindly. "We all need help from time to time." She dragged out a bucket of older apples. Some were brown and had soft spots. "I was planning to use them to make an apple cake, but I'm afraid they're getting too old. Please take as many as you like."

Rachel knew that the older apples were still fine for baking. Her own mother used older apples when she made sharlotka. Rachel appreciated the woman's kindness. "Thank you, ma'am." She picked one apple from the bucket.

"Just one? Are you sure?"

"Yes, ma'am. I'd best be on my way."

"If it's not rude of me, can I ask where you're going?"

Rachel didn't want to lie to the nice lady. She waved her hand, pointing to nowhere in particular. "The wide world." Rachel took off down the country lane. She ate half the apple and saved the rest for later, wrapping it in a dirty piece of paper.

Twenty minutes later, Rachel found herself in the center of downtown Princeton. She recognized the movie theater. It felt like forever since she had been there with Helmut. Had it only been the previous night? She was so much younger then.

The Dubinskis were not a wealthy family, far from it. But her father had always managed to earn enough money to put food on the table. And when money was especially tight, her mother could turn table scraps into a feast. For the first time, Rachel understood the difference between little money and no money. There were many eateries in the downtown district, but none of them were managed by a kindly farmer's wife.

Her eyes were drawn to a fabulous ice cream parlor on Nassau Street. She stood outside, her nose pressed against the windowpane. From behind her, she felt a hand reach out and touch her shoulder. She jumped, bumping her nose against the windowpane.

"I'm sorry, miss. I didn't mean to startle you."

When Rachel saw the man's face, she jumped again. This time, her nose avoided contact with the glass. "You're…you're…"

"Yes," the famous man said. "I am. Would you like a cup of ice cream?"

Chapter Thirty-Seven

2023

"WELCOME," Ben announced, reading the sign at the side of the highway, "TO WEST VIRGINIA."

"What was that?" Olivia was startled. "I must have fallen asleep."

"I'm sorry. I didn't mean to wake you. It's just, I've never been to West Virginia before."

"And?"

"I don't know. I guess I always pictured West Virginia differently."

"Different than what?"

"Less literate." Ben chuckled.

"Don't be a snob, Ben. It's not one of your better features."

"You're right." Ben kept his eye on the highway. "It's just, you know…West Virginia."

They were on their way to FCI Berryville to pay a visit to inmate Abby Jackson.

"How much further?"

Ben examined the GPS. "We should be there in a few minutes."

Olivia shook the sleep out of her eyes and pulled a manila folder from her briefcase. "Find a spot to pull over. I want to get myself ready."

Ben pulled into a truck stop. "Do you want something to eat?" He knew Olivia's soft spot for greasy burgers and soggy French fries.

"Maybe on the way home." Olivia sat up straight in her seat. "I'm queasy enough as it is."

"What's the matter?"

Olivia wondered if her husband was just playing dumb. "I can't believe I let you talk me into doing this."

"You need to relax."

"We're about to step inside a federal correctional institute under false pretenses in order to question a convicted seditionist about the whereabouts of her husband, who is also a convicted seditionist and who may be complicit in a mass murder. Do I really need to point out to you the number of ways things could go wrong?"

"I never could have done this without you." Ben leaned over and kissed his wife. "So what do I need to know so I don't screw up?"

"Well, for starters, I told the prison that you're here as my legal assistant."

"Got it. What does a legal assistant do anyway?" Ben grinned. "Other than sleep with the boss?"

Olivia smacked him on the arm. "Don't be stupid, Ben. This is serious."

"I'm sorry. Just walk me through this one more time."

Olivia skimmed the notes in her manila folder. "I'm visiting Mrs. Jackson today in my capacity as the executor of the last will and testament of a recently deceased client. Mrs. Jackson's husband, Tom, has been named as a beneficiary. Unfortunately, I've been unable to locate Tom Jackson."

"That part is true."

"Yes, Ben, that part is true."

"And that's enough to get us inside a federal prison?"

"That, and a bit of expert legal maneuvering."

Charlie was warming to the task ahead. "Are we going to be deposing her?"

Olivia laughed. "Do you even know what that means?"

Ben's face reddened. "No, not really."

"Okay, well, first of all, you're not doing anything. And all I'm doing is asking Mrs. Jackson to help me locate her husband so I can give him a substantial sum of money. I've made it clear that this is not a formal proceeding, and she's under no obligation to talk. She doesn't need an attorney, although she can have one present if she so desires. She doesn't even have to agree to see us."

"You mean, we may have made the trip for nothing?"

"It's possible, but I don't think so." Olivia checked her phone. "Not when there's money on the table."

Ben drove the last few miles. He spotted another road sign, FCI BERRYVILLE, TURN LEFT INTO THE PARKING LOT.

A security guard directed them to the main entrance. The federal prison was a large concrete structure. It reminded Ben of a warehouse complex, a very scary, very intimidating warehouse complex. He gulped. "Let's do this." They were met at the front entrance by another security guard who reviewed their identifying documents and their visit paperwork.

"It says here that you're an attorney," the security guard said.

Olivia knew that as an attorney, she was likely to get both more attention and, at the same time, more leeway. She was counting on it.

The guard took a closer look at the documents. "But you're not Ms. Jackson's attorney."

"That's right."

"So, this is not actually an attorney visit."

"Not in the sense that you typically mean. But I am an attorney, and I am visiting."

The security guard grinned. "Yes, that's true. If I understand the legalese, she stands to inherit…" and he whistled at the sum "quite a chunk of change."

"To be precise, it is her husband who stands to inherit the money."

"Yes, I see that. Can you please confirm that your visit has nothing to do with January 6?"

"I can confirm that."

The security guard pointed to the other end of the lobby and the entrance to the Visiting Room.

"You'll have to go through a metal detector. Your assistant can wait for you here in the lobby."

"That will be fine."

She turned to Ben and, in her best professional manner, told him to wait in the lobby. "I won't be long."

She stepped through the metal detector into the Visiting Room. The door closed behind her.

Chapter Thirty-Eight

1934

They settled into a corner table in the ice cream parlor. The famous man ordered two cups, vanilla for Rachel and black raspberry for himself. He watched as Rachel wolfed down her serving.

"Doesn't that give you a headache?"

Rachel looked up from her bowl. "Excuse me?"

"Eating ice cream fast like that. Doesn't it make your head hurt?"

"I don't think so. Should it?"

"If I ate ice cream that fast, it would give me a headache." He smiled and showed Rachel his half-eaten bowl of black raspberry. "I guess it's all relative."

He picked at the remaining ice cream. "So tell me all about yourself."

"I don't know what to say."

"Perhaps we should start with the simple things. Do you know who I am?"

"You're Dr. Einstein, the famous physicist. Everyone knows who you are."

"Then you have me at a disadvantage." He smiled impishly. "I don't know who you are."

Rachel turned red with embarrassment. "I am Rachel Dubinski."

Dr. Einstein stood up and bowed. "It is an honor to make your acquaintance, Miss Rachel Dubinski. He stood there for a moment and then sat back down, awkwardly, at their table. "And do you live here, Miss Dubinski?"

"Here, in the ice cream parlor? I should say not."

It was Dr. Einstein's turn to blush. "I mean, do you live here, in Princeton? I moved here recently myself."

"No, I don't live in Princeton."

"And yet I found you, a young woman, alone in Princeton, your nose pressed up against the window of an ice cream emporium." Einstein rubbed his chin and shook his head like she was a mathematical equation with too many unknowns. "I imagine you have a story to tell."

"Please, sir, no."

"Where will you be going when we finish up here?"

Rachel looked like she was about to cry.

"Then you will come with me."

"Thank you, sir."

Dr. Einstein smiled warmly. "My friends call me Albert."

"I could never. But I will try."

The famous scientist nodded. "When you're ready."

They stepped out onto the street. Dr. Einstein pointed to an old car. "The Institute has provided me with an automobile."

"Where are we going?"

"I should have been home an hour ago. Elsa worries if I'm late."

"Elsa?"

"My wife." He paused, mulling over an idea. "You might be more comfortable telling your story to a woman."

Elsa was waiting on the front porch for her errant husband. She was a handsome woman, looking older than her years, with kind eyes and a cautiously genuine smile. It was her self-appointed task to protect Albert from sycophants, con artists, and loose women. Rachel didn't seem to be any of those, but Elsa knew she could never be too careful. "You're late, dear."

Albert shrugged his shoulders. "I was rescuing a damsel in distress. I believe the ice cream may have lifted her spirits."

Elsa nodded her head. Ice cream and pretty women were two of her husband's favorite things. It's no wonder he was late coming home. She examined Rachel more carefully. The shift she was wearing was well-made but ill-fitting. A bruise was fading, but still visible on the young woman's arm. Her hair was in desperate need of brushing. Elsa peered into her eyes and saw the pain that Rachel was trying so hard to hide. "Let's go inside. I'll make tea."

"I'll be in my study." Albert disappeared into his work. Elsa showed Rachel into the kitchen. She put up a pot of water.

"I would have imagined that you'd have a person to do that."

"I do," Elsa said, "me." She rummaged through her cupboard and located a tin of tea biscuits. The women nibbled at the biscuits while they waited for the tea to be ready.

"Did my husband behave himself?"

Rachel was surprised by the question. "He was a perfect gentleman."

"I want you to know that you are welcome to stay here in my home as long as you need." She smiled warmly. "You do need a place to stay, am I right?"

Rachel nodded. She was finding Elsa Einstein easy to talk to. Dr. Einstein was too important to be burdened with Rachel's story. She was beginning to think she might be able to trust Elsa with her tale of woe.

"Last night, I went to the theater to see *King Kong*."

Elsa poured two cups of tea and let Rachel tell her story without interruption. When Rachel got to the end, Elsa hugged her. By the time Rachel let go, the tea had grown cold.

"You will stay with us tonight. Tomorrow, I will drive you home."

Rachel panicked. "I have brought shame on my family. I cannot go home."

"You must not blame yourself, my dear. You didn't do anything wrong."

"I wish that were so."

"It is." Elsa's heart went out to this young woman. "You may stay with us for as long as you need to."

"Thank you." Rachel had one more request. "If it's not too much trouble, might I have a bath?"

Elsa jumped up. "Where are my manners? Of course." Elsa gave her fresh towels and lent her a nightgown and robe. She showed Rachel to the guest bedroom and ran a warm bath.

Elsa knocked on the door to her husband's study. "We need to talk."

Chapter Thirty-Nine

2023

A Visiting Room Officer pointed to an empty table. "Sit there. Inmate Jackson will be brought in shortly." Olivia looked around the room. There were visitors at two other tables, family members visiting with their incarcerated loved ones. There were no barriers separating visitors and inmates. Guards enforced the rules strictly, but without intruding. A door at the back of the Visiting Room clicked open. Inmate Abby Jackson walked in, flanked by two female security guards. Abby Jackson looked like the coach of a high school cheerleading squad. She didn't look capable of violence. Except, of course, when she was trying to overthrow the federal government. She sat down across from Olivia.

"Who the hell are you?"

One of the security guards chided the inmate. "Watch your language in the Visiting Room."

Abby Jackson ignored the guard and stared at Olivia. "I don't know you."

"No, you don't."

Jackson stood up and signaled to the guard. "We're done here."

But the guard wasn't ready to return to the unit. "Why don't you find out what your visitor has to say."

Olivia spoke up. "I have money for you."

Abby Jackson sat down. "Okay. You've got five minutes." Her voice tone was chilly, at best, but she wanted to hear about the money.

Olivia explained about the deceased client, the last will and testament, the not insignificant amount of money that Tom Jackson stood to inherit.

"If I can locate him," Olivia said.

"You must think I'm stupid."

"No, of course not. Why do you say that?"

Abby Jackson smiled. It was not a friendly smile. "If my husband doesn't want to be found, I'm certainly not going to help you find him. How do I know you're who you claim to be?"

"Given your circumstances, I can fully understand why you'd be cautious. That's why I'm here. So you can see for yourself that my intentions are honorable."

Abby Jackson wanted to believe her. "How much money are we talking about?"

"I'm sorry, ma'am. I'm only allowed to discuss the details with Mr. Jackson." She saw the skepticism in Abby Jackson's eyes and quickly added, "We're talking six figures."

Abby Jackson had one more test for Olivia. "I don't hear much news here. What's happening with the President?"

"President Biden?"

The security guard was suddenly on alert.

Abby Jackson scowled. "The real President. President Trump."

The guard stepped in. "That's it. You know the rules. Visit's over."

One guard escorted Abby Jackson to her cell. The other guard took Olivia back to the lobby, where Ben was waiting for her.

"How'd it go?"

"Not here, Ben." She gave him a kiss. "I need fresh air."

Ben was searching for something on his phone. "Do you think there's a motel in the area?"

They had driven seven hours to get to Berryville. They were not about to make the return trip the same day.

Five minutes from the prison complex, they found an inexpensive motel. There was nothing fancy about the place, but it was clean and in good repair. It appeared to be an affordable brand name affiliated with one of the big hotel groups. Ben and Olivia booked a room for the night.

The motel had an onsite restaurant. The menu was limited, but the food was surprisingly good. Olivia recognized a couple of the other diners from her prison visit. Ben and Olivia were sipping decaf coffee when a stranger approached their table.

"You had a visit today with Abby Jackson."

"Who's asking?"

"This is for you." He handed Olivia a piece of notepaper and turned, and walked out of the motel.

"What was that all about?" asked Ben.

Olivia unfolded the note. "An address."

Chapter Forty

1934

Albert put down his physics paper and turned his attention to his wife. "What's the matter, my dear?"

Elsa approached her husband. "Last night, a man had his way with Rachel."

"You mean...?"

"Yes." Elsa shook her head. "She thinks that it's her own fault."

"That's ridiculous."

"I know that, and you know that, but this poor girl is in distress. She has no way to get home, but even if she did, she's too ashamed to go home. She is unwilling to bring her own shame on her family."

"Where does her family live?" Albert stood up. "I need my coat."

"She told me her family lives on the canal." Elsa frowned. "But it doesn't matter. She's not ready to face her parents."

Albert sat back down and put his head in his hands. "The poor girl will stay here with us for as long as she needs to."

Elsa hugged her husband. "You are a good man, my Albert."

"Where is she now?"

"She's taking a bath. I've already shown her the guest room."

Albert was proud of his wife. "It sounds like you have everything under control."

It was Elsa's job to have things in their life under control. Her husband might be theoretically brilliant, but when it came to practical matters, she was the smart one in the family.

"Omigod!" She nearly exploded. "What about her parents?"

Albert was puzzled. "What about her parents?"

"They haven't seen their daughter in twenty-four hours! They don't know where she is." Elsa began to pace. "They don't know if she's alive or dead!"

"We can call them from the Institute."

"They don't have access to a telephone." Elsa shook her head. "I asked."

"Then we'll have to drive there." Albert checked the time. "We can get an early start in the morning."

"No. Imagine if you were her father. You'd be crazy with worry. I will not make these poor people spend another night in fear for their missing daughter."

"You are right, as always." Albert reached for his coat. "I better get started if I'm going to get home before nightfall."

Elsa loved her husband for his decency. "You are not a safe driver, my love."

Albert harrumphed. "I drove to the ice cream parlor today, didn't I?"

"Yes, you did. Three blocks and only one turn." She spoke softly. "I will drive. You will stay here with Rachel."

"Yes, dear. But how will you find the house?"

"Rachel said her father was a lock tender. If I follow the canal, I will find the house."

* * *

Elsa drove slowly, keeping the canal on her left as she drove out of town. The late afternoon sun sparkled on the water. She was unfamiliar with the countryside but trusted the canal to lead her to her destination. She heard the water rushing into the lock before she saw it. A man stepped outside before she managed to park her automobile.

"Are you lost, ma'am?"

Elsa looked at the simple clapboard house, the narrow planking that ran from the house to the lock, and the intricate array of rods and levers that controlled the lock. She knew she was in the right place.

"Are you Mr. Dubinski, the lock tender?"

"I am." Abe was startled that the woman knew his name. "How can I help you?"

Elsa climbed down out of the automobile. "Could we perhaps speak inside?"

"Where are my manners? Of course." Abe led her inside. "Miriam, we have a guest."

Elsa inhaled deeply. "Something smells delicious."

Manny came running down from the second floor. "Rachel?"

Abe shook his head. "Manny, this is..." and then he stopped, realizing their house guest had not introduced herself. He turned toward the guest. "This is my son, Emmanuel."

Elsa smiled warmly. "It's a pleasure to meet you, Emmanuel."

Miriam stepped out of the kitchen. "I'm making flanken. It's my daughter's favorite." Miriam examined their guest. "Please tell me you have news about my daughter."

"That's why I'm here. Earlier today, my husband found your daughter alone in Princeton."

Miriam was grateful and, at the same time, confused. "It is good of you to drive all this way to bring us this news of our daughter. But if I may ask, why didn't you bring her with you?"

Elsa told the Dubinskis what she knew. She did her best to hide her own emotions, reporting the facts as she knew them, rushing through the uncomfortable parts. "I'm so very sorry. Your daughter is too ashamed to see you."

"Where is she now?"

"She is at my home in Princeton."

"She belongs here, with her family."

"I agree, Mrs. Dubinski."

Miriam looked at Abe. "You must drive to Princeton and bring our daughter home."

Elsa could feel Miriam's agony. "Please, you have to trust me. I believe if you try to see her before she is ready, you will only succeed in driving her further away."

Abe wanted to trust this woman who had driven all the way from Princeton to bring them news. "My daughter can be quite stubborn once she has made a decision." He hoped his wife wouldn't hate him for what he was about to say. "I will give Rachel two days. If she doesn't come home of her own accord in two days, I will come get her."

Elsa was relieved by Abe's decision. She turned to face Miriam. "Your husband is a wise man."

Miriam smiled sadly. "Not knowing has been agony. Knowing and having to wait is going to be even worse. But I trust my husband's judgment. I will wait."

Elsa stood up and prepared to leave. "I must be on my way. As it is, it will be dark before I get home. I wish we could have met under better circumstances."

"With all due respect, ma'am, we haven't met, not properly."

"I'm sorry. I guess I was nervous about having to deliver this news. I have completely forgotten my manners. Please excuse me. My name is Elsa Einstein. My husband's name is Albert."

Chapter Forty-One

2023

When Charlie Levenson moved into the lock tender's house, his intention had been to lead a quiet life, alone and undisturbed on the canal. It was still his intention, but it no longer seemed possible. He had somehow become the center of attention in the canal community. He couldn't decide whether Mr. Pisswater was friend or foe, but, apparently, the two men had formed some sort of partnership. "I think perhaps we can help one another," Mr. Pisswater had said to him. Charlie didn't know what help Mr. Pisswater was offering nor what he might expect in return.

Mr. Pisswater, aka Hank Morgan, was an enigma, a man with no apparent identity. The police had led Charlie to believe that Mr. Pisswater was the shadow head of a domestic terrorist organization with a cell in the village. Mr. Pisswater had implied that he was, in fact, an undercover officer who had infiltrated the local cell. Charlie didn't know what to believe and changed his mind several times a day.

There was also the matter of Mr. Plaid Jacket, aka Tom Jackson, who had served time for his role in the January 6 insurrection and who seemed to be a member of the local terrorist cell. Mr. Jackson had disappeared after the fire at the bridge tender's house. The investigators were now calling that fire a case of arson. Was Tom Jackson responsible for setting the building ablaze? Charlie had seen Mr. Plaid Jacket and Mr. Pisswater together at the bridge tender's house days before the fire.

It all meant something. It had to. Charlie didn't believe in coincidence. Perhaps, if he could clear his head, he might make sense of it all. The weather was sunny and warm with a mild breeze. What better place, he thought, to clear his head, but floating on the canal.

Charlie pulled his canoe down to the landing. He tossed a bottled water and a bag of potato chips into the canoe, grabbed his paddle and seat cushion, and set off up canal. He paddled lazily, doing just enough work to make progress against the slow-moving current.

He paddled past the bridge tender's and continued heading up canal. This was not a section of the canal that Charlie had spent much time exploring. He could see more houses along this stretch of the canal, and more roads, but surprisingly fewer people. An old man was sitting in a lawn chair, dangling a fishing pole in the water. Two teenage girls were smoking cigarettes and giggling as they walked along the towpath. A dog ran in circles around them. One boy sped by on his bicycle. Charlie imagined it must be a bumpy ride at the spillway. He turned the canoe, stowed his paddle, and let the canoe drift lazily down canal. He munched on his potato chips and dipped his hands in the canal to wash off the grease.

As he neared the lock, Charlie could see a man waiting for him. When he drew closer, he recognized Detective Warren. The detective called out to him. "What a fine day to be out on the water."

"That it is," Charlie shouted back.

The Detective motioned for Charlie to dock the canoe and join him on land.

Charlie sighed. If only the canal were larger, he thought, he could live his life on a houseboat. "I'm coming."

Chapter Forty-Two

1934

Abe Dubinski turned to his son. "I want you to follow Mrs. Einstein until she is back in Princeton. Then come straight home."

Elsa appreciated Abe's concern but dismissed it out of hand. "That won't be necessary."

Manny was proud that his father trusted him to drive the car after dark. He was not about to allow the opportunity to be of assistance to the wife of the famous scientist pass him by. "I'll start the car."

"Thank you, son." Abe turned to Mrs. Einstein. "I wouldn't want my wife alone on these roads after dark. I'm sure your husband feels the same way."

Manny wondered whether Albert Einstein would feel the same way. His brain was not like any other brain on the planet. If he thinks like no one else, Manny reasoned, he might also feel like no one else. It would give Manny something to contemplate while he drove.

"Perhaps if Rachel eats my flanken, she will realize she belongs here with us." Miriam handed a plate of food to Elsa Einstein. "And give some to your husband Albert as well."

Elsa smiled and said her goodbyes.

By the time Manny got the Model T started, Mrs. Einstein was well on her way. She was a fast driver, Manny noted, for a woman. The weather threatened. Perhaps, at the pace she was setting, they would beat the storm.

Suddenly, a few hundred feet ahead of him, Mrs. Einstein stopped her car.

Manny heard men's voices but could not make out what they were saying. Manny resisted the urge to speed up. Instead, he stopped the Model T and slowly walked forward, hidden in the trees that lined the country road.

"That's not her," one man said.

"But she was at the Jew house," a second man said.

The two men argued, and while they argued, they stood in the middle of the road, preventing Elsa Einstein from continuing on her way.

"Helmut told us to keep an eye on the Jew house. To watch for the daughter."

Manny crept closer.

"But this one is not the daughter."

The two men laughed. "Helmut has no use for an old Jewess."

"No. But we will need more cars when the camp opens."

The first man spoke directly to Mrs. Einstein. "We have decided to let you go, but we will be taking your car."

Elsa sat in the car, silent and still.

"Get out of the car, or I will drag you out." The first man reached for Elsa's arm.

Manny sprung from his hiding spot in the trees, knocking over one of the men and rushing the other. "Take your hands off of her!"

Manny's attack caught the men unawares. He managed to inflict a bit of damage before the men got their bearings. One of the men managed to secure Manny's arms. The other punched him in the gut. Manny doubled over. He was in pain and out of breath. He took a second blow, this one to the head. He focused on Elsa, still sitting in her car.

"Go," he gasped. "I'll be okay."

Elsa didn't move.

Manny managed to break loose from the thugs. He ran to Elsa's car and shook her. "Go!"

Elsa put her foot on the gas pedal.

As the men pummeled Manny, he raised his head in time to see Elsa drive away. Storm clouds blanketed the night sky. With a thunderclap, the heavens released their rain. The two men left him in a puddle at the side of the road.

Manny hoped that Mrs. Einstein would get home safely in the storm.

The men took off, on foot, heading back the way they came. Manny could hear bits and pieces of their conversation.

"...must be the Jew's..."

"...not as nice as the other one..."

They must have come upon the Model T.

"...better than nothing..."

"...you do it..."

Manny heard one of the men trying to crank the engine.

"...dammit..."

"...piece of crap..."

Manny listened as the voices faded in the distance. He pictured them, on foot, soaking wet, arguing about what they were going to tell Helmut.

When Elsa Einstein told the Dubinskis about Rachel, she didn't know the name of the man who had taken advantage of her. Rachel had omitted that detail from her account. Manny had no doubt it was Helmut who had defiled his sister. He made a promise to Mrs. Einstein, to himself, and especially to his sister that he would find Helmut and he would make him pay.

Chapter Forty-Three

2023

"You watched your granddaughter for a couple of days. Were her parents out of town?" Detective Warren did not appear to be happy, waiting for Charlie to dock his canoe, sweating in the afternoon sun.

"Yes, my granddaughter came for a brief visit. Why is that any of your business?"

"So far, Mr. Levenson, you have only had to deal with the friendly Detective Warren. I believe that's about to change." The detective scowled. "So I will ask you again, were her parents out of town?"

"Yes, my son and his wife wanted to get away for a few days."

"That's better. Do you know where they went?"

Charlie Levenson shook his head. They hadn't actually told him where they were going, and it was not in his nature to pry. "They have a place on LBI."

"But they didn't go to Long Beach Island." Detective Warren puffed himself up to his full gargantuan size. "They went to West Virginia."

Charlie started to laugh, but he realized he was laughing alone. Apparently, Detective Warren didn't get the joke. "I'm afraid to say this, but I believe that you've made a mistake."

"My only mistake was giving you a chance to come clean." Detective Warren pulled a sheet of paper from his pocket. It was a copy of a ledger of some sort. He showed it to Charlie. "Do you see any familiar names?"

There were only a few entries on the sheet. It took Charlie a moment to identify the signatures of his son and daughter-in-law. "What am I looking at?"

"That's a copy of the visitors log at FCI Berryville."

"FCI?"

"Federal Correctional Institute."

"I don't understand."

Detective Warren allowed himself the tiniest of smiles. "Neither do I. Perhaps you could explain why your son and your daughter-in-law paid a visit to an inmate by the name of Abby Jackson."

"I don't know."

"They told the authorities they were there about an inheritance."

"That doesn't make any sense."

"It didn't make sense to me either until I made the trip myself to Berryville and paid a visit of my own to Mrs. Jackson." Detective Warren pulled out a handkerchief and wiped the sweat from his forehead. "Your daughter-in-law posed as the executor of the estate of an anonymous deceased client. She told Mrs. Jackson that she needed an address for Tom Jackson in order to release the funds."

Charlie had nothing to say, so, for a change, he said nothing.

"Mrs. Jackson swears that she didn't give Olivia an address. The Visiting Room Officer confirms Mrs. Jackson's account of the visit."

Charlie started to say something, but Detective Warren interrupted. "You've been looking for Tom Jackson?"

"Yes."

"Did you send Ben and Olivia to Berryville?"

"No."

Detective Warren had been on his feet for too long. "Come with me." He walked over to Charlie's front porch and took a seat on one of the two chairs. He motioned for Charlie to sit on the other. When Charlie sat down, Detective Warren continued.

"We're about to have a serious conversation. Quite possibly the most serious conversation in your entire life. I would advise you to be honest with me."

"Do I need an attorney?"

"Only you know the answer to that question, Mr. Levenson." He softened his tone. "What you do right now may very well dictate the future of your son and your daughter-in-law."

"I don't understand."

"You don't have to understand. You just have to be honest."

Detective Warren gave Charlie time to consider his warning before proceeding with a new line of questioning.

"We've had eyes on a house in south Jersey for the last few weeks."

Chapter Forty-Four

1934

The sun had barely begun to rise when someone knocked on the Becker's door. Otto and Gertrude were early risers, so it was not a problem having someone appear at their home at such an early hour, but it was unusual.

"I hope it's nothing serious, mein Barchen," said Gertrude. "I have heard that the Dubinskis have had their share of trouble in the last few days.

"Let me see, mein Liebling. I'm sure everything is okay."

Otto opened the front door to find Helmut standing on his front porch. "May I come in, Herr Becker?"

"Of course, my friend. What can I do for you?"

When Gertrude saw that it was Helmut, she hurried to put up a pot of coffee.

"Can we talk?"

Gertrude nodded. "I will come back to pour the coffee when you are finished talking."

When Gertrude left the room, Helmut complimented Otto on his wife's behavior. "She is a good woman. We need more women like Frau Gertrude."

Otto doubted that Helmut had knocked on his door at dawn for the purpose of giving his wife a compliment. "What can I do for you?"

Helmut grew serious. "Two of my friends ran into trouble on the road last night."

"Are they okay?"

"They are now." Helmut shook his head in apparent dismay. "They were walking along the road last night when they were nearly run over by a woman driver."

"I can see why that might cause them some distress."

"Let me finish. When the car nearly hit them, my friends tried to have a polite conversation with the woman. She wouldn't listen to reason. I shouldn't be surprised. The woman was coming from the Dubinskis."

"That is unfortunate."

Helmut shook his head again. "It gets worse. Suddenly, the Dubinski boy comes out of a hiding place in the trees and attacks my friends. They were fortunate to avoid serious injury."

"I don't know what to say. I have always found the Dubinski boy to be well-mannered."

"You know how Jews are. They do not take responsibility for their shortcomings and are quick to blame others for their troubles."

Otto had heard such complaints before, and perhaps it was true about some Jews, but it did not hold true to what he knew about the Dubinskis.

"But that's not why I came to speak to you this fine morning. I came to let you know that I am opening my camp today right here along the canal. I have a job for you...that is, if you still want it."

Otto had no money in the bank. He had closed his small account after the crash and had never re-opened it. His cash reserves were approaching zero. "Thank you, Helmut. I am in your debt."

Helmut smiled. "I'm glad to hear you say that. There is one more thing we need to discuss."

"What is that, my friend and benefactor?"

"It has been brought to my attention that there has been an unfortunate turn of events in the life of the Dubinski girl and that she may, in fact, be missing."

Otto recalled a recent conversation with Manny Dubinski. The young man had been looking for Helmut.

"Missing? That is indeed unfortunate."

"I am embarrassed to tell you this, but I have heard rumors that the girl has taken up an unrespectable life."

"I find that hard to believe."

"In my experience, Jews, girls, in particular, have a limited grasp of morality." He stared at Otto. "But that is not the unfortunate part. What is especially distressing is that my name has been attached to the rumors. As if I had something to do with the Jewess's depravity!"

Helmut was finally reaching the point of his visit. "If you are going to work for me, I need to know that you will stand with me if the Jews make trouble.

Chapter Forty-Five

2023

"We've had eyes on a house in south Jersey for the last few weeks," Detective Warren said a second time. "It's an interesting house, more of a shack, to be precise, built in a salt marsh."

Charlie Levenson struggled to make sense of the Detective's new line of questioning. "What does this have to do with me?"

Detective Warren waved him off. "I'm getting to that. It's not far from the parkway, but you have to know what you're looking for. When you get off the parkway, you follow the new county road until you spot an unmarked turn for the old county road. The old county road dead-ends at the water. There's an elevated wooden walkway that extends out over the salt marsh. At the end of the wooden walkway, there's a narrow footpath that winds through the marsh. At the end of the footpath, there are a handful of abandoned shacks. It's the sort of place you'd never find unless you knew it was there."

The more the Detective explained, the less Charlie understood. "I'll ask you again, Detective, what does this have to do with me?"

"Your son Ben found the place."

"I don't believe you."

"Like I said, we've had eyes on the place. Also, cameras."

"None of this makes any sense."

Charlie had been less than forthcoming every time they'd talked. Detective

Warren resisted the urge to believe him this time. "You haven't asked me the most obvious question. It makes me think you already know the answer."

"Why have you been surveilling the house? That's the term, isn't it, surveilling?"

"Yes, that is the term. And that is the question." Detective Warren grinned. "We have reason to believe that Tom Jackson has been holed up in that shack."

"You believe that my son went to Berryville and got an address from Mrs. Jackson. That address turned out to be a shack in the salt marsh. You believe my son drove to the shack to do what? To confront Tom Jackson?"

Detective Warren rubbed his chin. "That's where things get a bit confusing. Tom Jackson was hiding out in the shack. We're certain of that. But he's gone missing again."

"That's one helluva surveillance team you put on the case. I would have thought they would have seen Tom Jackson when he left."

"Don't get smart with me." Privately, the detective felt the same way. "I have a team processing the house for evidence."

Charlie pulled his cell phone out of his pocket. "Let me call Ben. I'm sure there's a logical explanation."

Detective Warren reached out and took the cell phone. "That won't be necessary. Even as we speak, my partner is questioning your son at the station house."

"Ben is the most honest person I know." Charlie slumped down in the chair. "He's not under arrest, is he?"

"Not yet. But I believe he will be before the day is over."

"On what charges?"

Detective Warren pulled out a sheet of paper and reviewed it before answering. "For starters, your son and your daughter-in-law submitted fraudulent documents in order to gain access to a federal correctional institute."

Charlie thought that didn't sound too bad.

"Second, they have impeded a combined state and federal investigation into continuing criminal activities in the aftermath of January 6."

Charlie gulped. He knew the authorities were not about to go easy if the focus of their investigation related to January 6.

"Third, depending on what we find out from the forensics, it's entirely possible your son will be charged with the murder of Tom Jackson."

Chapter Forty-Six

1934

By the time Elsa Einstein got home, she was angry. What was wrong with men, thinking they could harass and abuse women at their will? She was fortunate to have Albert. He was not perfect, no man was, but he was good, and that was good enough for her. She sat in the car, regaining her composure before going inside. She would not tell her husband of the encounter on the road. She had no intention of giving up her independence. She didn't want him to worry every time she went off without him. She fixed her face and walked inside.

"I'm home."

Even at this late hour, she expected to find her husband in his study. She was surprised to find Albert and Rachel sitting in the parlor, eating ice cream. She had so many questions, she didn't know which one to ask first.

"You're eating ice cream."

Albert grinned. "I had the most fabulous idea. I called a taxicab."

"You arranged for a taxi to drive you to the ice cream parlor?"

Albert's grin grew impossibly large. "No. It took a bit of explaining, but finally, the cabbie understood. I got the pistachio, and Rachel asked for a hot fudge sundae."

"Are you telling me you convinced a cabbie to deliver ice cream to our house? You never cease to amaze me."

"This is one of my best ideas yet." Albert raised the bowl of nearly melted pistachio. "Here. Have some."

Elsa thought it looked drippy and messy and absolutely delicious. She took a spoonful. "Thank you, Albert."

"You're welcome, Elsa."

Rachel watched in wonder that there were people who lived like this, eating ice cream in their sitting room. It truly was amazing, and she was lucky to be there, but she felt a momentary pang of regret. It was lovely, but it wasn't home. "If you will excuse me, it has been a very long day. I should prepare for bed."

"Of course." Elsa had allowed the ice cream to distract her from her responsibilities. "Please let me know if you need anything."

"I'm sure I'll be fine. You have done so much already."

Elsa waited until Rachel was settled in her bedroom. She looked at her husband and smiled. "I expected to find you in your study."

"We have a guest. It would have been impolite to leave her alone while I poured over my lecture notes." Albert had a reputation for abandoning guests in favor of physics.

"You like her."

"I am enjoying having a young house guest."

They sat on the sofa, slurping what remained of the hot fudge sundae.

"She cannot stay here. She needs to be with her mother."

* * *

Rachel slept well on a four-poster bed with clean sheets and a multitude of pillows. In the morning, she took her second bath since arriving at the Einsteins, got dressed in clothes that Elsa had laid out for her. She walked downstairs. In the kitchen, she found a note. Elsa and Albert had stepped out. They would be home shortly. Next to the note was a platter of fresh muffins, a tin of jam, and a small pot of black tea. It was wonderful, but it was not like home. She missed her mother's coffee cake. She missed dipping the cake in a steaming hot cup of coffee. It was even better on the second day when the cake was no longer fresh. She missed home.

The Einsteins were old enough to be her grandparents, and she was beginning to think of them that way. Bubbe and Zayde. They would miss her, but they would understand when she announced that she was ready to go home.

She was spreading jam on a second muffin when she heard Elsa and Albert on the front porch. They were arguing. Rachel prayed they were not arguing about her. When they stepped into the house, nothing in their voice tone, nothing in their expressions, nothing in their posture hinted at a recent argument.

Elsa smiled. "I'm glad to see that you're eating."

"Yum. The muffins are delicious. Did you bake them yourself?"

Elsa blushed. "I have found a talented baker in Princeton. He keeps me well supplied in baked goods. My own attempts at baking are not so successful. Albert tells me I have to measure my ingredients with more precision."

Albert grinned. "My wife is precise in everything that she does, with the exception of baking."

"Baking is a mystery to me."

Rachel doubted that anything was truly a mystery to Elsa Einstein. "If you like, I can teach you how to make a foolproof sharlotka."

Albert answered for his wife. "We would both like that very much. Now, if you will excuse me, there are mathematics questions that need my attention."

Elsa turned to Rachel. "He will be in his study the rest of the day. Now how about that sharlotka."

Rachel checked the cupboard. "It appears that you have all of the necessary ingredients except for the apples."

Elsa took her by the arm. "There is a nearby farm with the most wonderful apple trees. Let's go pick a few apples. I'll drive us there."

Rachel recognized the farm when Elsa turned her car down the lane. The farmer's wife was tending to her apple trees. If she recognized Rachel, she didn't let on.

"We need six apples please."

"Tart or sweet?"

Elsa waited for Rachel to answer. "Tart."

"The Granny Smith are ripe this time of year."

"Granny Smith will be perfect. Thank you."

The farmer's wife placed six beautiful apples in a brown paper bag. "That will be twelve cents."

Rachel turned to Elsa. "When I was hungry, she gave me an apple even though I had no money."

The farmer's wife blushed. "It was the Christian thing to do."

Elsa reached into her change purse and counted out fourteen cents.

They drove straight back to the house. Elsa put on an apron and handed another to Rachel.

Rachel peeled and cored the apples, cutting them into small bites and mixing them with lemon juice. Step by step, Rachel showed Elsa how to prepare the batter.

Elsa poured the batter over the apples and put the cake pan in the oven. While the sharlotka baked, the women talked.

"If you don't mind my asking, how did you meet Albert?"

"Albert is my cousin."

"Do you love him?"

"It is, for both of us, our second marriage. And, for both of us, it is better than our first." Elsa paused, realizing she hadn't really answered Rachel's question. "Yes, I love him very much."

"It is obvious that he loves you as well." Rachel paused. Can I tell you something?"

"Anything, my child. Anything at all."

"You and Albert are the only Jews that I know."

"There are no Jewish families in your village?"

"No, just me, my parents and my brother."

"I don't understand."

"I went out on my date with Helmut because there are no Jewish boys in the village. My brother warned me, but I didn't listen."

"It's not your fault."

"I let him take me to the movies. I let him get us seats in the balcony. I let him, omigod, I let him put his hand inside my blouse." Rachel began to cry.

"You didn't do anything wrong."

"When I said no, he wouldn't stop."

"It has been my experience that once a man gets started, he rarely stops."

"Did it…"

Elsa interrupted Rachel before she could finish her question. "Isn't it time we check the sharlotka?"

Rachel opened the oven a crack. The smell of baked apples filled the kitchen. Carefully, she removed the cake pan from the oven. "We should let it sit for an hour."

"That may not be possible."

"How come?"

Albert walked into the kitchen, a smile on his face. "I could smell that all the way in my study." He picked up a knife and cut a piece of the cake.

Chapter Forty-Seven

2023

Detective Massoud knocked on the door of Ben Levenson's ranch house in the suburbs. It was a modest home, well-maintained, with a fresh paint job on the exterior. Ben Levenson opened the door and smiled. "Good morning."

"Good morning." The Detective showed Ben her badge. "I'd like to ask you a few questions."

Ben Levenson's eyes widened, for just a moment, before his placid demeanor returned. "Of course. Come in. I have a pot of coffee in the kitchen."

Detective Massoud had a better idea. "I have a pot of coffee at the station house. We can talk there."

"Is that really necessary?" Ben pulled his cell phone out of his pocket. "I'd like to call my attorney."

"When we get to the station house." Detective Massoud pointed to the neighbors who were watching them talk. "I don't want to embarrass you in front of your friends." She paused. "But I will, if I have to."

Ben Levenson nodded. "Let me, at least, turn off the coffee pot."

Detective Massoud nodded.

The coffee unplugged, Ben walked with the detective to her sedan. They didn't speak at all during the short drive to the station house.

When they arrived at the station house, Detective Massoud led Ben to the detective squad and pointed to a chair next to her desk. "Sit."

Ben sat.

"I'm going to have a cup of coffee. It's not like the double mocha Frappuccino I smelled at your house, but it's not half bad. Would you like a cup?"

Ben declined. His bladder was creating more than enough havoc without adding a cup of coffee to the experience.

Detective Massoud poured one coffee and sat down at her desk. She took her time, shuffling papers while drinking the coffee. Finally, she put down the cup and smiled at Ben. "Let's get started."

"Am I in some kind of trouble?"

"That depends." The detective picked up her papers and rifled through them. She selected one sheet, a photo, and showed it to Ben. "What can you tell me about this photo?"

"That's me and my wife." Ben studied the image. "I don't recognize where we were when this was taken."

"I believe you were checking into a motel in West Virginia."

"That doesn't seem possible. I've never been to West Virginia."

Detective Massoud scowled. "Let's review what we know. One. That's you and your wife in the photo. Two. The camera that snapped the photo is mounted above the registration desk at a motel in West Virginia."

Ben was not about to give in without a fight. "I'm no techie, but even I know that images can be doctored."

The detective spoke quietly, nearly spitting out the words. "Are you suggesting that I doctored this image?" She stood so that Ben would have to look up at her. "Before you answer, I should tell you that the federal prison takes photos of all of their visitors." She pulled another image from her stack of papers. "Is this one also doctored?"

"I don't think I should say anything more without my attorney."

Detective Massoud smiled. "If, by your attorney, you mean your wife, that will save me the trouble of asking her to come down to the station house." She waited to see whether Ben understood what she meant. It appeared that he didn't, so she offered a bit more of an explanation.

"When a private citizen such as yourself uses fraudulent documents to gain access to an inmate in a federal prison, that's a problem, but it doesn't necessarily have to be a big problem. Especially if the private citizen cooperates with the police. But when an attorney, an officer of the court, engages in the same activity in a federal prison, that is a big problem, a very big problem. If that's what you and your wife did, you're likely to get a slap on the wrist, but your wife will lose her license. She very well might get jail time herself."

For the first time, Ben understood what he had pushed his wife to do for him. "Yes, we went to Berryville. But it was all my idea. If I cooperate, can we keep my wife out of this?"

"We can certainly try." Detective Massoud smiled. "What say, we start over?"

Ben Levenson exhaled deeply. "I'd like that."

"I know that you and your wife went to the women's federal prison at Berryville. I know that your wife managed to arrange a visit with inmate Abby Jackson. I know that Mrs. Jackson is serving time for assaulting a federal officer during the insurrection on January 6. What I don't know is why your wife wanted to meet her."

"Again, before I answer, I want to state for the record my wife had nothing to do with this. It was all me."

Detective Massoud didn't bother to point out it was his wife who had actually spoken to Mrs. Jackson. There was no point in upsetting him just when he was starting to talk. "So noted."

"I was hoping Mrs. Jackson would tell us where we could find her husband."

"So you made up a bogus story about an inheritance." The detective frowned. "And it must have worked because, just three days later, you showed up at Tom Jackson's hideout in the salt marsh."

"I need to correct one thing. Mrs. Jackson didn't give us her husband's location."

Detective Massoud checked her notes. "Yes. She denies telling you where to find her husband."

Ben nodded his head. "That's the strange part. When we left the prison, we checked into a motel for the night. I guess you already know that. But that night, during dinner, a stranger approached us and handed my wife a slip of paper. It was an address."

Detective Massoud scribbled on her notepad. Ben thought it was a good sign. Perhaps he had brought the detective a new piece of information.

Detective Massoud looked up from her notes. "Do you know who the man was? Could you identify him in a photo?"

"He was a big man, almost as big as your partner, and he had close-cropped hair. I figured him for a prison guard."

"Why is that?"

"Well, for starters, like I said, he kinda looked like a guard. I guess I've always assumed that prisoners use the guards to carry goods and information in and out of prison."

"That is certainly something I'll be looking into. Anyway, you got the address, and you paid Tom Jackson a visit."

"Again, I'd like it to be clear that I made the drive down to the salt marsh all by myself."

"Okay. What happened when you got there? By the way, since we're being so upfront with one another, let me tell you, for the record, we've had eyes on that shack for days."

"So, you'll know if I'm being less than honest. Is that your point?"

Detective Massoud nodded.

"When I knocked on the door, no one answered. I peered in through a window. The place looked empty. I waited for an hour, and then I drove home."

"You never went inside?"

"That's right."

"So, we might find forensic evidence, the front door, for example, proving that you were at the shack, but we won't find anything indicating that you went inside?"

"Yes, that's it exactly."

"And when we find evidence of foul play, that evidence won't lead back to you."

"I promise." Ben paused. "Are we done?"

"Almost, Mr. Levenson. There's still one thing we haven't discussed."

"And that is?" Ben looked forward to answering the detective's final question and then heading home.

"Why was it so important for you to speak with Tom Jackson?"

Chapter Forty-Eight

1934

Elsa and Rachel were in the kitchen eating leftover sharlotka for breakfast.

"It's even better the second day," Elsa announced.

Rachel grinned. "The longer it sits, the gooier it gets."

"It won't sit much longer, not the way my Albert has been enjoying it."

"In your home, time doesn't act the way it does elsewhere. One moment can span a lifetime, and a lifetime can be captured in a single moment."

"There are more things in Heaven and Earth, Horatio, than are dreamt of in your philosophy."

"Shakespeare said that." Rachel was proud of herself for recognizing the quote from Hamlet.

"Have you read it?"

Rachel nodded. "Hamlet, Macbeth, The Merchant of Venice."

"Most girls your age read Romeo and Juliet."

Rachel didn't bother trying to explain. She had a mouthful of sharlotka. Rachel needed to face a hard truth. It was easier after the apple cake.

"I think it's time for me to go home."

"I think you are correct. Albert and I will miss you, of course." Elsa smiled. "Perhaps you will visit us from time to time."

"I would like that very much."

Elsa put the dirty dishes in the sink. It will take me a few minutes to clean the kitchen. Then I will take you home."

"Thank you. That will give me time to say goodbye to Albert."

Rachel rushed out of the kitchen and barged into Albert's study without knocking.

Albert looked up from his papers. "My child, what is the matter?"

"I just wanted… what I meant to say is…thank you for saving me."

"All I did was buy you a cup of ice cream." Albert was surprised at the depth of emotion he felt for this young woman. "So you've decided to return home?"

"I have."

"Then you'd best be on your way." He took out a handkerchief and wiped a tear from his eye. "I've got work to do."

* * *

Elsa didn't tell anyone that thugs had stopped her on the drive home from the Dubinskis. She promised herself, if the same men were on the road, this time she would run them down. She would not stop her motorcar. She would protect Rachel with her life if necessary. She kept a keen eye out for anything out of the ordinary, but the road was empty. The trip was uneventful. Elsa was grateful when she spotted the lock tender's house.

"We're almost there."

She snuck a peek at Rachel, who seemed nervous about the homecoming.

* * *

Miriam was the first to spy the motorcar approaching their home. She was sitting on the front porch, resting after a brief dizzy spell. Miriam yelled to Abe who rushed outside and helped his wife get up from the chair. He held her tenderly around the waist and waited. He recognized the Einstein's motorcar. He identified Elsa as the driver. Then he spotted the passenger. He picked Miriam up in a hug. "Our Rachel has come home!"

Abe put his wife down and did a jig on the porch. "Our Rachel has come home!" He ran to meet the car. "Let me help you."

Rachel allowed her father to help her get out of the car. "Papa!"

Miriam was making her way slowly toward the car. Rachel ran to her. "Mama!"

Elsa sat in the car, proud of her role in bringing about this moment. Rachel was right, she thought, sometimes a lifetime can be encapsulated in a single moment in time.

Her thoughts were interrupted when Abe came around to her side of the motorcar. He lifted her out of the car and smothered her in a hug. "Thank you, Mrs. Einstein. Thank you for bringing our daughter home!"

Miriam watched a red-faced Elsa Einstein locked in a hug with her husband. "Abe, you're embarrassing Mrs. Einstein."

Abe put her down and backed away. "I'm sorry. It's just, I'm so relieved to see my daughter, I don't know what I'm doing."

Elsa laughed. "It's alright, Mr. Dubinski."

"Please, let's all go inside. This calls for a glass of Slivovitz."

Abe led the way into the house. He retrieved the bottle of plum brandy and four glasses. He gave one to Elsa, one to Miriam, one to Rachel, and kept one for himself.

"You're giving our daughter a glass?" Miriam was stunned. "Well, maybe just this once."

While they sipped the Slivovitz, Elsa told Miriam about the sharlotka.

Abe Dubinski sat back in his chair, allowing the three females to chat, unencumbered by a man's opinion.

"My Rachel is a talented baker." Miriam beamed. "Are there men her age in Princeton?"

Elsa understood that by men, Miriam was asking about Jewish men. "I believe there are."

"Perhaps one day, you could introduce my Rachel to a young man at your synagogue."

"Albert and I are not religious. People in Princeton would be surprised to find us at temple." Elsa chuckled at the thought. "We shall see."

Rachel remembered something that Elsa had said that morning. "There are more things in heaven and Earth, Horatio than are dreamt of in your philosophy."

"Touché, my child. Touché."

Abe Dubinski excused himself and stepped outside. When women were talking, Abe knew, sometimes it was best not to be present. He took the opportunity to wash Mrs. Einstein's motorcar.

A short time later, Mrs. Einstein came out of the house. Her car was sparkling in the afternoon sun. "Thank you, Mr. Dubinski. That was not necessary."

"No, Mrs. Einstein, thank you. Thank you for bringing my daughter home. She seems to have survived her ordeal thanks to your care and attention."

"She does seem to be doing remarkably well, but I must tell you, I believe she is going to need a good deal more care and attention than I could possibly offer. She needs the care that only a mother and father can provide."

Elsa started her car and headed back to Princeton. Now that Rachel was safely home with her parents, whatever dangers had been lurking on the country road seemed to have disappeared.

Chapter Forty-Nine

"Do you know who my mother is? Who she was?" Ben couldn't explain his interest in Tom Jackson without first acknowledging the murder of his mother.

Detective Massoud had done her research. "The B'nai Shalom murders."

"Yes. My mother was Zoya Aziz."

"Surely, we belong to Allah, and to Him shall we return. May Allah grant your mother, Jannah." The detective bowed her head in silent prayer. "May her memory be a blessing."

"Thank you, Detective."

"Are you saying that Tom Jackson had something to do with the B'nai Shalom murders?"

"My father believes that is so."

Detective Massoud made a quick note before stepping away from her desk and placing a call to her partner. "Hey, are you still talking to Charlie Levenson? Ask him about his wife's death." She returned to her desk and resumed her questioning.

"According to the case files, the police believed the shooter had an accomplice. Do you believe that Tom Jackson was the accomplice?"

"I don't know. That's why I wanted to speak to the man."

"And after you spoke to him, then what?"

"I never had the chance to find out."

Detective Massoud was not satisfied with Ben's response. "Surely you had thought ahead. Did you plan to take revenge against Tom Jackson?"

"I will tell you that there were nights when I couldn't sleep. I imagined what I would do if I found Bobby Ray's accomplice. In the light of day, I am ashamed to admit, I didn't fantasize about justice."

"You wanted revenge."

"Yes."

"And now, what do you want now?"

Ben Levenson didn't have an answer. "It would seem that my opportunity has come and gone."

* * *

Detective Warren hung up the phone. "My partner wants me to ask you about Zoya Aziz."

Charlie looked up at the Detective. "Why?"

"Why not?"

Because it's none of your damn business.

"In Persian, Zoya means Alive, Loving, and Caring. She was that, and a good deal more, until she wasn't anymore."

Detective Warren didn't want to trample on Charlie Levenson's memories, but he had a line of questioning to pursue, and he couldn't allow Charlie's loss to stall the case. "I am sorry for your loss. Please understand I have a job to do. Your wife was the one Muslim fatality at the mass shooting at the Jewish temple last spring."

"Yes."

"What does that have to do with Tom Jackson?"

Charlie forced himself to remember what he saw, how he felt. "I was in the crowd of onlookers in the immediate aftermath of the shooting."

Charlie fell silent. Detective Warren waited until he was ready to continue.

"I didn't realize it at the time, but I saw Tom Jackson in the crowd. There was no reason for him to be there."

"You didn't realize it at the time?"

"No."

"So when did you figure it out?"

"Do you remember the fire at the bridge tender's?"

"Of course. I questioned you about it. You were not what I would describe as forthcoming."

"No, I guess I wasn't. But I did tell your partner that I had seen the plaid jacket at the bridge tender's."

Detective Warren scanned his notes. "Yes, I see that you did."

"It wasn't until after Detective Massoud questioned me that I realized that I'd seen the same plaid jacket in the crowd outside the temple."

"You've been looking for Tom Jackson ever since."

"Yes."

"You believe he is the unidentified accomplice?"

"Yes."

"How much did you tell your son?"

"Did my son hunt down Tom Jackson?" Charlie put his head in his hands. "Omigod. What have I done?"

Detective Warren was finding Charlie to be oddly sympathetic. "I don't know."

"Please, if he did anything wrong, he did it for me."

Chapter Fifty

1934

The first car arrived shortly after sunrise, a brand new six-cylinder BMW 303 with its distinctive kidney grille. The car stopped at the side of the road, between the canal and an empty field. A teenage boy stepped out of the rear seat, dressed in a three-piece tweed suit with a matching flat cap. By mid-morning, cars were streaming into the village. A few had New Jersey license plates, but most were from New York and Philadelphia. Otto recognized Baurs and Biecherts, Opels, and Karmanns. He spotted a brand new Adler Trumpf. Curious villagers lined the road in wonderment. It might have been a parade. All that was missing was the marching band.

Teenage boys climbed out of every car, some wearing suits, others in overalls, all of them blond-haired and blue-eyed. Within an hour of their arrival, all of the boys were dressed in brown shorts and military-style shirts. Some of the boys spoke German fluently, others tried to, but most of the boys chatted nervously in English. All that they knew for certain was that their German American parents had sent them away to camp.

Helmut divided the boys into two large groups. While one group erected a tent village, the other group would learn how to march. At a designated time, the groups would switch places. Helmut's hand-picked staff supervised each activity. When Otto arrived, Helmut assigned him to oversee the tent assembly. It was important that each tent be a sturdy structure able to withstand both wind and rain. Helmut promised Otto forty-five cents an hour for one day's work. Two men were in charge of marching. Otto recognized them. They were the same two men who had thrown a rock through the front window of his home and painted a Star of David on his wall. Otto would need to be careful. Still, he was grateful to have the work.

It was the boys' responsibility to erect their own tents. Otto's job, according to Helmut, was to show them one time how it was done, making certain that the swastika was properly displayed on the canvas wall, and then to punish the slackers. For a man who had a childless marriage, Otto was overwhelmed with some thirty teenage boys. It was not in his nature to punish these boys, who might have been, under other circumstances, his own. Not only did he show the boys what to do as many times as they needed, he helped with the task as long as Helmut wasn't watching.

Otto snuck a peek, from time to time, to watch the marchers. The two staff members had embraced Helmut's instructions. Boys were yelled at, individually and as a group, in English and German. If a boy was out of step, he got slapped. If he stumbled, he was kicked. If he was deemed to be insufficiently blond-haired or blue-eyed, staff were generous with their beatings. But the staff was merciful. The unworthy would be allowed to perform special tasks to prove their allegiance. These special tasks would be revealed over time. Only the blondest of hair and the bluest of eyes were deemed worthy from the start. They would be allowed to perform special tasks of a different sort. In the meantime, they marched up and down the towpath. The two staff were sure to point out the Jew lock tender's house as they marched past.

When all the tents were erected, and all the boys had mastered the rudiments of the march, Helmut called for them to assemble on the empty field behind the tents. A small stage had been hastily assembled. Helmut ascended the stage. The boys stood in rows before him.

"Sons of the Fatherland," he began. "Welcome to this momentous occasion."

The assembled boys roared.

Helmut extended his right arm. "Sieg Heil!"

The boys extended their right arm and responded as one, "Sieg Heil!"

"Sieg Heil!" Helmut said again.

"Sieg Heil!" the boys replied.

Helmut gave the boys time to settle down before continuing.

"Tonight, in New York City, our friends and colleagues will be rallying to restore our values and to establish a true and faithful alliance between Germany and America. I'm sure that many of your parents will be there."

The boys cheered.

Helmut extended his arm. "Sieg Heil!"

"Sieg Heil!" they shouted in unison.

"Perhaps some of you are unsure why your parents have sent you to me."

The boys quieted down, eager to hear Helmut's explanation.

"Our Fuehrer wants all the German children to come unto him that we may make the Fatherland a thing of glory once again!"

The crowd roared.

Helmut drew himself up and extended his arm. "Heil Hitler!"

"Heil Hitler!" the boys proclaimed.

"And how, you may be wondering, are you to come unto our Fuehrer, who is occupied with our glory away in Europe? How will you know him, and he will know you?"

No one said a word, waiting for Helmut to answer his own question.

"You shall come to him through this camp. You will come to him through me."

One of Helmut's thugs jumped up onto the stage. He looked at Helmut lovingly, extended his right arm, and saluted. "Heil Fischer!"

The boys proclaimed, "Heil Fischer!" repeatedly until their throats were hoarse.

Helmut stood on stage, warmed by their loyalty and love.

There would come a day, and it would come soon when Germany would control the entire world. Helmut could already imagine a Nazi America led by an American Fuehrer. These boys would be his first regiment.

When the rally came to an end, the boys returned to their tents. The boys did their best to settle down for the night, but they were far too excited to go to sleep. Helmut sent word to the tents, instructing the boys to head off into the woods and to return to the open field with dry branches and twigs. His specific instructions were "to return with anything that will burn."

Gangs of boys roamed up and down the towpath in the dark. They nearly destroyed the swing bridge, dismantling the A-frame structure. They did destroy the lock, ripping apart the miter gate and the wickets. Within an hour, the boys had assembled a grand bonfire in the open field. At its peak, the fire reached fifty feet in the air. The fire raged until morning.

In the lock tender's house, Abe Dubinski barricaded the door to his home from the inside and waited nervously for the light of day.

Chapter Fifty-One

2023

When Detective Massoud offered to drive, her partner agreed enthusiastically. Detective Warren didn't like to drive. The passenger seat in Massoud's truck was big enough to comfortably seat a man of his size. That would keep him in a good mood on the long drive to the salt marsh. So he was less than pleased when she pulled up, not in her new truck, but in her aging sedan.

The sedan was old enough to have a front bench seat. The first time she picked him up in the sedan, she told him the bench seat would give a man of his size more space than a modern bucket seat. And that, by itself, was true. Massoud neglected to mention that she had to pull the seat up as far as it would go for her feet to reach the pedals. And a bench seat didn't provide separate controls for the driver and passenger. Warren felt like the sedan was a clown car, and he was fourteen clowns.

"I'm sorry, partner. My husband took the truck today."

It was not the best way to start the trip to the salt marsh. Detective Warren added it to his growing list of complaints about the case.

"We were supposed to have eyes on the place."

"We did."

"No, I mean, we should have had our own guys watching the shack instead of relying on the locals."

Detective Massoud refused to take the bait. "Sometimes things go wrong.

You know that. Anyway, you'll understand when we get there."

"What I understand is there's only one way in and one way out. How hard is that to surveil?"

"You're not going to let it go."

"No."

"Okay, here's the thing. There's only one road in or out. But you can't see the shack from the road."

"So one guy takes the road, and the other takes the shack. Easy peasy."

"Easy peasy my ass. You're just in a bad mood because you're crammed into the front seat." Massoud sighed. "That's my bad. But there's nothing we can do about that now, so let's just get to our destination, get your ass out of the car, and do our damn job."

Massoud was right, of course, but Warren wasn't about to give her the pleasure of admitting it. "Whatever."

They'd been in the car for almost an hour when Massoud exited the parkway. "Keep your eye out for a turn."

"Okay. What am I looking for?"

"Like I said, a turn."

Warren was beginning to get aggravated all over again. "Yeah, I know. But what's the road sign? What's the landmark?"

"No road sign. No landmark."

"No shit."

Massoud found the turn and drove to the end of the unmarked road.

To Detective Warren, it wasn't just the end of the road. It seemed like it might be the end of the world. "Where to now?"

Massoud pointed ahead. "Do you see that wooden walkway?"

"Do you mean that rickety thing that extends out over the salt marsh?"

"Yeah. That thing." Detective Massoud opened the trunk of her car and grabbed a pair of Wellies. "It's likely to be wet back there."

Warren groaned. "My day just keeps getting better."

The detectives made their way out onto the old wooden walkway. There were a couple of houses built along the walkway. "Here?" Detective Warren asked hopefully.

Massoud laughed. "Keep going."

At the end of the walkway, Detective Massoud pointed to a narrow path cut between the sedge grasses. "That way."

As they made their way deeper into the salt marsh, Detective Warren spotted an abandoned shack festooned with crime scene tape. "Please tell me this is the place."

Massoud smiled. "This is the place."

They stepped inside. The shack was a single room with a hot plate and a microwave on one wall, and a bed on the other. Detective Warren looked around, taking it all in. "Do people really live like this? In New Jersey? In the twenty-first century? My god. There's no bathroom!"

Detective Massoud pointed to an outhouse behind the shack. "I don't think anyone lives here year-round. I expect that someone sleeps here when they come down to fish."

The shack had already been processed by the crime scene guys. The detectives liked to give the techs a hard time, but Warren and Massoud had learned to rely on their expertise. Two things had been marked for the detectives' attention. First, and obvious to anyone with or without crime scene training, there was a circle of dried blood on the floor. Massoud had already spoken to the techs. The blood was a match for Jackson. Second, a small hole in the wall. Detective Warren made himself a note to follow up on the stray bullet.

"So what do we know? Tom Jackson was hiding out in the shack. Charlie Levenson believes that Jackson was complicit in the murder of Levenson's wife. Levenson's son tracked him here. But there's no evidence that Ben Levenson found him. There's no evidence that Ben ever set foot inside the shack. So, unless the blood or the bullet says otherwise, Levenson appears to be a distraction. There's also the matter of the arson investigation. Jackson was pulled out of the fire before he disappeared. Maybe he set the fire. Maybe not. But I'm willing to bet my next paycheck that Jackson knows something about the case."

Detective Massoud let her partner finish.

"The thing is, I don't see why that would send Jackson into hiding. I sure would like to know who Tom Jackson was afraid of."

The detectives went through the shack looking for anything the crime scene guys might have missed. They came up empty.

"Let's check out the marsh," Detective Massoud suggested. "Maybe the local cops will have something for us."

"My shoes are going to get ruined."

"Yeah, probably. Next time, remember to bring your boots."

The detectives followed the narrow path, heading ever deeper into the salt marsh. A detail of local officers were helping out, conducting a grid search, to the extent it was possible in the salt marsh. At low tide, they were hoping to find new evidence. Detective Warren expected to find Jackson's body.

In her Wellies, Detective Massoud joined the officers in the wettest part of the marsh. Detective Warren hung back along the edge. It was dirty, wet, tedious work. The local officers had been out there in the salt marsh for hours without complaint. Detective Warren was growing tired of listening to himself whine. To hell with his shoes, he had a job to do. He caught up with his partner, up to her ankles in brackish water.

"Glad you could join me."

"Let's do this," replied Warren.

Suddenly, one of the local officers shouted, "I think I found something."

The officer bent down for a closer look. "It's a gun." Working carefully, the officer picked up the gun, along with bits of sedge grass and wet sand, and placed it all in an evidence bag.

Detective Massoud examined the gun. She was not a weapons expert, but to her, it appeared that the gun had only recently been disposed of. "Good work, Officer. Let's get that to forensics right away."

They had blood evidence. They had a stray bullet. Now they had a gun. Before the day was over, perhaps they would have a body. With enough evidence, Warren knew they didn't really need a theory of the crime. The detectives doubled down on the grid search.

Detective Warren's foot snagged on a low shrub. He took a nasty spill. He struggled to regain his footing, landing on his butt in the wet marsh. But they continued searching. They continued until it was too dark to see. They found no additional evidence.

Detective Warren's body ached. His shoes were ruined. His knee was bruised. His pants were drenched. He was crammed into the front seat of his partner's car. It was, he announced, a near-perfect day of police work.

Chapter Fifty-Two

1934

Early the next morning, Sheriff Anderson paid a visit to the Nazi youth camp. By the time he arrived, teenage boys were already practicing their marching. The Sheriff marveled at the tent village that had sprung up in the past twenty-four hours and the mass of boys who inhabited the village, dressed in their identical camp uniforms, with their identical blue eyes and blond hair and their identical holier-than-thou sneer. Boys of a certain age have a nasty habit of confusing uniforms with power. Give one of them a uniform; he thinks he's the king of the universe. Give a group of them uniforms; they think they're God's own security detail. The Sheriff never wore a uniform. He rarely bothered to carry his badge. After all, everyone in the village knew Sheriff Anderson. One of the blond-haired, blue-eyed boys decided to intercept the Sheriff.

"Who goes there?"

"Excuse me, lad. I didn't realize the camp had posted sentries."

The boy stammered. A small group of campers gathered to watch.

The Sheriff patted him on the head like he was a lost child or perhaps a pet. "There, there. Just tell me where I might find Helmut Fischer."

The boy continued to stammer.

"That's alright, son. If you can't talk, perhaps you can point."

The boy pointed in no particular direction. One of the bystanders yelled, "You can find Herr Fischer over by the mess tent."

"Thank you." The Sheriff strolled past the boys and stopped the first adult he spotted. The adult was an older version of the campers.

"Good morning. I'm looking for Helmut Fischer."

"Then you found him." Helmut had that same holier-than-thou sneer. "What can I do for you?"

"I'm Sheriff Anderson. I mostly came by to say hello. It's not every day that a group your size materializes unannounced in our little village."

"I have permission to be on this land."

"You're not from around here, are you?"

"I don't see how that matters."

"It's just, in these parts, we like to know our neighbors. It would have behooved you to stop by my office yesterday and introduce yourself."

"I was very busy yesterday."

"I know. I would have thought that setting up a camp of this size would have kept you plenty busy, but there you were last night, setting off a bonfire that had most of the villagers worried the whole area would go up in flames."

"My boys got a little over-excited."

"Their over-excitement, as you call it, may have been responsible for sending one of our villagers to the hospital." Sheriff Anderson took another look at the row after row of identical boys. "Just what is your business here?"

"My associates and I have opened this camp to teach the boys about their German heritage. It is our hope that this may strengthen the bonds between our two great nations."

"How long do you intend to stay here?"

"As long as it takes. We especially want to teach the boys how to defend themselves against those who would oppose a German-American alliance."

Sheriff Anderson was curious. "Who might those people be?"

Helmut shook his head in dismay that the Sheriff would need to ask. "The Jews, of course. Surely you know that the Jews are responsible for all that is evil in this world and beyond."

Sheriff Anderson scuffed at the dirt with the toe of his boot. "The thing is, we don't get many Jews in these parts, so I won't pretend to be an expert on Jewish evil. We only have one Jewish family in the village—the Dubinskis—

and they have never caused any trouble. In fact, they have been exceedingly helpful. Abe Dubinski is, or at least was, the lock tender until the company shut down the canal."

Helmut grinned. "It was the Jews who shut down the canal."

Sheriff Anderson was losing patience. "I wouldn't know about that. But I can tell you, sure as I'm standing here, the Dubinskis didn't close the canal."

"Are we done here? I have to finish setting up the mess tent. Boys can't march properly on an empty stomach." Helmut pointed to a group of boys trying to erect a large, communal mess tent.

The Sheriff watched as one man tried, with limited success, to maintain an orderly work crew. "Is that Otto, the bridge tender?"

"Otto is a good man, but he has a tendency to be too easy on the boys." Helmut turned his attention to the disarray at the site of the half-assembled mess tent. "Boys need discipline. Don't you agree?"

"Do you mind if I hang around for a while? I'll stay out of everyone's way."

"Certainly, Sheriff. After all, it's my camp, but it is your village."

"Thank you. Can I also offer you one piece of advice?"

"Of course."

"When I got here this morning, the boys were marching. I saw that you have two local men, in addition to Otto, supervising the boys."

"Yes, I like to hire local men when that's possible."

"The thing is, I know those two men. They're troublemakers."

"Thank you for the warning, Sheriff. I will keep my eyes on them." Helmut smiled. "I wouldn't want them to do anything that might reflect badly on the camp."

"I'm glad to hear that. I'll be on my way then." The Sheriff took his leave. He took several steps before looking back at Helmut. "I can see that you are busy, but I'd appreciate it if you would stop by my office sometime this afternoon. And bring a copy of the papers that give you permission to use this property."

Chapter Fifty-Three

2023

Wh. "I brought you a cup of coffee."

"Thanks. I didn't sleep well."

Massoud knew that when her partner wasn't sleeping, he was close to cracking a case. "So where are we?"

"No further than we were when we left the salt marsh. Except I've spoken to the lab. When they dusted the shack, the only prints they lifted belonged to Tom Jackson. And they confirmed that the blood sample belonged to Jackson. Whoever shot him knew what they were doing."

"What about the gun?"

"Glock, 9mm."

"And the bullet they pulled out of the wall?"

"It's a match."

"So now we just have to track down the gun owner."

"I'm working on that now." Warren pointed at his computer screen. "You'd be amazed how many Glocks have been bought and sold in the last couple of years."

Detective Massoud nodded in agreement. "It's a freakin' epidemic."

"And that's only counting the ones that we know about."

"You'll find it." Massoud flashed a quick smile at her partner. "Even if it's just so you can get back to sleeping through the night."

"Amen, sister." Warren took a gulp from his coffee. "What are you working on?"

"I'm going back through the arson files."

"That's still the only obvious connection." He took a second gulp of coffee. "Even if neither of us likes it for Jackson's murder."

"I need, at least, to rule it out."

Warren knew that there were days when police work was exciting. But most days, even if the case was exciting, the work itself consisted of mind-numbing drudgery. They were making progress on the Jackson case, but if they were going to bring it to a close, they needed to go through files, both digital and paper, trusting that somewhere in the mess that passed for a system, something would get their attention.

Three hours and a dozen phone calls later, Detective Warren hit paydirt. "Hey, Massoud, drop what you're doing."

"What've you got?"

The Glock was bought at a gun show in Pennsylvania. I spoke to the dealer. He wasn't especially helpful, but I leaned on him…"

"With your not inconsiderable weight."

"Exactly. And when this body leans on you, you say uncle. The gun was bought by an Eddie Matthews."

Detective Massoud sat down at her computer. "Okay, partner. Let's see what we can find out about our Mr. Matthews."

It didn't take her long. "Hey, Warren, what year did Mr. Matthews buy the Glock?"

Warren checked his notes. "2021. Did you find something?"

Detective Massoud had most definitely found something. What exactly, she wasn't sure. "Eddie Matthews died of end-stage cancer in 2019."

Chapter Fifty-Four

1934

"Take your sister and go upstairs."

Manny wanted to stay downstairs, but one look at his father's expression, and he knew that this was no time to argue. "Let's go, Rachel. We can play a game."

"I'm not in the mood for games."

"I know, but it will help keep our mind off the troubles outside. I'll set up the checkerboard. It's been too long since the last time we played."

The first game of checkers, Rachel was distracted. Manny won the game quickly. "You're a better player than that. Let's play again."

This time, Rachel kept her focus on the checkerboard. Within minutes, she was able to look at her brother and say, "King me."

Moments later, she said it a second time. The game came to a rapid conclusion.

"Are you satisfied, Manny? Did I play better?"

"Yes, I guess you did."

"Then leave me be." Fully clothed, Rachel climbed into bed and pulled her blankets up to her chin.

Manny didn't know what Rachel wanted from him. Was he supposed to leave the room, or did she just want him to stop annoying her? His twin sense was failing him. He sat on a chair in the corner of Rachel's room and chanced one final remark. "Everything will be alright."

Rachel realized her brother had no idea what being alright entailed for a woman. She was doing far better than that horrible night when Helmut had raped her. She was glad to be home with her family. But she was not alright. She would not be alright ever again.

She was with child. It was too early to know for sure, but she did know. The father was a Nazi. She had been raped by a Nazi. And now that Nazi threatened to burn down their home. "I want to be alone."

"When things get a little scary, it's not a good idea to be alone."

"Please. Just go."

Manny's twin sense was starting to tingle. "We've always been together. Always."

"Not now, Manny." Rachel held back the tears. "Please."

Manny was torn. Should he stay upstairs and be there for Rachel, or should he respect his sister's wishes and leave her alone with her grief? He went downstairs to sit with his parents. When things get a little scary, it's not a good idea to be alone.

Alone, Rachel allowed herself to cry. She cried, and then she prayed, and then she cried some more. What good was a God that didn't answer her prayers? Rachel would answer her own prayers.

She climbed out of bed. She retrieved an implement from its hiding place in her wardrobe. She walked to the bathroom. In a moment, it was done.

She stifled a scream. She tried not to think. She walked back to her bedroom. She wiped off the implement and put it back in its hiding place. She climbed back into bed.

She tried to ignore the blood. She told herself it would stop soon.

She would call for help if things got any worse.

She tried to call out. She was too weak. She lay in a puddle of blood.

* * *

Downstairs, Manny was having a difficult time. Maybe it was the horde of Nazis setting things on fire just outside their door. That would certainly be sufficient to explain his discomfort. But there was something else, something

196

Manny couldn't articulate.

"I thought I heard something." Manny stopped to listen, but whatever it was, was gone. "I'm going to check on Rachel."

Abe was proud of his twins, the way they looked out for one another.

When Manny reached the top of the stairs, he knew that something was wrong. He looked into Rachel's bedroom and yelled for his parents. Miriam and Abe rushed up the stairs.

"What is it?" asked Abe.

Miriam took one look and knew. She turned to Abe. "Get me a bucket of water and lots of clean towels."

"What is it?" he repeated.

"Just go. Now!"

Abe turned and headed for the kitchen. Manny remained standing at the top of the stairs. "What should I do?"

"Go downstairs."

"Is that all?"

Miriam paused just long enough to see her son's anguish. "Say a prayer."

Abe was already returning with the water and the towels. "Both of you. Downstairs."

Miriam turned and entered Rachel's bedroom, closing the door behind her.

"Rachel," she said softly. "I'm here."

"Mama." It was barely more than a whisper.

"I'm here, child. Mama's here."

While she spoke, Miriam's hands were busy checking Rachel's injuries. Thankfully, the bleeding had largely stopped. Gently, Rachel washed her daughter and held a clean towel against her. They stayed that way until morning, Miriam crooning to her daughter, holding her close, cleaning her wound. Slowly, Rachel began to rally. Her voice gained a bit of strength, more a murmur, less a whisper. Her eyes began to focus on her surroundings.

"Mama," she asked, as her thoughts began to take shape. "What did I do?"

"It's alright, my Rachel. It's alright."

"But I…"

Miriam interrupted her daughter. "We'll have none of that."

Miriam began to sing. *When my sugar walks down the street.*

Rachel managed to sing her part. *All the little birdies go tweet, tweet, tweet.*

"That's my girl. You see, everything is going to be alright."

By morning, Miriam called to her husband. "I think Rachel could sip a bit of tea."

Abe thought those were the best words ever spoken. "I'll put up the water."

It took forever to come to a boil. But a few minutes later, he was able to bring a tea kettle and two cups upstairs. Manny tried to follow him, but Abe told him to wait downstairs. He didn't want to overwhelm Rachel.

Rachel sat up in bed and smiled weakly. "Papa."

"Yes, my child, it's Papa. I've brought you a cup of tea."

"Thank you." Rachel was exhausted by the effort.

Abe had never loved his daughter more. "Lie down. Rest."

He turned to Miriam and asked a question with his eyes.

"Let's talk in the hallway." Miriam touched Rachel's cheek. "We'll be right back."

In the hallway, Abe voiced the question. "Is she going to be alright?"

"Time will tell. When the sun comes up, we need to take her to the hospital."

Chapter Fifty-Five

2023

Detective Massoud jumped up from her desk. "Eddie Matthews was a Senior."

Detective Warren wasn't sure why his partner was so excited, but it was obvious that she was. "A Senior citizen? Am I missing something?"

"Not a Senior citizen. I mean, yes, he was a Senior citizen, but that's not what I'm talking about. He was a Senior. There's an Eddie Matthews Junior!"

Detective Warren's bulk prevented him from jumping up as well, but he was equally excited. "Junior must have bought the gun. We need to find him."

"I'm already on it. He lives in Lancaster County."

Detective Warren pulled up a map on his cellphone. "That's Amish country. Would an Amish man buy a Glock?"

"I don't know. But I think we need to find out."

Warren was re-checking his map. "It's a two-hour drive. Are you sure about this?"

"I'll drive." Massoud grinned. "Don't worry. I've got the truck today."

When they crossed the border from New Jersey into Pennsylvania, they were treated to billboards advertising fireworks, guns, and peanuts. As they continued driving, the billboards changed to promote the authentic Amish experience. Perhaps Eddie Matthews Junior straddled both Pennsylvanias.

Detective Massoud checked her GPS. "We're almost there. How do you want to play this?"

"He's Amish. Let's take things slow and easy."

The first thing they noticed when they arrived at the address was a car parked in the garage. The next thing, electricity. Detective Warren shot a glance at his partner and then rang the doorbell.

A man came to the door, wearing black pants held up with suspenders, a blue cotton shirt, and a straw hat. He certainly fit Detective Warren's notion of what an Amish man would look like, down to the chin beard. "Can I help you?"

Detective Massoud showed her badge. "We're looking for Eddie Matthews Junior."

"That's me." He opened the door wider. "Please come in."

The home was modest, but surprisingly modern. There was a television in the family room and a radio in the kitchen. Detective Warren could hear the whirr of an air conditioner.

"You've had a long drive on a hot day. Can I offer you a glass of lemonade?" Mr. Matthews poured three glasses of lemonade, put them on a tray with a box of tea biscuits, and pointed to a seating arrangement in the family room. "How can I help you."

Detective Massoud took the lead. "We're investigating a shooting in New Jersey. The gun was purchased in Pennsylvania."

"What does that have to do with me? As you can see, I am neither a gun buyer nor a gun seller."

"The gun was bought at a gun show not far from here. According to the dealer, the gun was bought by your father, Eddie Matthews Senior."

"That's crazy. My father was a pacifist. He would never set foot in a gun show, let alone purchase a gun."

Detective Massoud checked her notes. "I'm glad to hear you say that. We don't think your father was the buyer. If you could verify the date of your father's death, it would be helpful."

My father died March 2, 2019, after a lengthy battle with cancer. I'm sorry you had to come all this way for nothing."

Detective Warren joined the conversation. "We are sorry for your loss.

There is one more thing."

"What is it, Detective?"

"Did you purchase the Glock?"

Most men would be angered by such a question, but Eddie Matthews didn't appear to be angered, not even for a moment. "The apple doesn't fall far from the tree."

"Excuse me."

"I'm a pacifist, detective. Like father, like son."

"I'm sorry, I had to ask."

"I understand you have a job to do. If I were in your position, I would ask the same question."

"We appreciate your cooperation."

Eddie Matthews had a question of his own. "Can you tell me when the gun was purchased?"

Detective Warren nodded. "2021."

"So, after my father died."

"Yes."

"That's why you had to ask if it was me."

"Yes."

"Have either of you ever had to bury a parent?"

Detective Massoud nodded. "My mother."

"So you know that feeling, for months afterwards when the post office delivers mail for your deceased parent."

"I know what you mean. It always put me off when I'd find a letter to my mom in my mailbox."

"After a couple of months, it pretty much stops, but every now and then, you still get a piece of mail."

Detective Massoud could tell that this was leading somewhere. She only wished Mr. Matthews would get there already.

"I hadn't gotten anything for my father for several months, and then, a couple of years after he died, there was a flurry of junk mail. Ads for gun shows. Offers for gun magazines. Requests for donations from gun-loving politicians. What do you think that means?"

Detective Massoud answered first. "It means whoever purchased the Glock used phony identification."

Detective Warren finished the thought. "And then the scumbag dealer sold his list of buyers to the gun lobby."

Eddie Matthews Junior had chores to attend to. "If that is all detectives?"

The detectives stood up and prepared to leave. "I do have one last question," Detective Warren said, "if it's not rude to ask."

"What is it, Detective?"

"I always thought Amish weren't allowed to have modern things. You know, cars, electricity, air conditioning."

"Yes, I have been asked that question many times." Eddie Matthews chuckled. "We're not Amish. We're Mennonite."

Detective Warren pretended to understand. "Thank you. Anyway, we'll be on our way."

In the truck, Detective Warren looked at his partner. "I guess I'll take another run at the gun dealer."

"I'll see if it's possible to reverse engineer the phony identification."

"Sounds like a plan."

Detective Massoud started up the truck. "You don't know what a Mennonite is, do you?"

Warren grinned. "Let's go home."

Chapter Fifty-Six

1934

With Manny's help, Abe pushed the cabinet away from the doorway. The barricade, which had seemed essential to their safety during the Nazi bonfire, felt like an overreaction in the light of day. The sun was shining. The sky was blue. There was a cool breeze. The bonfire was out. The Nazis had retreated to their tents. His daughter had survived the night. Life, he reminded himself, is always a blending of the sour and the sweet.

Abe started the Model T. Then he went back into the house. He wrapped Rachel in a clean blanket, carried her down the stairs, and placed her gently in the rear seat. Miriam sat next to Rachel, cradling her daughter in her arms.

Manny wanted to be with them at the hospital, but Abe would not leave his home empty, with the Nazis next door, even in the light of day. Manny waved from the front door as his family drove off in the Model T. Manny had faith in modern medicine, but as the motorcar drove off, he had a premonition that he would not see his sister again.

With every bump in the country road, Rachel cried out in pain. Miriam sang softly in her ear private mother-daughter songs that she had sung when Rachel was an infant, songs that would make the pain go away.

An orderly met them at the hospital entrance and transferred Rachel from the car to a wheelchair. Abe insisted on pushing the wheelchair into the building. Rachel was assigned to a bed. Abe and Miriam were allowed to sit with their daughter while they waited for a doctor. It felt like forever, but it was actually just a few minutes. He was an older doctor, balding with tufts of white hair above his ears, crow's feet, and the slightest tremor in his hands.

Dr. Tidwell took one look at Rachel and asked the Dubinskis to go to the waiting room. "I will send a nurse to sit with you, if you like."

"That won't be necessary. Will you come talk to us when you have completed your exam?"

"Of course."

Abe shook the man's hand. The tremor was hardly noticeable. "Take good care of my daughter. Please."

* * *

Abe had spent his entire life never needing a hospital. This was his second visit in a matter of weeks. He looked fondly at Miriam sitting next to him in the waiting room. She was doing better. His daughter was alive because of Miriam's care. Now, it was up to the doctors.

Abe was a fortunate man, beset by a plethora of misfortune. When the canal closed, he lost his job, and unless things took a turn for the better, soon enough, it would cost him his home. Antisemitism, never far removed from his thoughts, was on the rise in his little village. A Nazi had raped his daughter. Her very survival was in question. Thugs beat his son. The thugs themselves might not be Nazis, but they were doing the Nazis' bidding. In the last twenty-four hours, nearly one hundred Nazi youth had moved into tents next to his home. The Nazi bonfire had nearly set his home ablaze.

Abe was a fortunate man. He took his wife's hand in his own. "It is time for us to find another place to live."

"We will make a new home."

They sat in the waiting room, each lost in their own thoughts, praying for good news from the doctor. Several hours passed before the doctor returned.

Abe was the first to spot Dr. Tidwell walking down the hall. He was not alone. He was deep in conversation with a young woman in a white coat. She didn't look like a nurse.

They approached the Dubinskis. The doctor introduced his colleague, Dr. Nordquist.

Abe was astonished. "You are a doctor?"

"You'll have to excuse my husband. He's never met a woman doctor." Miriam shook her hand. "Neither have I."

"She is the first woman doctor at the hospital," explained Dr. Tidwell. "Given the circumstances of your daughter's case..." Dr. Tidwell didn't finish his thought, leaving the explanation to his female colleague.

"Do you mind if I sit down?"

Abe jumped from his chair. "Where are my manners? It's just.... Please, sit down."

Dr. Nordquist sat down and turned to Miriam. "I'd like to talk woman-to-woman."

Dr. Tidwell took Abe by the elbow. "Let's leave the women to talk."

"It must have been a harrowing night."

Miriam was grateful to have a woman to talk to. "I did what I had to. I did what any mother would do given the circumstances."

"I have not been blessed with a child, but I think I know what you mean. Taking care of children is the essence of being a woman." Dr. Nordquist smiled warmly. "It is, perhaps, what has made me a good doctor."

"Is my daughter going to be alright?"

"Before we go further, there is something I need to say. There are things about your daughter that I don't need to know. There are things in the law, if I know about, then I have to do something. Do you understand?"

"I understand."

"Your daughter lost a lot of blood. You did a good job controlling the bleeding. I went in this morning and cleaned up after you."

"Cleaned up?"

"Your daughter should make a full recovery."

"Cleaned up?" she asked again.

"I am sorry to have to tell you this, but your daughter will not be able to have children."

Taking care of children is the essence of being a woman.

"Cleaned up?" Miriam knew it would come to this. She knew it from the moment she stepped into Rachel's bedroom in the middle of the night. But until the doctor said the words, she had held out hope. What is life without hope? What is life without children?

Taking care of children is the essence of being a woman.

Miriam broke out in tears in the hospital waiting room. Her daughter would never be a mother, and there was nothing Miriam could do to change that.

There was nothing Dr. Nordquist could do to change that either. "We will keep Rachel here until tomorrow to make sure she is healing properly. You can take her home tomorrow."

Chapter Fifty-Seven

2023

Detectives Warren and Massoud were in the squad room. The air conditioning in the station house was on the fritz. Despite the heat, Massoud was drinking her regular cup of coffee. Warren had switched to a water bottle.

"I called the gun dealer, but I couldn't pry anything out of him. Told me I should consider myself lucky that he gave me a name. I told him the name he gave me was bogus, and he should consider himself lucky that we were talking on the telephone."

"We just need to connect a real person to the bogus name." Massoud had an idea. "These days, there's video surveillance everywhere. You can't go anyplace without being caught on camera. Maybe I can find something."

"Good idea. In the meantime, I'm gonna double back on Ben Levenson." Detective Warren returned to his desk and pulled his file. He placed a call. "Ben Levenson? This is Detective Warren."

"What can I do for you, Detective?"

"Detective Massoud and I paid a visit to the shack."

"Did you find anything?"

Detective Warren knew better than to give out information without getting something in return. "Nothing, really. I'm calling in the hope that you've remembered something since we last talked. Some small detail that might help move the investigation along."

The detective decided to dangle one more piece of bait. "The good thing, at least the good thing for you is we didn't find anything that would contradict your account."

"Are you saying that I'm no longer a suspect in Tom Jackson's murder?"

"Yes. That's what I'm saying."

"Then, you're right. That is good news...for me."

"There's still the matter of your activity at the federal prison." Detective Warren allowed that to sink in before continuing. "Of course, without a murder charge hanging over your head, we should be able to resolve that matter without too much difficulty."

"Without involving my wife?"

"If all goes well, then yes, without involving your wife." Again, he gave Ben time to appreciate what the detective was offering. "Can you come to the station house today?"

"I'll be there in an hour."

Detective Warren hung up the phone and got himself another cup of coffee.

* * *

Detective Massoud finished off a bottle of water while hunting for surveillance cameras in the vicinity of the gun show. She started with the organization that had sponsored the gun show. The dealers themselves wanted to know as little as possible about their customers, but the sponsor organization might have a stake in knowing who was in attendance at their events. It didn't take her long to track down the name of the organization and their contact information.

The gentleman who answered the phone was shocked, shocked, he repeated, at the possibility that a gun transaction occurred at one of their events without proper documentation. "You understand, I'm sure," he continued, "that we merely sponsor the event. The dealers are responsible for the actual transactions."

"Yes, of course. It is always someone else. Do you get copies of any of the documentation from the dealers? Do you save images of anyone's identification? Do you, perhaps, take photo or video images?"

The gentleman sounded deeply hurt when he responded. "I can assure you we do everything that is required by law."

"And nothing more."

"I need to say goodbye now, Detective. I hope you find what you're looking for."

Detective Massoud hung up the phone. The call had gone about the way she had expected. Time was when the gun lobby had supported the police. She identified the various traffic authorities with jurisdiction in and around the site of the gun show. It was a long shot, but with a bit of luck, she might see something of interest. One by one, she contacted them, verifying the roadways, intersections, entrances, and exits where they had video surveillance. In a few cases, she was able to watch the video remotely, but most either wanted her to come to their office or to produce a warrant allowing them to release the tapes. She watched what she could and put the remainder on hold for the time being.

Detective Massoud was missing something. She updated her partner on her progress, or lack thereof. Detective Warren was getting ready to sit down with Ben Levenson. Massoud needed a break from video dead-ends. "Is it okay if I sit in?"

Warren quickly briefed Massoud. He had already reached out to his contact at the feds. If Levenson was no longer a murder suspect, they all wanted the federal charge to go away. No one had the time or the stomach to deal with something that, in effect, was little more than a dumb prank. Prosecuting Levenson would raise more questions than it would answer. If Ben was willing to cooperate, they would make the federal charge go away.

Under the circumstances, knowing that Olivia's license to practice law would not be jeopardized by his antics, Ben Levenson was ready to cooperate. Warren asked him again if he remembered anything more about the place.

"Nothing. Sorry." Ben Levenson rubbed his chin, as though it might stimulate his thinking. "I didn't think places like that existed in New Jersey."

Detective Warren agreed. "I know. I mean, how does anybody live without indoor plumbing?"

Ben nodded his head. "Tell me about it. I had to take a dump. It was awful."

Detective Warren stared at Ben Levenson. "You took a dump in the outhouse?"

"Yeah."

"You're sure?"

"You don't forget a thing like that."

Detective Warren pulled open a file. "Anyway, thanks for coming in."

When Ben Levenson left, Massoud gave her partner a puzzled look. "What was that about?"

"Did anyone process the outhouse?"

"Huh?"

"Did anyone process the outhouse?"

"I don't understand."

"Maybe Ben Levenson wasn't the only person to use the outhouse recently."

"I'll make arrangements to send a team back there." Detective Massoud grinned. "But you can be damned sure I'm going to tell them it was your idea."

Chapter Fifty-Eight

1934

"I've come to a decision, and when I tell you what it is, I don't want an argument." Miriam and Abe rarely argued, but she knew this was likely to anger her husband.

"Of course. What is it?"

Miriam steeled herself. "When Rachel is discharged, I don't think she should come home."

Abe said nothing. Miriam began to wonder whether Abe had heard her. "When Rachel is discharged, I don't think she should come home."

"I heard you the first time."

Miriam had never seen her husband looking sadder than he did at that moment.

"I agree with you, my Miriam. I don't think it's safe for her with the Nazis nearby."

Miriam was relieved that her husband understood. "I will need to go with her. She needs her mother now more than ever."

Abe nodded. "Of course."

"The only question remaining is where Rachel and I should go."

Abe thought about the options. They had had no contact with his parents or hers since before the twins were born. They could not ask for family help now. Their only real friends were the Beckers. It would not be fair to ask the Beckers. And in any case, it wouldn't be safe. There was only one place for them to go, but Abe would be embarrassed to ask. "What about the Einsteins? They seem to care deeply for Rachel."

They sat in silence, waiting for Rachel's release.

Dr. Nordquist stopped in to see Rachel, before sending her home. She was surprised to find that the wound had re-opened. There was a small, but significant stream of fresh blood. Rachel didn't appear to be upset. The doctor decided not to ask Rachel how the wound had come to re-open. Instead, she simply repaired the damage and held her in the hospital for one more night.

When she returned the next morning, Rachel was quiet. The wound had closed properly. Her color was good. There was no evidence of an infection. "I'm going to discharge you today."

"Thank you." Rachel was appreciative but didn't seem to be especially excited about the prospect of leaving the hospital.

"Is everything alright?"

"Yes. Everything is fine." Rachel's affect was flat, belying her words.

Dr. Nordquist decided it was time to speak up. "I already mentioned this to your mother, but I think it is important for you to hear this as well." The doctor paused, choosing her words with care. "I myself am childless. It is not the curse that you currently imagine it to be. My work here at the hospital is important. It leaves me little free time, but what time I have, I spend with my nieces and nephews. I lead a full and happy life."

"Can I confide in you, doctor?"

"Of course."

"A man took me against my will."

Dr. Nordquist nodded. "I suspected so."

"The man is a Nazi. Do you understand? I could not permit myself to have a Nazi baby."

"You did what you had to do."

"I did. And I'm glad that I did, but my father is a lock tender. Do you understand?"

"No, Rachel, I'm sorry, but I don't."

"Am I destined to grow up to be a lock tender?"

"Of course not."

"So there is no reason for me to assume that the baby would grow up to be a Nazi." Rachel wiped a tear from her cheek. "I will never know for sure. But I am going home today."

* * *

Miriam helped her daughter find a comfortable position in the rear seat of the Model T. Abe started the motorcar but didn't drive. Abe turned to his wife for advice. Miriam looked back at Abe and began to laugh. Neither of them knew where they were going.

From the rear seat, Rachel spoke up. "Go ahead. I'll tell you where to turn."

Abe was astonished. He turned to Miriam. "Did you tell her?"

"No." Miriam turned to Rachel. "How?"

It hurt when Rachel laughed. She laughed anyway. "I know how Papa is. 'It's not safe for Rachel at home' or something like that. Am I right?"

Abe's cheeks reddened. "Something like that. Anyway, I'm taking you and your mother to the Einsteins. Hopefully, they will agree to let you stay with them for a few days."

"Mama, too?"

Miriam took her daughter's hand. "Me too."

Several short blocks and three turns later, Rachel pointed out the house. Abe parked the car. "Wait here."

He walked up to the front door and knocked. Elsa answered.

"Mr. Dubinski." She spotted Miriam and Rachel in the car. "Is everything alright?"

Abe had rehearsed what he intended to say, but he couldn't get the words to come out in a coherent order. Still, he managed to say hospital and Nazis and a few other keywords.

Elsa didn't need to understand. "Of course, you are welcome here. Help the ladies climb down from the car. I'll tell Albert we have guests."

Elsa turned and walked inside, leaving the front door open. By the time the Dubinskis stepped into the house, Albert was waiting anxiously in the parlor.

Abe stared at Albert. He was in awe of the great man. "I'm so sorry to take you away from your important work, Dr. Einstein."

"Please, call me Albert." He smiled broadly. "Is our Rachel ill?"

Elsa interrupted her husband. "I told you…"

"Yes, my dear, you are correct." He turned to Rachel. "Sit down," he said, pointing to a particular chair. "I put an extra pillow on that one so you would be more comfortable."

"Thank you." Rachel smiled weakly. "If it's not too much trouble, may I have a glass of water?"

Once everyone was settled, water for Rachel, lemonade for Miriam and Elsa, and brandy for Abe and Albert, Miriam explained why they had come. When she was finished, she looked at Elsa. "I do hope we're not intruding."

"Intruding? Of course not. If you hadn't asked, I would have insisted that you stay." Elsa turned to her husband. "We left Switzerland to get away from the Nazis. And now, they are here, in the Dubinski's backyard. It is unacceptable!"

Abe spoke up. "If Rachel and Miriam can stay here for a few days, that should be enough time."

Miriam heard something in her husband's voice, something that suggested he was not thinking about Rachel's recovery time. "What do you have in mind, my dear husband?"

"I intend to reason with Helmut. Surely, he will understand that his behavior and the behavior of his campers cannot be allowed in our little village."

Albert Einstein shook his head. "In my experience, Nazis do not respond to reason."

"But I must try. I have to believe that human beings are fundamentally decent."

"I wish I shared your belief. Still, I agree. You must try." Albert paused, collecting his thoughts. "It might be a good idea to bring several men with you to emphasize your desire to come to a peaceful resolution."

Abe stood up. "The sooner I get started, the sooner this will all be over."

Chapter Fifty-Nine

2023

Detective Massoud interrupted her partner. "Where exactly was the gun show?"

Warren had a copy of the gun show flyer. "Tomatum, Pennsylvania."

"No. I mean, what building?"

Warren took another look at the flyer and read off the address of the venue.

Detective Massoud jotted down the address in her notebook. "I wonder who owns the building?"

Warren put down his own work. "What are you thinking?"

Massoud was still working it out in her head. "The gun dealers won't cooperate. Neither will the organization that sponsored the gun show. But what about the owner of the building?"

"Of course."

"Some guy owns a building. He rents it out for trade shows, warehouse sales, baseball card shows, all sorts of events. I'll bet the owner gives a damn about who is coming and going at these events, if for no other reason than controlling the cost of his insurance premiums."

"That makes sense. But the landlord's not standing at the entrance checking IDs."

"No, he's not. But he might have a security camera, maybe several."

It didn't take long for the detectives to determine the name of the company that owned the venue. The facilities manager confirmed that they did, in fact, have a camera mounted in the parking lot, aimed at the building's entrance.

"If it was up to me, we wouldn't rent space to the gun lobby. But baseball cards, remaindered books, patio furniture, well, they only fill so many days on the calendar. So if some group wants to host a gun show, we'll rent them space. Of course, we check all the organizations that rent from us to make sure they're legitimate."

He had no qualms about sharing the tape. "If you can drive out here to Tomatum, I'll introduce you to someone on our security team. They'll be happy to set you up in front of a video camera."

"Thank you. But it's a two-hour drive each way. I'll make the trip if I have to, but I could better use that time viewing tape. Would it be possible for you to send the day's video to my computer?"

"Let me check with my boss."

"Thank you, Mr...."

"Grissom."

"Thank you, Mr. Grissom."

"Please, call me Gerry."

While Massoud waited to hear back from Gerry, she checked in with the crime scene technicians who had been dispatched down to the salt marsh. The supervisor was none too happy.

"We've already processed the place once. What are we looking for this time?"

"Shit."

"What?"

"Shit. Piss. The usual."

"The usual?"

"Your team processed the shack for us, and they did their usual thorough job, but none of us thought about processing the outhouse."

"Shit."

"Exactly."

"I assume this is a rush job."

"Aren't they all?"

"I'll have someone there first thing tomorrow morning."

By the time Massoud had finished with the crime scene guys, she had a message from Gerry. "I spoke to my supervisor. He said it's okay. I need you to email me from the address where you want the file sent. I need your name and badge number in the request and the date of the video."

Detective Massoud sent off the email. An hour later, the video arrived as a file attachment. Her shift was almost over. She ordered a couple of pizzas, grabbed a hold of her partner, and settled in, in front of her monitor. It was going to be a long night.

Three hours and two pizza boxes later, Detective Warren leaned into the monitor. He shouted, "Stop the tape!"

Massoud halted the video. "What is it?"

"Rewind.... Good, there it is."

Detective Massoud did her best to examine the grainy image of a man wearing a hoodie. "Who is he?"

Detective Warren leaned back in his chair. "That's Mr. Pisswater."

"Who?"

"I'm sorry, Hank Morgan."

"Are you sure?"

Warren picked up a slice of pizza and waved it in the air as a sign of victory. "As sure as I'm gonna eat this slice of pizza, we just found Eddie Matthews Senior." He chomped down on the pizza for emphasis. "In the morning, I'll send a couple of uniforms to pick him up."

"Where exactly do you plan to send them? As I recall, Mr. Morgan proudly lives off the grid."

Chapter Sixty

1934

"I have an idea," Elsa started, "if it's okay with your mother. After you have recovered, when things get back to normal, Albert and I would like to hire you to be our housekeeper."

Rachel was still too weak to jump up and down, but in her mind, she was jumping. "Can I, Mama? Please?"

Miriam didn't want to say no to her daughter, not after everything she had been through, but she was not ready to say yes.

"We thought she could stay with us here in Princeton several days a week and spend the rest of the week home with you and your husband. The specific days don't matter. Whatever works for you and your husband." Elsa gauged Miriam for a reaction. "We would pay her, of course, thirty-five cents an hour."

"Oh, Mama. Then Papa wouldn't have to worry so much."

Miriam looked from Elsa to Rachel to Albert and then back to Elsa. "That is very kind of you. Yes. I believe I can get Abe to agree."

Miriam watched as Rachel and Elsa began running through a list of the chores that Rachel might be able to help with. Housekeeping, of course. Some cooking. Some laundry. Shopping. Elsa smiled. "This will be a very big help to me. Taking care of Albert, by itself, is a full-time job."

Albert shrugged. "I have been known to be a bit messy."

Elsa laughed. "A bit?"

"Everything is relative." Albert always had an explanation or at least an excuse. "One man's mess is another man's treasure."

Rachel thought this might be the perfect time to make a suggestion. "If I might add one more task to the list, strictly as time permits, and I wouldn't expect any payment, but perhaps Albert, you would allow me to be your research assistant. I promise you I can handle the material."

Albert didn't believe that he was in need of an assistant. If he did, he would do well to ask the Institute to send someone over.

Rachel pressed ahead. "Currently, I'm reading *Im Kopf eines Geometrikers.*"

"That is quite a book for a young woman." Albert Einstein whistled in amazement. "Recently, a young man, a handyman of sorts, expressed an interest in becoming my assistant. I gave him my copy of that very book and told him to come back in a month. I haven't heard from him since. To be frank, he seemed more eager than capable."

"His German is not very good. Between you and me, he is having trouble comprehending the book."

"You know this boy?"

Rachel grinned. "He is my twin brother."

Albert let out another prolonged whistle. "You Dubinskis are full of surprises! So tell me about your brother. Won't he be angry if I hire you?"

"I don't believe Manny would be angry. Jealous, yes, but not angry."

"But he wanted badly to be my assistant."

"You are my son's hero," explained Miriam. "He has always talked about becoming a scientist when he completes his schooling."

"Some days, my brother wants to be a scientist. Other days, he wants to be a professional hockey player. My brother is a very good person, but I fear he will not be either."

"What do you think he will be?"

Rachel knew exactly what her twin brother would be. "He will be a wonderful husband and father. He will be a tradesman and earn enough money to take good care of his family. He will be loved by many and respected by everyone."

Albert listened carefully. "And what will you be?"

"I will be a mathematician."

"Have you finished reading *Im Kopf eines Geometrikers*?"

"No, but I have made a good beginning."

"Then you must tell me about the book. To do anything else would not be fair to your brother."

"Certainly. The book explains the relationship between theoretical and practical geometry."

"Yes. That is true, but what does that mean?"

Rachel took a moment to organize her thoughts. "Practical geometry is the study of real shapes that exist in the real world. It allows us to understand concepts like area and volume. It is the geometry of everyday life."

"Yes, yes," Albert said impatiently. "Go on."

"There are other shapes that do not exist in the real world. They exist only in our imagination. Most people are unaware of their existence."

Albert nodded. "In my experience, most people are kept busy trying to imagine how they will pay their rent. They do not have enough imagination left over to consider shapes that do not exist anywhere but in the imagination. I am surprised that you know about these imaginary shapes."

"I have never been enamored of the real world."

"I have only one more question. Why should we bother studying these imaginary shapes?"

Rachel knew she was about to become Albert's assistant. "Because we can use them to construct worlds that exist only inside the human mind. And then we can apply what was only in our imagination to solve practical problems in the real world."

Albert stood up. "Come with me, Rachel. We have a lot to talk about."

Rachel followed Albert to his study. Miriam and Elsa sat in the parlor, stunned.

"Your daughter, she has a brilliant mind."

Miriam didn't know what to say. Her own schooling had ended in the third grade. Here, her daughter was engaged in a discussion of advanced mathematical concepts with Dr. Einstein himself. "May I ask you a question?"

"Of course."

"You and Albert are Jewish, am I right."

"Yes."

"But you are not religious."

"If you mean, do we follow Jewish law, no, we do not. Albert and I believe in God, but not so much in religion."

Miriam rushed ahead. "I do not want to offend you. My Abe and I are not devout Jews, but we are observant. In our home, we light Shabbos candles."

"I understand. I will discuss this with Albert. I believe we would not be offended if Rachel were to light Shabbos candles in our home." Elsa grinned. "Of course, we do not have any of our own. Rachel will have to bring them."

Chapter Sixty-One

2023

Detective Warren didn't know where to find Mr. Pisswater, but he knew where to start: with Mr. Pisswater's gun-loving friends. At the bridge tender's, the police had collected identifying information from each of the men who had brought a weapon to the demonstration. They had pressed charges against Dickie Simpson, the one man who had discharged his weapon. With a gun charge hanging over his head, Detective Warren figured Simpson was likely to cooperate. After checking Simpson's record, Detective Warren paid an early morning visit to Simpson's farmhouse.

The early morning sun was beginning to burn through the haze. Detective Warren knocked on the door. The man who answered was unwashed, half-dressed, and had yet to run a comb through his hair. Detective Warren loved showing up before the man had had his first cup of coffee.

"Dickie? Dickie Simpson?" Detective Warren flashed his badge. "Can I come in?"

"Do you have a warrant?"

"Do I need one?"

Dickie Simpson stood in the doorway. "I know my rights."

"And I know that you're facing jail time. I would be happy to tell the district attorney that you were cooperative." Warren grinned. "That is, if you decide to be cooperative."

Simpson stepped aside, allowing the detective to enter his home. In the kitchen, Simpson stared lovingly at his coffeemaker.

"Go ahead Dickie. It's okay. Pour yourself a cup."

Dickie grabbed a second amendment coffee mug from a cabinet and poured himself a cup. He didn't offer one to the detective.

Warren waited until he'd had his first sip. "I need to talk to Hank Morgan."

"Who?"

"Cut the shit Dickie."

"If I tell you where to find him, can you make my jail time go away?"

"That's up the DA."

"But it's possible."

"Yes, Dickie. It's possible."

"And you'll tell the DA that I've been cooperative?"

"Didn't I just say that I would?"

"I'm just making sure."

"Yes, I will tell the DA that you've been cooperative."

"I don't know where Hank Morgan lives."

"What about a job?"

"I don't know if he has a job."

Detective Warren was growing frustrated. "What do you know, Dickie-boy?"

"A bunch of us like to drink at a bar just outside of town."

"Does the bar have a name?"

"You won't tell Morgan how you found the bar?"

"It'll be our little secret."

Dickie Simpson didn't want his friends to know he had cooperated with the police. But more than that, he didn't want to go to jail. "The Alehouse."

"Now that wasn't so hard." Detective Warren smiled. "I'll let myself out."

The Alehouse wouldn't open until noon. Even if Pisswater was a day drinker, it was too early to head for the bar. In any event, he wanted to give the crime scene guys time to process the outhouse, before confronting Hank Morgan. The supervisor had promised Detective Massoud he'd have a team inside the outhouse first thing that morning. Warren didn't want to think about the guy who got that assignment, up to his hips in shit and salt water.

Detective Warren drove to the station house and waited. At noon, he drove to the Alehouse, a classic old man bar on the other side of the canal. The detective stepped inside. The Alehouse was poorly lit, with ripped faux leather barstools, a well-worn wooden bar top, a grainy image on the television screen, tuned to a sports talk show, the volume turned off, illegal electric cords hanging from the TV and from the light fixtures, and, half a dozen old men, drinking bourbon backed with beer. There was an aroma in the Alehouse that reminded Warren of the outhouse.

The detective approached the barkeep. In another few years, he would be old enough to join the regulars on the other side of the bar. He didn't need to see a badge to know that Detective Warren was on the job.

"What can I do for you, Detective?"

Warren pulled out a photo of Mr. Pisswater. "Do you know this guy?"

The barkeep studied the photo. "Third barstool from the rear, most days at 5:00."

Detective Warren thanked the barkeep. He turned and headed for the exit. Clean air called to him from the other side of the exit door.

The detective killed an hour driving aimlessly along both sides of the canal. He had grown up in the village. In his lifetime, he had always believed it to be a nice little village. The villagers didn't always know their neighbors, didn't always like the ones they did know, but they had always respected their neighbor's right to live whatever law-abiding life they chose. Times were changing, and not for the better. Suddenly, Detective Warren stopped the car. An idea had come to him in a flash, and he didn't like it. Were the times really changing, he wondered, or had he simply been blind to the bad parts.

Detective Warren had always been the right color, the right gender, the right religion. If he were to ask his partner, what would she tell him? Did she feel like an other? What did that feel like, living your life as an other, in your hometown?

He pushed the thought down, filing it away for later, and returned to the station house.

Detective Massoud was waiting for him. "I just got off the phone with forensics."

Detective Warren liked that his partner was all business. It saved him from the need to make small talk about big issues. "Did they get anything?"

"They brought back a sample of, their words, the miasmal sludge in the bottom of the pit latrine."

Detective Warren took a moment to picture the tech who had to retrieve that sample. He imagined the tech, in full hazmat suit, ripping up the floorboards, climbing down into the hole, poking around in the decomposing human waste, emerging like the creature from the black lagoon, dripping with all manner of sludge. "And?"

"And they're skeptical that lab tests of the sample will identify anything that we can use. But he managed to lift a few fingerprints from the door and also from the toilet paper roll. They're running the prints through the system now."

"Excellent. I have a lead on Hank Morgan. We should be able to pick him up for questioning today at 5:00. Any chance we'll get word on the prints before then?"

"I'll make a call."

Detective Massoud placed the call. After a few short minutes, she disconnected. "I told him it was urgent."

Detective Warren could see where that was leading. "And?"

"He reminded me that everything is urgent."

Detective Warren re-checked his notes. "That's okay. Even without the prints, we've got plenty to discuss with Hank Morgan."

* * *

It was happy hour when the detectives arrived at the Alehouse. At the Alehouse, it would have been more accurate to refer to it as ever so slightly less depressed hour. Warren scanned the room. Three seats from the back, Hank Morgan was nursing a whisky. The detective strolled over and gave Mr. Pisswater a jovial slap on the back.

"You look damn good for a man who's been dead for four years."

"I'm afraid you've got me mistaken for…" Hank Morgan swiveled around on his stool. "Detective! What are you doing here?"

"My partner and I need to ask you a few questions."

"Here? In the bar? Have you no manners?"

Detective Massoud spoke up. "You're absolutely right. We don't want to embarrass you in front of your friends. So finish your whisky, get up off your ass, and come with us to the station house."

Hank Morgan puffed himself up. "All I have to do is say the word, and my friends, as you call them, will turn this place into a war zone."

Detective Warren drew his weapon. "Turn around and put your hands on the bar." While Warren cuffed Mr. Pisswater, Massoud stared down the drunks in the bar. Most of them were so deep into their whisky they hardly noticed.

Detective Warren put Mr. Pisswater in the back seat of the car. The two detectives climbed in front. For a change, Warren was behind the wheel. From the backseat, Hank Morgan had a question. "What is this all about?"

Detective Warren kept his eyes facing front, on the traffic. Detective Massoud didn't bother to turn around. Hank Morgan could talk to the back of her head. "Like my partner told you in the bar, we have a few questions."

Hank Morgan gave up. They would tell him what this was about when they were good and ready.

At the station house, Detective Massoud went to check on the fingerprints. Detective Warren removed the cuffs and put Hank Morgan in the interview room. "Sit down."

Hank Morgan sat.

"My partner and I are investigating the death of Tom Jackson."

"He's dead? I guess that explains why he hasn't been in the bar recently."

"This is not the time for you to be a wiseass." Detective Warren read him his rights. "Just a formality," the detective explained.

"Then here's a little formality of my own. I want a lawyer."

"Then you shall have one. I can get a public defender here sometime today."

"You'd like that, wouldn't you? Anyway, I've got my own attorney."

"No skin off my ass," the detective replied. "Make your call."

After Hank Morgan got off the phone, Detective Warren cuffed him and left him in the interview room. He caught up with his partner.

"Any news yet on the fingerprints?"

"Not yet. Are you getting anywhere with our suspect?"

"He lawyered up."

"Perhaps he'd be interested in hearing what we know about the case."

"We can't talk to him."

"But we can talk in front of him."

Detectives Warren and Massoud returned to the interview room. Warren took the cuffs off their suspect. "While we all sit here waiting for your attorney, my partner and I are going to discuss the case. Feel free to ignore us."

Detective Massoud opened a manila folder and pulled out her notes. "Let's see. We found Tom Jackson's blood on the floor of a shack in the salt marsh. We found a stray bullet in the wall of the shack."

"That's right." Detective Warren compared his case notes. "We found a Glock in the salt marsh behind the shack. The bullet in the shack was a match for the Glock."

Detective Massoud picked up the thread. "The gun belonged to Eddie Matthews Senior. Mr. Matthews purchased the weapon at a gun show in Pennsylvania in 2021."

Detective Warren kept his eyes on his partner, two detectives reviewing their case file, no more, no less. If Hank Morgan chose to listen, that was on him. "Here's the interesting part. Eddie Matthews Senior couldn't have bought the gun."

Detective Massoud played along. "Why not?"

"Because he died of end-stage cancer in 2019."

The two detectives and their suspect sat silently in the interview room, waiting for the attorney.

"I almost forgot," Detective Warren said as if out of the blue. "We have video evidence indicating that Hank Morgan attended that very same gun show on the day the Glock was purchased."

The room lapsed back into silence. An officer knocked on the door. Mr. Morgan's attorney had arrived. "By all means, bring her in. Mr. Morgan has a right to representation."

A petite woman in a power suit marched into the interview room. She carried her briefcase like it was an explosive. She introduced herself as Beverly Benitendi.

The detectives stepped out of the room, allowing Hank Morgan plenty of time to confer with his attorney. When they returned to the interview room, Ms. Benitendi made quick work of the matter. "My client may know something about Tom Jackson's death. By the way, you don't actually have a body, do you?" She didn't wait for a reply. "Anyway, my client may have information that you would find useful."

"What is the nature of the information?"

"You are looking for evidence that someone, perhaps, hypothetically speaking, my client, shot Tom Jackson and left him, somewhere, dead. I'd like to suggest that the essential question is not who killed Tom Jackson. Rather, the question you may want to ask is, who hired someone, perhaps my client, again, speaking hypothetically, to murder Tom Jackson."

Another officer knocked on the door. Detective Massoud had an important phone call. She stepped out and, after a brief conversation, returned to the interview room. "Since we're speaking hypothetically here, I'd like to clarify one thing. Did your client just confess to doing the murder?"

The detective didn't give Beverly Benitendi time to reply. "That phone call was from forensics. They lifted a set of fingerprints from the outhouse." She drilled her eyes into Hank Morgan. "By chance, did you have need of the outhouse when you killed Tom Jackson?"

Beverly Benitendi conferred with her client. "My client wants it known for the record that if he did do the murder, he could tell you who it was that hired him. Of course, that depends on the terms of a deal." Beverly Benitendi found plea deals tedious. That was, perhaps, why she was so good at them. In a matter of minutes, she had hammered out a mutually acceptable plea deal.

"According to my client, he was hired by Abby Jackson, the victim's wife."

Chapter Sixty-Two

1934

Manny, at home, was eagerly awaiting news about his sister. His twin sense told him that she was going to be alright, but he wouldn't be sure until he saw her. When he heard the Model T, Manny ran outside. He was disappointed that it was only his father in the motorcar.

He pestered his father with questions. "Your sister is healing." Beyond that, Manny would have to wait until Papa parked the car, went inside, washed off the road dirt, and had something to eat. Finally done, Abe lit a pipe and sat down for a serious conversation with his son.

"Did you have any trouble while I was gone?"

"No, Papa."

"There were no more bonfires?"

"No. The boys spent all day marching and singing and listening to speeches."

"Have they made any threats?"

"Sometimes, I see boys pointing to our house. I hear them talking about the kikes."

"And you. What did you do?"

"Nothing, Papa. I wanted to punch them in the face, but I promised you I would not engage with them."

"You're a good boy."

"I'm not a boy anymore."

Abe looked at the young man who was his son. "You are right, Emanuel. You are a good man."

The two men, father and son, sat silently, each lost in their own thoughts. Finally, Abe turned to his son. "I am going to speak to Helmut tomorrow."

"But Papa, is that safe?"

"I am going to reason with the man. I believe I can show him the error of his ways."

"But Papa, Helmut is a Nazi. I don't believe that Nazis can be swayed by reason."

Abe stood up and began to pace. "I believe that all men desire to do what is good and right. Some men need to be shown what that good and right thing is, but once shown, they will naturally change their ways."

"Do you really believe that?"

Abe stopped pacing. "I have to. Otherwise, what is the point of living?"

* * *

What is the point of living? Manny had no answer. He had done poorly on his exams. It was unlikely that he would become a scientist, let alone Dr. Einstein's assistant. He kept the bad news from his parents. They had enough to worry about without worrying about his future.

He had only ever wanted to be two things—a scientist and a hockey player. The first was no longer realistic, and the second, he finally had to admit, never had been. If there was anything special about being Emanuel Dubinski, it was that he was a twin.

Manny had always said that Rachel got the looks, and he got the brains. The truth is, Rachel got the looks and the brains. She could be whatever she wanted to be. And then that Nazi had taken her to the movie theater and defiled her.

Abe Dubinski wanted to reason with the Nazi. Emanuel Dubinski wanted revenge.

That night, neither Dubinski slept well. Abe's sleep was marred by dreams of Nazis goosestepping on the towpath. At the end of one row of marchers, Abe spotted Otto goosestepping along with the rest of the Nazis. He woke in a cold sweat. Manny dreamt of dead Jews, riddled with bullets, lying in a puddle of blood. As happens in dreams, the location was totally unfamiliar and, at the same time, instantly recognizable.

Manny was up before the sun. He went downstairs and found his father sitting at the kitchen table, swirling a spoon in a bowl of kasha, pretending to eat.

"There's more on the stove," Abe said, pointing to the pot of buckwheat groats.

"I'm not hungry."

Abe put down the spoon and pushed the bowl away. "Neither am I."

"Can I come with you?"

"No."

"Papa, can I ask you a question?"

"Of course."

"What will you do if Helmut doesn't want to be reasonable?"

* * *

When the time was right, Abe and Manny stepped out of the house. As Abe expected, the towpath was empty. At that hour, the boys would all be in the mess tent having breakfast.

"Wait for me here."

No one stopped Abe as he approached the mess tent, but one hundred pairs of eyes were trained on him when he pulled back the tent flap. Abe announced his intentions. "I'm here to speak to Helmut Fischer."

Helmut was eating eggs and bacon at the head table. He stood up and walked over to greet his uninvited guest. "Good morning, Mr. Dubinski. I do not wish to be rude, but Jews are not welcome here."

"Good morning to you as well, Mr. Fischer. Isn't it a splendid morning?"

"I don't know what Jew trick you are planning, but I tell you again, you are not welcome here."

"I have come here to talk to you, only to talk. When I am finished, I will leave."

"Follow me, Hebe." Helmut Fischer stepped outside. Abe followed him out.

"Now, what is it you have to say?"

"It is such a nice day. Let us walk on the towpath while we talk, man to man."

"You Jews think you are so clever. Why would I agree to go for a walk, where I would have no advantage? If we talk here, I have one hundred who will come to my aid."

"You will walk with me because we are both reasonable men. You will walk with me because you want to hear what I have to say. And finally, you will walk with me because, in your arrogance, you believe that a Jew could never best you in any contest."

Abe walked toward the towpath. Helmut signaled to the mess tent and then joined Abe.

"Spit it out, Jew, and then be on your way."

"Be patient, my friend. Let us take a moment to enjoy this beautiful day."

"I will enjoy the day when you are gone."

Abe smiled. "You see, we are not so very different. I, too, will enjoy the day when you are gone."

"You think you are clever." Helmut spit it out. "The day is coming when such an insult will result in your imprisonment...or worse."

"I regret that you see my comment as an insult. That is not my intention."

"I have wasted enough of my day on you already."

"When you came to this village, it was winter. Do you remember?"

Helmut said nothing.

"My wife and I were skating on the canal, right about here, when the ice cracked. You helped save her life."

"To my eternal shame and regret."

"Do you mean to say, if you had known then that we were Jewish, you would have let my wife drown?"

"The death of a Jewess would have been of no significance."

Helmut and Abe continued to walk on the towpath. They were approaching the bridge tender's house.

"And then, there is the matter of my daughter."

"Whatever she has said, I tell you man to man, she wanted it."

Without thinking, Abe slapped Helmut across the face.

Helmut roared in anger, more than pain. He pulled a gun from his pocket.

Otto stepped out of his house, brandishing a shovel.

Helmut looked up. "Herr Becker. It's about time. Please dispose of this trash."

Otto looked at Helmut, his cheek red with Abe's handprint, his hand pointing a gun at Abe's head.

With no regard for his own safety, Abe lunged at Helmut. The gun went flying toward the canal. They rolled on the ground, each trying to gain an advantage.

Helmut screamed at Otto. "You work for me!"

"Not anymore, I don't." He swung the shovel, catching Helmut with a glancing blow on the side of his head.

Otto pocketed Helmut's gun. He helped Abe stand up. "Come quickly, my friend."

"What about Helmut?"

"Leave him to his Nazis."

Otto and Abe ran to the bridge tender's house. Gertrude let them in and shut the door behind them.

"Thank you. Both of you. What do we do now?"

Otto placed the gun on a table by the front door. "We wait."

Chapter Sixty-Three

"What exactly did Abby Jackson hire you to do?"

"She hired me to keep an eye on her husband while she was in jail." Now that the deal had been struck, Hank Morgan just wanted to answer the questions and be done with it.

Detective Massoud obliged. "Why did she need someone to keep an eye on him?"

"I don't know. Maybe she thought he was going to take advantage of her jail time to fool around with other women."

"And did he?"

"Have you ever heard of insurrection groupies?"

"What?"

"There are women who will sleep with a man just because he was at the Capitol on January 6."

"Of course there are."

"And if you served time, it's like being a rock star." Hank Morgan laughed at the thought. "Tom Jackson was a rock star."

"So when he got out of jail..."

"Exactly. With his wife serving time, Tom Jackson had his pick of the litter."

Detective Warren had a question of his own. "So, you're not one of those right-wing gun nuts? Are you saying that you infiltrated Abby Jackson's organization in order to keep tabs on her husband?"

"In my line of work, we take guns very seriously. There's no good will come of these irresponsible assholes and their second amendment bullshit."

"What, for the record, is your line of work?"

"I'm an independent contractor."

Detective Warren turned to Ms. Benitendi. "Could you remind your client that we have a deal?"

Beverly Benitendi conferred with her client. "For the record, we are prepared to stipulate that my client is a hired gun."

Detective Massoud jumped back into the conversation. "Why did Abby Jackson hire a hitman, if all she needed was someone to surveil her husband?"

"All she needed, at first, was surveillance. But it was always understood it might lead to something more before the job was done. Why hire two contractors when one can handle all of it?"

"When did she hire you?"

"Four months ago."

"When did she order the hit?"

"Last week."

"How did she communicate with you?"

"There's always ways to get messages in and out of prison."

"What changed?"

Hank Morgan didn't understand the question. "What do you mean?"

Detective Warren thought the question was self-explanatory. "What changed last week? Why did she order the hit?"

"You'll have to ask her that."

"I'm asking you."

"To the best of my knowledge, it had something to do with money."

"Can you be more specific?"

"Someone visited Abby Jackson in prison. A lawyer, I think, looking for a way to contact Tom Jackson."

Detective Warren already knew about Olivia Levenson's trip to Berryville. He decided to slow play his hand. "Why did the lawyer need to find Tom Jackson?"

"Something about an inheritance."

"An inheritance?"

"Tom Jackson stood to inherit a tidy sum of money."

"Do you know how much money?"

"No."

"But it must have been a big enough number for Abby Jackson to get greedy."

"Tom Jackson was on the outside while his wife was still inside, doing time. Abby Jackson knew, by the time she got out, her loser husband would have blown through the cash."

Beverly Benitendi decided she had allowed her client to say enough. "We're done here, detective."

"A deal's a deal. Stand up, Morgan."

Hank Morgan stood up.

"Hank Morgan, you are under arrest for the murder of Tom Jackson." Detective Massoud turned her attention to Jackson's attorney. "We will try to expedite your client's processing."

"Thank you."

Later, in the squad room, Detective Warren complimented his partner on her work.

One thing troubled Detective Massoud. "Do you believe his story about the wife?"

Detective Warren had given that a lot of thought when they were in the interrogation. "I don't have any great confidence in Hank Morgan's truthfulness, but I've dealt with Benitendi on other cases. I trust her completely."

"Still, what's the expression? Trust, but verify."

Detective Warren groaned at the thought of the long drive. "Maybe we don't need to make the trip."

"What do you have in mind?"

"The feds would love to pin a murder charge on Abby Jackson. Why don't we leave it to the feds to verify."

"I'm good with that. I'll be in the video room. Let me know what happens."

Detective Warren reached out to his contact at FCI Berryville. As he expected, the feds were happy to add murder to Abby Jackson's record. They would take over the case.

Detective Warren disconnected the call and went in search of his partner. He found Massoud cataloguing the video evidence from the gun show. "We keep Hank Morgan. The feds get Abby Jackson. Case closed."

Chapter Sixty-Four

1934

It didn't matter that Papa had told him to stay in the house. A man has responsibilities. Manny was no longer a boy. He waited until his father walked up toward the mess tent, and then he stepped outside. He picked a spot along the canal where the foliage was growing wildly and settled in to watch and wait. It wasn't long before Papa and Helmut came out of the mess tent and began to walk toward the towpath. Manny sunk back deeper into the foliage.

He was perhaps fifty feet away when he saw his father slap Helmut across the face. He began to make his way closer when he saw Otto Becker knock Helmut senseless with the shovel. He watched as Otto and Papa made their way to the bridge tender's house.

Manny saw one more thing that no one else noticed. Ahead, in the foliage, one of Helmut's thugs, pointing a gun at their backs. It was one of the same men who had accosted Elsa Einstein and beaten Manny. He would have his revenge. Manny picked up a rock from the edge of the canal. He took aim and let the rock fly. He heard the thud and watched the thug collapse. Then Manny turned and ran.

The Model T didn't start the first time, didn't start the second time, but the third time, when he cranked the engine, it coughed, sputtered, and wheezed, and then it roared to life. It was a short drive to the Sheriff's office.

Manny's breathing was as erratic as the Model T's engine. He forced himself to take long, slow breaths and, by the time he arrived at the sheriff's office, he managed not to look or sound entirely like a madman.

"Papa tried to reason with the Nazi. He's in great danger."

"Where is your father now?"

"Helmut pulled a gun on Papa. Mr. Becker came to the rescue."

"Where is your father now?"

"At the bridge tender's. Hurry!"

The Sheriff grabbed his rifle. "Let me round up a few more men, in case of trouble."

* * *

Helmut lay on the towpath. His head throbbed. The shovel had left a nasty bruise. He pulled himself up to his knees. Where was the man he'd instructed to keep watch? The man was a moron. Him and his brother, one dumber than the other. Looking at them, he should have known. They obviously were not part of the master race. But they had nasty tempers and violent natures, and Helmut thought they would be useful. Helmut would not make that mistake again.

He managed to stand. From the higher vantage point, he spotted the thug unconscious in the underbrush. His gun lay on the ground just beyond the reach of his outstretched hand. Helmut picked up the gun, shook the asshole until he came to, waited for the man to grasp his situation, and then shot him between the eyes.

Helmut would have liked to have discharged the entire magazine into the asshole, but he would need the firepower when he caught up with the Jew and his Jew-lover friend. Helmut dragged himself down the towpath to the Jew house. The house was empty. The car was gone. The Jew was on the run.

Later, he would organize the boys into teams. They would have a hunt. Whoever returned with the Jew would win a prize. First, he would deal with the Jew-lover.

Helmut turned and walked to the bridge tender's. It was a short walk, but

Helmut was not at his best. His back hurt from the fight on the towpath. His head hurt from the shovel. He stopped repeatedly to catch his breath and rub his legs.

He stood on the swing bridge and called out. "Herr Becker, you have been judged, and you have been found guilty. Come out and face your punishment like a man."

There was no response from inside the house.

"If you come out now, I will spare your wife."

Otto Becker could not allow Gertrude to be put in any danger.

"I will come out."

Gertrude blocked his way. "Do not believe him. If you are dead mein Barchen, then I am dead as well."

Abe Dubinski could not abide that he had put his only true friends in jeopardy. "I will go outside."

Abe called out to Helmut. "If you leave the Beckers alone, you can have me."

Otto gasped. "No Abe. No."

Gertrude peeked out the window. "He is on the bridge."

Abe called out again. "I am coming out now." He slipped the gun in his pocket. Slowly, he opened the door and stepped out onto the porch. Abe was prepared to die for his faith. He was prepared to kill for it as well.

From the swing bridge, Helmut taunted him. "Go ahead, Jew. I will give you the first shot."

Helmut waited. Abe didn't make a move.

"Don't worry about your precious morals, Jew. You are defending your God. He will forgive you. If you don't shoot, I will."

Silently, Abe said a prayer. He aimed the gun and pulled the trigger. The bullet ricocheted off the top of the king post and landed in the canal.

"You brag that you are chosen. Perhaps your God has chosen you to die." Helmut slowly walked toward the bridge tender's house. "Are you frightened, my Jewish friend? You should be." Helmut walked ever closer.

Abe's world narrowed to the Nazi standing some twenty feet away.

Abe didn't hear motorcars racing toward the bridge tender's. He didn't hear the Sheriff shouting at them both to drop their weapons.

He heard two shots. One from Helmut's weapon. One from his own. He didn't hear the third shot, the one from Sheriff Anderson's rifle.

He watched Helmut fall to the ground.

Abe had killed a man. He stood on Otto Becker's porch and sobbed.

Sheriff Anderson walked up to Abe.

"You saw what happened. I killed Helmut," Abe said. "You must arrest me."

Sheriff Anderson took the gun from Abe's hand. He emptied the remaining bullets and threw the gun into the canal. "Your first shot hit the king post. My deputies and I will do a thorough search. I expect to find your second shot somewhere in the foliage."

"But…"

"Listen to me carefully. I don't know much about Jews. To be honest, I don't know much about Nazis either. But I know you, Abe Dubinski. I know that you are not a killer."

A sheriff's deputy ran up to the house. "We found one of Helmut's thugs dead in the underbrush."

The Sheriff turned his attention back to Abe. "Did you also shoot him, Mr. Dubinski?"

"No, of course not."

"That's right. Because you are a good and decent man."

Manny Dubinski ran up onto the porch and hugged his Papa.

Sheriff Anderson nodded at Manny. "In case you're wondering what brought me out here, it was your son who came to get me."

Abe looked at Manny and smiled. "I thought I told you to stay inside."

Sheriff Anderson looked up towards the campsite. "If you will excuse me, I have to figure out how to send one hundred boys back to their families."

* * *

Abe was exhausted, both mentally and physically. Manny wanted to take his father home, but first, Abe needed a moment with Otto. The two men stepped inside the house to talk privately.

Abe smiled at his friend. "I am sorry I dragged you into this."

Otto dismissed Abe's apology. "I only wish I had done something sooner. I am embarrassed to admit that I was more worried about my job than I was about my friend."

"Nevertheless, when I needed you most, you were there."

"I can find another job." Otto looked at the picture that hung by his front door, the one he had hung to impress Helmut Fischer. "I guess I don't need this anymore." Otto ripped the German Chancellor's picture off the wall.

The two men stepped out into the sunshine. Manny helped his father into the Model T and drove the short distance home. He helped Abe out of the motorcar and into the house. He poured his father a glass of cold water. Abe asked instead for a brandy.

"Two brandies. Now that you are a man."

Abe and Manny sipped their brandies. When they were finished, Abe had one more request. "Can you drive to Princeton and bring home your mother and your sister? I believe the danger has passed."

"Will you be alright?"

Abe smiled weakly. "I need to be alone with my God. We have some things we need to discuss."

Alone in the house, Abe spoke to his God.

"Blessed art Thou, o Lord our God, who commandeth me to kill in thy name."

Sheriff Anderson had made it clear that Abe was not responsible for Helmut Fischer's death. But the Sheriff was only talking about Abe's aim, not his intention. From the moment Abe stepped out onto the Becker's porch, he was ready to kill Helmut Fischer. More than just ready, he wanted to kill the Nazi. The Nazi had dishonored his family and defiled his daughter, and for that, he must die.

If Abe's aim had been better, Helmut Fischer would have been dead before the Sheriff arrived on the scene.

In that moment, facing the Nazi, Abe's intention had been clear. He wanted to see the Nazi die. No, he had to admit, it was more than that. He wanted to be the instrument of the Nazi's death. Was Abe's God so puny that he needed Abe to kill in his name? Is that what God wanted from His chosen people? Is that what it meant to be chosen?

Abe's intestines were roiled with agony. He didn't want to think. He didn't want to feel. He wasn't sure that he wanted to live. He only knew that his pain was the fault of his God.

"I renounce you!"

Abe waited for God to smite him, but no smiting came.

"I renounce you!"

"I renounce you!"

"I renounce you!"

Abe waited and prayed, but he was not struck down.

"Blessed art Thou, o Lord our God, who commandeth me to kill in thy name."

It was nearly sundown. Always, the Dubinskis had lit the Shabbos candles and said the Shabbos prayer. He would never again allow Shabbos candles to be lit in his home. He would never again allow God to command him to do anything.

Abe rummaged through the cupboard and found the Shabbos candles. What was he to do? He wanted to pray, but that was merely a bad habit. There was no God left for him to pray to. Whether he was unworthy of his God, or his God was unworthy of his prayers no longer mattered. He placed the two candlesticks in a box. He took the box outside and buried it in his yard. There was a flash of thunder and lightning. The heavens opened, and the rain came down in a torrent.

"Blessed art Thou, o Lord our God, who commandeth me to kill in thy name."

Chapter Sixty-Five

2023

Mr. Plaid Jacket was dead. Mr. Pisswater was in jail. Charlie Levenson was sitting in his canoe, drifting down the canal. After an early morning shower, the sky had cleared, white puffy clouds dotted the sky, the sun sparkled on the water. The frogs, turtles, and birds sang songs that allowed Charlie to pretend that he was floating through an animated movie.

The star of the movie was an animated Jami, racing along the towpath, Ben and Olivia doing their best to keep up.

Charlie had forgotten his ballcap. He could feel the sun on his bald spot. A bit of sunburn was a small price to pay for paradise.

He was nearing the bridge. Jami ran to the middle of the bridge. As the canoe passed beneath her, Jami sprinkled flower petals on her grandfather.

Charlie waved to a couple who were strolling on the towpath. He would make more of an effort to get to know his neighbors.

He would make more of an effort to appreciate living.

Charlie shoved his paddle into the canal, allowing the canoe to pivot. A few quick strokes, and the canoe was on its way toward home. Jami, on the towpath, raced ahead. By the time Charlie pulled the canoe onto the landing, his granddaughter was waiting with two fresh glasses of lemonade. He picked his granddaughter up in his arms and danced on the edge of the lock.

"Be careful, Grandpa."

"Always." Charlie kissed his Jami. "Always."

Ben and Olivia were sitting on the front porch. They had prepared a picnic lunch. Hot dogs, potato chips, all the essential food groups. Olivia and Jami disappeared into the kitchen. They returned carrying a tray.

"What did you make?"

Jami showed him. "Persian almond cookies."

A tear came to Charlie's eye. "Mamani's favorite."

Jami smiled. It was Zoya's smile on Jami's face. "Would you like one?"

"Please."

Jami examined the platter, looking for the best cookie. She took a bite and then handed the cookie to Charlie.

Olivia helped herself to an almond cookie. "When you bought this place, I have to admit, I thought you were crazy."

Charlie laughed. "Maybe I was."

Ben had a better explanation. "You just see things a little differently than the rest of us."

"Zoya taught me that."

"I miss her." Ben wiped his eyes with a napkin.

"Me too. But she is never far away. I see her in you and especially in Jami."

"We need to get on the road. Will you be okay?"

"I'll be fine." Charlie hugged his son. "Thanks for coming."

* * *

"Mr. Plaid Jacket is dead?"

Charlie had been expecting Zoya. "Yes."

"Is that enough?"

"It has to be."

"I can't believe it's been a year."

"It hurts like it was just yesterday, but I'm learning to live with the pain."

"Stay focused on the love, and the pain will recede."

"What did I ever do to deserve you, Zoya?"

"You sat at my lunch table."

"I did, didn't I?"

"You were brave and strong and ate lunch with the girl who said Howt."

Charlie chuckled, remembering high school.

"I want you to do me a favor, Charlie."

"Of course."

"I want you to light the Shabbos candles."

"I don't have any."

"Yes, you do. Remember the box you dug up?"

Charlie had nearly forgotten the box that had been buried by the last lock tender.

He retrieved the box from his closet and removed the Shabbos candlesticks. He placed them on the kitchen counter and waited for sundown.

* * *

Blessed art Thou, O Lord our God, Ruler of the Universe, who sanctifies us with His commandments and commands us to kindle the Shabbos light.

* * *

"In my lifetime, I have had the great good fortune to belong to three amazing families. My parents, Leila and Karim Aziz, who loved me so much that they sent me away. The Barookhian family, who loved me enough to let me in and, of course, the Levensons.

When my parents sent me away, they entrusted me to Allah. Allah is love, and love is light. I have always believed that it was Allah who brought me to the Barookhian family. It was Allah's love that saved me. Without Allah's love, I would never have become a Barookhian. I would never have learned that Jewish love is no different than Muslim love. When the Barookhians lit the Shabbos candles and said the Shabbos prayer, we weren't celebrating what made us different. We were celebrating what made us one. We were celebrating love."

Acknowledgements

Writing is a solitary activity, but it would be a mistake for you to conclude that I do this alone. I've benefited from the support of many authors, editors, publishers and readers in the crime fiction community. I'd like to take this opportunity to thank just a few of them—Ann Aptaker, A.J. Sidransky, Rob Creekmore and Lanny Larcinese.

Ann Aptaker graciously accepted my invitation to read an early draft of the novel and responded with several pages of detailed, thoughtful notes. A.J. Sidransky and Rob Creekmore didn't wait for an invite, each of them insisting that they needed to read a copy. A.J. has gone out of his way to introduce me to individuals and organizations who can help get the word out about the book. Lanny Larcinese is one of those guys that you want to sit down with and talk about the art of storytelling. The first time I read an excerpt from my then work-in-progress was at a literary salon in Lanny's home. I will always be grateful to Ann, A.J., Rob, and Lanny for their early and enthusiastic support.

In October 2023, I sent an unsolicited manuscript to Level Best Books. Twelve days later, Verena Rose offered me a contract. I'd like to thank the team at LBB—Shawn Reilly Simmons, Deb Well and Verena Rose—for their support of *The Other*.

About the Author

Jeff Markowitz is the author of six novels, including the award-winning dark comedy, *Death and White Diamonds*. Jeff spent more than forty years creating community-based programs and services in New Jersey for children and adults with autism, including twenty-five years as President and Executive Director of the Life Skills Resource Center, before retiring in 2018 to devote more time to writing. In October 2021, a puzzle hunt based on Jeff's novella, *Motive for Murder* raised more than $1 million for at-risk children in NYC. Jeff is a past President of the New York Chapter of Mystery Writers of America. He lives in Monmouth Junction NJ with his wife Carol and two cats, Vergil and Aeneas.

AUTHOR WEBSITE:
https://jeffmarkowitz.com

SOCIAL MEDIA HANDLES:
Facebook: jeff.markowitz.3
Twitter: @JeffMarkowitz1

Also by Jeff Markowitz

2024 "Her Hips Were the Face of El Vizir" in *Mystery Tribune*, Issue #21

2022 "The Black-and-White Cookie" in *Jewish Noir II*

2022 "No Outlet" in *Mid-Atlantic Tales: Short Horror and Mystery Stories*

2021 "The Third Date Rule" in *Asinine Assassins*

2021 *Motive for Murder*

2020 *Hit or Miss*

2018 "Twelve Steps" in *Plague of Shadows*

2014 *Death and White Diamonds*

2009 *It's Beginning to Look a Lot like Murder*

2009 "State Home for the Holidays" in *woman's corner magazine*

2009 "The Sound Bite" in *woman's corner magazine*

2009 "Gilligan Finds a Body" in *Mysterical-e*

2007 "The Old Bitch" in *Mysterical-e*

2006 *A Minor Case of Murder*

2004 *Who Is Killing Doah's Deer?*